River Roots

River Roots

Mary Kuykendall-Weber

Texas Review Press
Huntsville, Texas

FIRST EDITION, 2009
Requests for permission to reproduce material from this work
should be sent to:

Permissions
Texas Review Press
English Department
Sam Houston State University
Huntsville, TX 77341-2146

Acknowledgements:

The author expresses her graitude to the following publications, in
which many of these stories initially appeared: *Hard Row to Hoe*,
Byline Magazine, *Rambunctious Review*, *Goose River Press Anthology*,
Tall Grass Writer's Outrider Press Anthology, *Mountain Girl Press
2007 Anthology*, *Tapestries Anthology*, *Cup of Comfort*, *Christmas
is a Season 2008*, and *Anthology of Appalachian Writers*.

Library of Congress Cataloging-in-Publication Data

Kuykendall-Weber, Mary, 1938-
  River roots / Mary-Kuykendall-Weber.
    p. cm.
  ISBN-13: 978-1-933896-29-8 (pbk. : alk. paper)
  ISBN-10: 1-933896-29-9 (pbk. : alk. paper)
  1. Hampshire County (W. Va.)--Fiction. 2. Potomac River,
South Branch (Va.-W. Va.)--Fiction. I. Title.
  PS3611.U94R58 2009
  813'.6--dc22

                                    2009006031

River Roots

Table of Contents

For my parents

Jim Tot

There were probably twenty of us, ages ten through fifteen, working for old man Jim Tot, who ran Mr. James Stump's sugar corn packing operation along the South Branch of the Potomac River in the eastern Panhandle of West Virginia. He was in his 80s now and had been retired from the harder field work to keep us in line. A warning sign that we were not doing the job the way he wanted it done would come when the short and stout feisty old Scotsman would stroke his handle-bar mustache. Our older brothers, who had been sent to the fields to work with the men, warned us to be wary of Jim Tot when he stroked his stache. They were considered old enough to know which ears of corn to pull by hand and toss them in long, narrow sleds being pulled through the cornrows by mules.

The sound of an approaching sled meant we younguns, as Jim Tot called us, had about five minutes to bag up the corn pile we were working on before the pickers dumped another load for us to bag. We played a game of trying to get all of the corn bagged before another sled got there so we could take a quick dip in the river which was just a ball-field run away from our packing site under the sycamore trees. As usual, when we lost, Jim Tot would egg us on. "We'll beat the next one in, see the pile is smaller than the last one ye wuz workin on when the men came in." If we complained, he would tell us we had it better than our older brothers and the men. "They are out there in the hot sun with no chance fer a break whilst ye younguns are under these nice trees thinkin bout swimmin."

Then he would explain that sugar corn didn't wait on anybody to ripen and that it was important to get it to market as fast as you could and as early in the season as you could. "There's a bunch of kids south of here that started baggin corn two weeks before ye younguns," he would add. "But the price is still good this early in the season. Ye can rest more when the men pick the fields over the third time when it takes longer to find good corn and the price haint so good. We do a good job now and Mr. James, he become mighty relaxed."

I can still hear Jim Tot laugh when we could hear the approaching men telling the younger ones how to pick corn. He knew they were repeating his talk to us when we started at sunup, "Look at the corn tassels. See if they are dry. Make sure the hair coming out of the ear has turned brown. Snap the ear straight down. It won't pull right from the side. If you see worms, leave it for the hog corn pickers."

My older cousin in the field would tell me later that they mostly yelled those instructions when they knew that Jim Tot could hear. They wanted this venerable old man's approval just as we did. Occasionally they would pretend to do something wrong just to see him signal his ire by stroking his bushy mustache which he kept healthy and sturdy by buttering it up to eat corn, a habit he admonished us was more sanitary than our using our hands and one that was more efficient in spreading the butter. Our parents, upon hearing this, glad that we were not old enough to grow beards, merely winced when we proclaimed that he never spit out loose hairs as he twirled the cob through his buttered mustache.

Lunch time, of course, was looked forward to constantly as a time to rest and hear stories by Jim Tot, who would take out his pocket watch with the long silver chain twisted around his suspenders, to announce the time. In fact, it was right before lunch and at the end of the day, trucks in all sizes would come lumbering down the mountainside road and through the fields to pick up the corn. Mr. James not only rounded up all the farmers' kids and paid us a $1 a day to bag corn, but he also paid our parents to rent their cattle or pulpwood trucks when the corn came on. We would cheer when we saw the trucks coming because it would be a sure chance to cool off and rest. To keep the corn cool on its three-hour trips to markets in Pittsburgh and Washington, the men would have to quit picking and scatter ice chunks among the bags with a layer on the top of the load.

As we sat down to eat our peanut butter and jelly sandwiches and get an ear of corn from the pot Jim Tot had boiling, he would tell us about the old days. On a particularly hot day, he would repeat how they used to saw the ice out of the river in the winter and store it in the heavy insulated shed by the river where it was buried deep in a pit in sawdust with maybe half of it surviving until corn picking. Then when the Rural Electrification Act brought in electricity in the 40s, Mr. James began buying huge ice blocks from the new icehouse in town. But it, like the river ice had been, was still buried in sawdust in the shed for daily use. When the ice shed was opened, we were allowed to run in for a quick romp in the damp sawdust as the men dug out the blocks for chipping.

The men would use sledgehammers to break the blocks, aiming for the white streaks caused by air pockets, which would produce quicker, cleaner breaks with fewer fast-melting chips. Then we would hang around and watch them load the trucks and pack the ice around the burlap bags we had filled that morning. By following the trucks over the bumpy field road to the county road, we usually managed to get bits and pieces of ice as it fell through canvas openings or through the truck rails. Jim Tot thought this was a better use of our energy than swimming, particularly when the ice was passed round for everyone. Mostly, the ice chips were used to soothe sunburns or gnat bites.

Years ago, Jim Tot had come up with the idea to Mr. James that we should store the burlap bags over the ice for further meltdown protection. Jim Tot had made hauling the bags in and out—and always having a jug of tea ready for storage—part of our jobs. Then with chilled tea and cool burlaps to sit on, we would open our brown paper lunch bags and pull out apples and mostly peanut butter and jelly sandwiches. We had 30 minutes to eat and hear Jim Tot tell stories.

Everyone wanted the latest news about the old boss man who owned all these fields, Mr. James A. Stump. None of us had been in his big four-story brick house near town but Jim Tot had. He would tell us how Mr. James still had his daddy's confederate rifle over the fireplace mantle… the very one that his paw had used to try to keep the Yankees from stealing his horses and hay . . . and how Mr. James A. had been shot right off that hay stack by them Yanks with the missus running out of the house to him and little Mr. James going right ahead of her . . . that Mr. James did what his paw told him as he lay dying. He hid the gun in the spring house. His daddy was still cursing the Yanks while his ma tried to help him at the bottom of the stack. But little Mr. James did what his paw said declared Jim Tot. He had hidden the rifle. The Yanks got the hay but they didn't find no gun. Then he would tell us that slaves used to work pulling sugar corn in these same fields and that they called these lower fields sugar bottom and that was why he called sweet corn, sugar corn. Then he would tell us that we had it much better than slave children because we could not be sold and that by working hard we could end up with a better future.

Jim Tot really had our attention when he told us that when he was our age, he was putting in the railroad across the river. He had ridden the ties down the seven-mile mountain trough of the South Branch of the Potomac River in high white water to get them to their positions for laying tracks. He had seen the railroad come and recently go in his 88 years and reckoned it was "whut they call progress." We knew we were in for a long explanation when he opened his tobacco pouch. He told how railroads replaced horses and the C&O Canal, and how trucks had now replaced our railroad because they were faster and cheaper in getting produce directly to their markets. But he was quick to add he didn't agree with such progress. He would point to the mountains surrounding us and tell us how all those people could no longer go down to a train stop to sell their produce or even get a ride to town. "They movin to town to make a livin and it hain't much of one," he would conclude.

Then he would talk about how he had heard those big corporate farms in California could get three crops a day and how hard it was getting for the small farmer to compete with one growing season. "That new Jolly Green Giant they got now haint so amusin." he would laugh. He did agree with Mr. James that trucks were better than the train since the faster corn got to the market the better it was because heat not only made it hard but it lost its taste. "That's also why we ice it. Only thing wurse than 2-day old sugar corn is week-old poke," he would declare as he chewed his plug and spit out tobacco juice. Then he would tell us how riding the ties over rough rapids could flatten you just like the train used to smash the Indian head on our pennies.

All too soon, the men would be back in the fields after prodding the mules away from the grassy bank along the river. As they went, my cousin would laugh as he and the others heard Jim Tot give us a running lecture on what to do: "Ye kids, don't ye forgit to feel fer dem worms . . . ye can feel em with yer hands . . . no shuckin it back . . . it will rot . . . ye can feel it if the ear is full . . . I want nothin but good eatin corn in these bags…the rest ye throw over there in that pile . . . that's fer hogs and lazy kids . . . an one last thing afore ye start fillin these bags . . . remember that the faster ye fill up these bags, the better the chance ye'll have to take a quick dip in the river. Those mules are gettin tired out there . . . the sun's way high and it gonna git over a 100. Some of em are gonna get stubborn nough they'll be hard to coax. So quit yer complainin that there are too many men and mules and sleds. Ye can beat em. But ye got to be smart."

Then we would start on the count of one with no talking because he didn't want us to lose track of how many ears were going in the bags. Jim Tot, and the other old men too old for the fields, would hold the burlap bags up with one kid on each side bending over one at a time picking up four ears of corn and placing them in the bag until the count of 15 had been reached. This endless procedure resulted in hundreds of burlap bags of five-dozen each ready for market.

At the end of the day, the field boss would then jostle with Jim Tot and ask him, "Are you getting them younguns ready for real work in the field?" and Jim Tot would rub his huge white mustache and tobacco stained whiskers and retort: "If ye all get any slower out dere, we're gonna start usin the ice for a tea party here. Howse bout sendin some corn in without the worms? I got nough bait here for the whole county to go fishin," he would grin as he pointed to the discard pile.

Jim Tot was always ready with a feisty answer. The men said this was because he grew up with just coon dogs to bark orders to. He was known throughout the eastern panhandle for his skill at training beagles to hunt coons. Some said that was because the dogs associated with him. Word had it that he used a lot of the discarded corn to make moonshine. When that happened, some said he would get down on all fours like a dog and was just as likely during this training to track a coon and find it hiding high in a tree before the dogs did. He would bark at the base of the tree to complete his dog training, setting off a howl from the dogs you could hear for miles. Those who bought coon dogs from him said those beagles never forgot Jim Tot, and if they got near his place they made a run for it; that they loved the old man, and that was why they always obeyed him.

Perhaps that was why we kids never disobeyed him either. If he saw we were under performing for the other old men holding bags, he would move us over to fill his bag and invariably stroke his mustache. The instructions would be repeated and attitudes quickly corrected if the ears were thrown in haphazardly.

One day he noticed that my younger cousin, Jack, had a clever way of not being the first one to place four ears of corn in the bag. He would chose girl partners and proclaim, "Ladies before Gentlemen." This resulted in Jack having one less bend per bag because it took just 15 handfuls to make five dozen

After partnering Jack up with another boy, Jim Tot watched to see what he would do and smiled when Jack would say, "go head, you're younger" or "old folks first." After that he was given the "honor" of always being first to fill the corn bag by Jim Tot.

Mr. James had thought it was funny but agreed with Jim Tot that Jack's parents ought to know about it so they could watch out for such tricky behavior—or as Jim Tot explained, "While Jack sure didn't fall off no turnip truck, it is best he not grows up and become one of them robber barons."

Revelations

"Reckon you won that one," said Clem as he turned Isaac's coke bottle upside down, spitting his chew on the sawdust covered floor in Dick Spurling's store. "Jeeze, it came all the way from Seattle," he declared as he, Rufus and Luke handed their dollar bills to Isaac.

Dick's store at the north end of the South Branch valley of the Potomac River was where the four loggers hung out. Dick always made sure he had plenty of pipe and chewing tobacco on the counter, that there was a full case of coke. Every Friday, after a week of cutting wood for the paper mill, Clem, Rufus, Isaac, and Luke would bet an hour's pay on who got the coke that was bottled the farthest away. First, they would toss their jackets on the woodpile behind the Morning Glory pot belly stove to dry out, be it from summer rain or sweat or winter sleet. Next they would stock up on tobacco for the week. Then Dick would kick-slide over a case of Coke to the four loggers as they sat on empty, upside-down coke crates around the stove.

Dick knew they were chasing the cokes down with some of Luke's homemade shine which he carried in an old mouthwash bottle. West Virginia was probably one of the few states left that was dry, gambling not allowed. Still no one could accuse Dick himself of breaking the law. No Siree! The logger's business was their business.

Isaac gave Dick one of his winning dollars for two cans of the more expensive Prince Albert tobacco. Tugging on his mustache that he was trying to style like the Prince on the can, Isaac sat upright on the case, declaring, "Now, when I get a top hat like the Prince here, I won't be needing none of your disrespect. But I will always take your money." It was his job now to do the honors with another round of cokes and Luke's brew.

When money and shine was passing, Dick always looked the other way so he could also watch to see if other customers were coming. The loggers had their own rules. By taking no more than two swigs to make room for Luke's lightning shine, then finishing the rest after what Isaac called "reviewing the week's events," it was bottoms up to see who had the coke bottled the farthest away. The one that won received a dollar from the other three, an hour's pay for back-breaking work, but, "What the heck, it was for a good Friday cause," reasoned Clem.

Dick figured it was not really gambling. "No Siree!" There was no middle man in between. A dollar was just exchanging hands among friends. That's what he had told the parishioners down at the Presbyterian Church where Van Meter creek ran into the South Branch. No more sinful than bingo games in the Sunday School room he had ventured. But the deacon had quickly pointed out to him that 10% of the bingo proceeds went to the Lord. Still, he and the other farmers had not suggested the logmen come to church even if they tithed. Dick knew the flatlanders had little use for mountain people.

Whenever Dick saw the four loggers finishing their spiked cokes and it was bottles up time, he would stand by his U.S. map, with ruler in hand, in case there was a debate. Clem won this round: they didn't need Dick to measure it on the map. Clem's bottle was from Texas while Isaac and Rufus had Virginia bottles and Luke had one from Maryland. Dick had gotten his map out of the old one-room school up the holler when it was closed some 20 years ago. When they first started the game, it had been put to the test many times to close an argument even though it showed only 48 states. Dick had figured they didn't make Coke in Hawaii and Alaska and he reckoned he must be right because in the ten or so years this had been going on, they had never gotten a bottle from there. Dick had even gotten to checking the cokes when they were delivered just to see for himself. If there was, he'd take it out. He didn't want no trouble in his store because something wasn't on the map. He had teased Clem when his granddaughter had come in for penny candy, looked at the marked up map and declared that her grandpa knew a lot more than her teacher did about where all the cities and states were located.

One time Rufus had tried to bribe Dick into stacking the cokes in his favor. But Dick had said, "No Siree!." He was an honest man. No drinking and gambling. He could hold his head just as high as all the folks did down at the river valley Presbyterian Church. But as Clem said, "That might be, but I don't see them invitin you to their private doins? You're still a holler man."

Dick knew that was true but that didn't bother him none.

He liked knowing everybody even if they didn't want to know him. Besides, the folks down at the church were showing a big interest in him these days. They wanted to know what was happening on all that mountain top land the rich man from New York had bought from the lumber company.

He was supposed to be building a mansion on the highest knob in the mountain area. It would not only overlook the upper end of their river valley but would even have a view into the Van Meter hollow where Dick's store was. Word had it that he was a big game hunter and that he was going to stock his 3000 acres of woodland with bear, wolves, wildcats and, by Jeesus, he might even bring back the buffalo,

The river valley people had invited the rich man to church but he had ignored them, saying he wanted to get away from it all and that included churches. The rich man had come in Dick's store several times for bullets and a snack or two. But as Luke was quick to point out the rich man only bought food in a can which should tell Dick something about what the rich man thinks of his meat counter.

The valley folks' sighting of the rich man in Dick Spurling's store had been enough for the deacon and the other farmers to extend their hospitality to Dick. Dick had even been asked to stay after church and join them behind the church where they discussed the trials and tribulations of raising crops despite a fickle mother nature. When Dick joined, the conversation would soon change to sightings of the rich man from New York and his drivers. So far they had counted three different Cadillacs going up the valley road. The drivers had been dressed in fancy suits. Only the rich man wore regular clothes so they assumed the drivers never went hunting with him.

Dick's main source of information was the loggers. He saw no gain for anyone in telling this to the churchmen. The rich man had hired the loggers to take care of four Arabian horses which he kept in an abandoned barn in the upland trough. For $10 a week, more than a day's pulpwood pay, all Clem, Isaac, Rufus and Luke had to do was make sure the horses had hay and water. They had not let on to the rich man how it would be an easy trip for them.

The lumber company had let them hunt and they had no reason to see why they should stop. They told Dick they even sometimes rode the horses up the old logging road to the best deer crossing spots. "Them Arabs might forget what its all about if they ain't rode some," Rufus told Dick.

But ever since the rich man's body had arrived in a long, black Lincoln limousine followed by four other cars with New York and New Jersey plates, rumors had been flying. One of the drivers had told Isaac that the rich man's will had called for him to be buried at the site of his mountain top mansion which had never gotten built, that his will called for him to be buried with his favorite possessions including his bow and arrows, a Roman sword and a safari gun which Isaac had seen and admired because it had tusk inlays from an elephant and was housed in a real leopard bag. "Now that guy has style," he had told them at the store as he waxed his Prince Albert mustache.

When the stretch limousine had not been able to make it up the steep, winding dirt road to the mansion on the hill that never got built, the pall bearers had carried the casket a mile up to the burial site. "Even those not carrying anything looked plumb tuckered out," said Rufus. Isaac reckoned that he would have been happy to have carried the engraved sword which the rich man had once told him was over a 1000 years old. But they figured they shouldn't disturb the funeral party.

That Sunday, Dick at the back of the church after the service repeated what he had heard about the burial, but the valley men didn't believe it. They joked that maybe the rich man was also taking his gold with him including the silver scales he weighed it with.

As months went by, people tired of talking about the funeral, puzzled over the gate across the road leading to the mansion on the mountain top which did not get built. It had a lock on it now. A check in the courthouse had shown the rich man had a son who inherited the land. But no one had met him. The taxes were being paid by mail. No one knew anything more. It was a stir that took some time to quiet down.

As usual Dick would ask the loggers every Friday night if they had seen anyone going up the road to the old rich man's place that never got built. "Lock on the gate is getting rusty and weeds are taking over the road," was all they would say.

The horses had been trucked out right after the funeral. So about all Dick could do on Sunday nights was tell the parishioners that the lock was getting rustier and brush taking over the road, that so far no one had seen anything of the son or the drivers or the fancy cars. Nothing. The lock had not been touched. Before long the road would wash out if somebody didn't keep it up.

Years later the rich man's mansion that never got built was seldom mentioned. The valley farmers were too busy worrying about a drought that was so severe they had to start selling off road and river frontage to the developers. A bangs plague had even hit their cattle and the government had ordered them to bury them to prevent the contagious disease from going airborne. If the rich man had built his mountaintop mansion, the view would no longer be of wheat, corn, and pasture fields dotted with cattle but that of rusty RVs by the river and trailer parks along the roads and into the fields. There were some jobs at the new Wal-Mart and chicken processing plant up the river. But most people were on welfare. The lumber company had sold the rest of their land to developers. Clem, Rufus, Isaac and Luke had moved out of the holler to live in trailers by the river.

In fact, the mountains today are looking as prosperous as the valley once did. Retired Washington people, looking to escape school and property taxes, continue to buy the scenic mountain land from the developers. They occasionally drop in to the old Presbyterian church now called the Assembly of God. They hang out at Dick's store.

Dick replaced the pot belly stove with electric heat, installed a window air conditioner for the summer and planted a herb and vegetable garden. The newcomers also like his imported organic cereal grains, teas and coffee beans which he weighs on his silver scales. "Never eat stuff out of a can," he advises his customers on their way to their mountain homes. He decorated his store with Native American artifacts, including a huge bow with arrows pointing to his shelf of dried meats, fruits and vegetables on sale.

Dick sympathizes with the Washingtonians when they complain that their fine views of the river and fertile farm valley are disappearing and how they don't like looking at rusty trailers parks.

But Dick flinches when some of them refer to the valley people as trailer trash. Still, he answers their questions about who they are and what do they do. He even got some of the newcomers in their gated mountain manors to visit the loggers along the river by telling them about their interesting collection of artifacts. They came back talking about the unusual gun collection they had seen and the ancient Roman sword that hangs over Isaac's fake brick fireplace. They had tried to buy the guns, the sword and a leopard skin pouch but the only thing the loggers would sell were old Coca Cola crates and bottles and a map of the U.S when it just had 48 states. They told Dick a guy named Isaac had figured there were some things they wanted to take with them, whatever that meant.

Nell and Mack

Nell would never forget that morning. It had started out as a typical warm summer day. Her pail was about half full of milk.

In sync with the splish-splash rhythm of Nell's gentle pulls, Guernie chewed on her timothy hay and Nell hummed.

Nell had planned a full day of chores. She would churn the milk to get cream, chop wood and weed the garden. And, as soon as the kids got off the school bus that afternoon, all of them would be busy picking green beans and then snapping them for canning. Her youngest child still had hands small enough to pack the snapped beans into the Mason jars. Her oldest son had just gone off to Viet Nam, leaving his young wife and young son in their care. It had been tough to let him go, but everyone knew there was no way for him to make a living on their small farm. The army would give him training, maybe pay for a college education.

Income from their family farm barely supported Nell and Bill these days. Nell used to make extra money sending eggs and milk with Bill when he went to the stock sales, but that had been stopped. The government didn't allow these to be sold for fear of sanitary production procedures, they said. Bill said it was big business taking over farming.

Nell didn't want to think about the odds of her son coming back alive from Viet Nam. It had been bad in both World War I and II. The only living reminder now from World War I was her great Uncle Mack Van Meter, who, 50 years later, was still taking his silent walks up and down the valley road. One in four of the valley sons had not come back from World War II. Nell had been grateful when her Bill returned. They had gotten married just as they planned. She had counted the months until Bill came home by putting a notch beside his name in her family's barn. Now she was doing the same for her son, Bill, Jr.

Nell had just poured her pail into the milk can and settled down for a refill when she felt the rising sun warm her back. She felt good. She amused herself watching the sun shadow her image on Guernie's glossy brown side. Maybe, she thought, the sun was shining on her son today too. Several wrens were darting back and forth gathering hayseed dropped by Guernie. The barn cat was not even bothering the birds, content to lap up milk Nell had given it.

Nell was taking it all in—the smell of warm milk, fresh hay, the chatter of birds, the peaceful farm animals, and the warm sun on her back—when she heard the footstep. She felt a chill. Someone or something was behind her. She was about to turn around when she froze with fear. Her image on Guernie's side had been overshadowed by that of a huge man with a raised hand.

Guernie jolted. Nell, frozen, tried to calm herself, noting that the shadow was not moving closer. But the stare at her back was running shivers down it. She was in a vulnerable position. She would test how much she could move. She had to be able to do something. She tried to continue pulling milk, but Guernie was not cooperating, swatting her tail furiously. "Stop it Guernie," said Nell. "There are no flies in here." She was glad to hear her own voice calming Guernie and maybe whoever it was behind her.

Still frozen in the depth of the shadowy figure with a hand up in the air, Nell saw the raised hand was not moving. He was not coming closer. Nell started on "You are my Sunshine" to buy time. She kept rhythm with her feet to see if they would work.

Nell wished she had taken her husband's advice of milking Guernie in the horse barn. He had admonished her for wasting time taking Guernie to the machine shed for milking. But Nell didn't like the dark barn. She still had nightmarish memories of the time she went into the stall and was trapped by a black snake eating eggs. She should have known the way the hen was carrying on nearby that something was wrong. She managed to step over the snake when it came out of the hen's nest beside her. She even talked herself back into the barn with a hoe to kill it even though her husband said they were better mousers than a barn cat. But cats didn't eat eggs. She remembered how her mother ruled that money made from all the eggs not found in the hen house boxes would be used for extras. In the 30s, there was still a theater in town that bartered. A dozen eggs got all of them in to see the movie. Her mother managed to raise Nell and her siblings all by herself. Nell could not remember her father. He was one of those who died in World War I.

After the snake scare, Nell did the milking in the shed. It was large and open on one end. She would tie Guernie along the back wall where she could easily drink water out of a trough and hay out of an old seeder box on the planter. She told her husband that Guernie seemed to enjoy the sounds and smells of the fresh outdoors as much as she did. The anxious cow often led Nell out of the stable to her milking site.

But in the barn, thought Nell, "I would not have my back to whoever is back there. I would have seen whoever it is coming. I could have gone out the other door. Just as Nell began the second stanza of "You are my sunshine," she saw the shadow move forward.

But she was ready. She gripped the milk bucket firmly. She turned quickly and had the pail ready to throw when she saw the shadow was her great uncle, Mack. Nell gasped. She swallowed hard. She said "Hello, Mack," as serenely as she could. She took another breath, and added "nice day."

Despite all the rumors and speculation, Nell felt he had never hurt anyone. Yet, his imposing frame and dark, vacant eyes and stone-cold silence alarmed everyone. Mack had not spoken a word to anyone since he came back from World War I in 1918. He seemed oblivious to everyone and everything.

Nell remembered the day Mack went to war and the day he came back. His whole family, including her mother, had been there when he got off the train.

Then, as now, Mack was a big man—over six feet tall with the broad shoulders and the large arm and leg bones that visually identified generations of the Van Meter family around the county.

He looked pretty much the same. He had lost weight, but so had most of the others soldiers who'd come back. The high school band was there to welcome all the survivors, everyone in a festive mood. But Mack did not flash his big grin or let loose with the hearty laugh that he'd left with four years earlier. He did not run up to join his relatives rushing toward him. He just stood there with hollow eyes that seemed to look through and beyond them.

Nell's mother told her how quiet it was when they took him home. They did not take him to the victory celebration. They could not get him to talk. He didn't show any recognition of his baby picture or the one of him graduating from high school. Standing in the back row where they put the tall boys, he was still taller than the rest. A newspaper article describing his going off to war with other valley boys didn't interest him at all. He just let it lay on the table. He stared blankly at it, just as he did the newspapers they put in front of him, trying to interest him in at least reading.

Wherever they led him, he would stand or sit if there was a

chair, without doing or saying anything. His father and brothers even took him to the corn fields and handed him a hoe to see if he would chop out the weeds like they were doing. He just stood there.

When his family built a new home in town, Mack Van Meter was left in his ancestral home which his family had rented to farm tenants. The tenants earned extra money to look after Mack. They tried to get him to break his routine of only coming out of the attic to eat when the bell rang, to go to the bathroom or to take an afternoon walk after lunch.

One caretaker family, who had three sons killed in the same war and another who committed suicide, was the most sympathetic. They quickly proclaimed him to be a victim of shell-shock and taught their kids not to fear him.

Another caretaker family decided he was just lazy. They made it clear that if they would've had the money they sure wouldn't be working six days a week, ten hours a day, for his family who they proclaimed were living in town because the country was not good enough for them. They reckoned Mack was actually the smartest one in the valley because he knew how to get out of hoeing corn.

A healthcare worker, who trained with the WPA after the depression, said Mack could be a victim of what a lot of World War I veterans suffered but nobody talked about, venereal disease. She did not appreciate it when Mack's caretaker joked that in high school all the ladies had chased after Mack and probably French women were no different, that maybe Mack had been caught by loose women in France.

The valley people were fearful of Mack when they saw him taking his daily walks along the valley road. Many were scared of his silence and to many, he became inhuman. Some kids accepted dare's to go up to him. Others taunted him. But Mack paid no attention and never stopped taking his walks—even the day the body of a man that everyone felt had killed his wife and molested his own children was found alongside that very road. He had been strangled by barbed wire from a nearby fence.

The investigating sheriff's older brother, now dead, had also been a survivor of World War I. The sheriff remembered his stories of the pitiful attempts of soldiers trying to protect themselves in their foxholes with barbed wire fences. Soldiers were shot and left to die hanging in the fences. The sheriff had a copy of Robert Service's poem about it called "On the Wire." He wondered about Mack.

As the sheriff and coroner were removing the body from the ditch by the road, Mack walked by. Looking up, the sheriff could have sworn that Mack saluted him but he could not be sure. Mack continued on, not breaking his slow, steady pace. The sheriff, knowing the history of the victim, decided this was a case best left unsolved.

As time went on and more people forgot about the old wars, things got worse for Mack. His health was failing and his walks got shorter. He would often be seen just resting by the road, staring out into the cattle fields, watching them by the hour. According to the teacher who had once taught at the one-room country schoolhouse and was now teaching at the school in town where all the kids were bussed, as soon as the word "pervert" came into the valley vocabulary, Mack was labeled with it. Despite the teacher's best efforts to teach the students about war casualties, Mack was the object of ridicule. Some of the new generations of his own family even started to throw stones. But not Nell. She still remembered her mother's stories.

Mack didn't react when Nell quickly choked back her gasp, smiled and put down the bucket. She instantly knew why he had his hand up. He was pointing into his mouth which was opened wide. Somehow, Mack had known that his niece, Nell, sometimes filled in for her aunt who was a dental assistant in town. Nell looked to where he was pointing and could see that he had tried to pull his own tooth and that it had broken off and was badly infected.

Sensing Nell's relief, Guernie relaxed and resumed eating. Nell pointed to the truck, and she and Mack left for the dentist office. The milking would wait.

After that the skies were a little bluer for Mack. The taunting stopped. He was human after all, they said. He had a toothache.

That night Nell cried before setting out to the barn to put another notch in the beam for her son. Her two-year-old grandson wanted to help. Nell brushed his hair out of his eyes as she lifted him up. He was so carefree now. And his father, her son, was still alive in VietNam. She managed a smile. And began to sing softly, " . . . Please don't take my sunshine away."

Big Dan and Carolina Rose

While Big Dan DuBois and his wife, Carolina Rose, were the first in West Virginia to get their house on the national historic register, they had trouble being accepted socially by the Sons and Daughters of the American Revolution and the Virginia Huguenots. Even, Carolina Rose—without the boisterous Dan - was ignored by the Colonial Dames.

Their problem was temperament. The blue bloods simply could not tolerate bad manners. Yet, Carolina Rose and Big Dan craved their attention.

They had no problem fitting in with most of the locals living around them. Constant squabbling and yelling was not unheard of plus Big Dan and Carolina Rose had lots of money and they didn't mind spending it.

Money, more than manners, is what made them different from the other farmers in the valley. Big Dan's ancestors were the first to claim land in the high Allegheny front, made up of craggy-faced mountain ridges that ran in bread-loaf formations for miles. As long as anybody could remember, the DuBois cattle were herded up there on top of a long, flat ridge for the summer grass; acres and acres as far as the eye could see.

Then, back in the forties, coal was discovered . . . mountains of it, under all that grass. Big Dan sold a huge strip of land to the massive Mount Storm 1,000,000kw power plant. The "whole affair," as Carolina Rose called the huge generating plant with its stacks and smoky plume on top of the main Appalachian ridge, could be seen for miles. It had become a tourist attraction as people drove up to watch Virginia Power Company's huge augur gather up the coal to fire up its boilers and feed its turbines. Each time Big Dan sold a few acres at a higher price he also got the power company to move the fence back to keep his cattle contained. He liked taking pictures of his big, black Angus cattle munching on green grass against the blue sky with the gigantic augur in the background gorging itself on black coal.

Big Dan and Carolina Rose lived several foothills below the mountain chain in the valley leading to the South Branch of the Potomac River, a valley dotted with churches and filled with reverent folks. Nevertheless, Big Dan found a few converts to his weekly poker game. His game was especially popular because he was not a particularly good poker player. Even the Hampshire County sheriff joined the clandestine meetings in the back room of Big Dan's historic house. It had once been a stagecoach stop for those going west and, despite Carolina Rose's objections, he insisted that he was only reliving history in the old house. He had found an 18th century circular chip dispenser in the basement and, as Carolina Rose always shouted out, he taught himself how to play.

Carolina Rose was hard of hearing. Big Dan, who had gotten used to shouting at her, didn't take the time to realize that other people could hear so both of them just settled down into railing at everyone. His poker games could be heard by the churchgoers driving by. But with the sheriff as a regular player, Big Dan had no problems with illegal gambling. For that matter, the sheriff was also very broad-minded about liquor. West Virginia might be a dry state but Maryland and Virginia, next door, were not. The sheriff often confiscated crates of it at the border from those who eschewed the local shine. He knew Big Dan had acquired a hearty taste for "Virginia Gentleman" bourbon, resulting in Carolina Rose loudly proclaiming he was not even a West Virginia gentleman.

The sheriff was useful in other ways, too. Carolina Rose, as well as Big Dan, liked cruising around the county in their big Buick. They got a new one each year. The dealer always mimicked the loud arguments they would have in the show room as to what color they wanted. Horsepower, however, was something Dan didn't consult Carolina Rose about. Once a dashing Steerman bi-plane pilot, he loved storming up and down the valley. When he hit a power line, he survived but the airplane didn't—but Big Dan still liked going as fast and straight as he could.

Carolina Rose always said the road banks used to be higher around the county before Big Dan plowed into them. People had learned to get off to the side of the road to try to avoid him when they saw him coming. But, as the sheriff liked to say, Big Dan was good for business so he made sure Big Dan always kept his license. There was just one car dealer, but the sheriff credited Dan with helping to support two garage repair businesses in town. He always paid for damages, even if he went through a broken-down rail fence.

When a car wash came to town, it didn't take Dan long to

pay a hefty bill there. Not being familiar with driving onto and staying locked on the steel rails which carried a car through the cleaning process, Big Dan revved up the engine when Carolina Rose screamed. The big 420hp engine had taken the rails with it when he bolted out of the car wash. Carolina Rose, whose window had been completely down, was soaked and soaped. Their tongue lashing lasted for days as they argued as to whose fault it had been: was it hers for not putting her window up and yelling like hell which he said caused him to rev the engine, or his fault for not realizing how drive-in car washes worked.

Whatever the reason, such incidents served to amuse—and endear—Big Dan and Carolina Rose to the locals. But not the blue bloods.

When it became obvious this rambunctious couple had worn out their welcome with their bickering at the county and state chapters of the heritage groups, the pair decided to attend a national meeting of the Huguenots. The "frogs" are considered the "creme de-crop," Dan told the Sons and Daughters of the American Revolution, who only had to be in this country during that war, while the Huguenots had to trace their ancestry to a 17th century settlement in America.

The Huguenots, who first settled in New Paltz, NY in the early 1600s could easily track their ancestry before the French Revolution and, some of them, like Big Dan, a direct descendant of DuBois, could go back to Charlemagne.

So when Marci Kuykendall, a niece of their first cousin, was working in upstate New York, got a call they were coming for a reunion of DuBois ancestors and were even going to bring her mother and two other relatives who also were eligible for membership, Marci was delighted.

This was the third time she had been tapped as their New York escort and it always proved to be an adventure. "Of sorts," her mother would add, always the first to be embarrassed when Big Dan and Carolina Rose made a "scene."

Marci remembered the first time she hosted the group to New York back in the late 60s. Yul Brenner was playing in "The King and I." It was Big Dan and Carolina Rose's 25th anniversary. They wanted to come back to what Dan called "the scene of the crime" which was their wedding in the Little Church around the Corner in lower Manhattan. The wedding gala had been paid for by the sale of the first fifty acres of the Allegheny front land to build the coal-burning power plant.

While making plans for this first trip in the 60s, Carolina had burst loudly into the phone conversation Marci was having with Big Dan to say they also wanted to buy the most expensive meal they had in New York City for everyone, including Marci. Big Dan, not one to just agree, had added that included drinks, too. He had not had a Manhattan since right before he got married up there and, by God, he might as well have some more as it didn't matter if he was hit by lightning twice as he was already damaged goods. This, as usual, led to a verbal battle between them until Marci could get back in the conversation to tell them she would meet them at the train station after she made sure the reservations at the Biltmore for all of them were confirmed. The check had already been sent and Marci agreed to Dan's request, "Don't let yer mother know," or she will "get it in her head" that she and the others should stay at a cheaper place. He also wanted everyone's rooms beside each other on the same floor.

When Marci commented that they might want some quality time for themselves since it was their 25th, Big Dan roared that that was what he was aiming for. He had "done 25 years of time with the Rose and it didn't qualify for much." Carolina Rose, a former teacher, yelled back into the phone: "make sure Dan has the best view possible of Yul Brenner. He could learn a lot from how the King became a real king."

As it turned out, Yul Brenner seemed to enjoy Big Dan as much as Big Dan enjoyed him. Marci, who had seen the play a month before, could have sworn that Yul had put on a much better performance as the rambunctious, single-minded king because Dan frequently roared out his approval. Anna seemed more amused than appreciative of the equally loud support she got from Carolina Rose.

Marci noticed her mother sat on the end, trying to appear as if she was not part of the group. The others, while enjoying the play, spent much time casting apologetic looks to the rest of the audience and shushing their hosts.

Big Dan was even able to make an impression on the noisy Times Square streets. When he spotted the marquee for The Best Little Whorehouse in Texas he declared, "See they advertise it up here . . . all the way from Texas, too."

The most expensive meal in the city turned out to average $125 each by the time Big Dan got through ordering a couple of Manhattans. Marci had calmed her mother before they went by telling her that she had made reservations at 6 p.m. at the Rainbow

Room. Dinner time to city people was 8 p.m. so they would probably have the place to themselves. She had also informed the head waiter that an unusual group would be showing up for an early dinner and, while a couple of them may be loud and boisterous as a result of poor hearing and manners, it would behoove the waiters to be considerate as the two loud ones also owned a coal mine and were known to be heavy tippers.

To Big Dan's delight, the menu was in French and he insisted on ordering for everyone. He had been in France during World War II. Carolina Rose, used to his pronunciations and dialect, helped the waiter by pointing to whatever he was ordering. Because the dining room was nearly empty, save one couple who left shortly after their arrival, the group soon had the undivided attention of the entire waiting staff. Even the chef came out to assure himself the meals were being enjoyed.

Marci, fearing that maybe she had overdone it with her description of the group, was relieved that the staff was clearly enjoying the event. She could detect no signs of condescension; only obvious interest in the culture of West Virginia and its coal mines. The service was superb. Even when Carolina Rose's meal—a delicate fish stew in a hollowed-out half of a cantaloupe arrived - there had been a slight uproar. Big Dan announced it was just like Carolina Rose to go for a $100 melon, getting a quick and loud rebuttal from Carolina Rose that she was not the one who ordered it.

It was then the chef invited Big Dan and Carolina Rose to tour his kitchen to sample the ingredients. Marci's mother quietly gave thanks to the chef for taking off with their hosts, giving the rest of them time to quietly enjoy the meal and view of the city.

Dan had been very generous with his tips, doubling the city's normal fifteen percent because of the kitchen tour plus the mango he had picked up on the way through. The chef had assured him it was edible.

Big Dan wanted everyone to take the subway back to the hotel. But he was voted down because of fear of riding it at night. Since they were going to the Little Church around the Corner the next morning, Marci suggested they wait and take it then. When Sunday morning came, Marci realized she should have been more familiar with the city herself. She knew the newspapers were crying foul when President Ford had declined coming to the aid of the city in its budget crises. One headline read, "Ford to City: Drop Dead."

What Marci failed to realize was the subways were not being cleaned up to save money and, even worse, the crew that used to take the Saturday night drunks and addicts off the train and put them in shelters had also been laid off.

When they got on the subway they had to step over several drunks lying on the floor. Marci's mother and the others demanded to get off at the very next stop and take a cab. But before they could do this, Carolina Rose, who had been watching one of the bums who was motionless and half-covered by a newspaper, was bending over to adjust his eyeglasses which were sliding off his face. Marci's mother pulled her away, telling her he could be dangerous while Big Dan suggested Carolina Rose give him her hearing aid since it didn't seem to do her any good.

When they finally made it to the Little Church around the Corner, Big Dan got so carried away with the sight of it squeezed between all those Wall Street skyscrapers, he kissed Carolina Rose and told her that they should get married again, that being struck by lightning twice might be just the thing he needed.

So when Marci got a call ten years later to be the host for the second time in New York, she was elated. This time it was for the reunion of the DuBois ancestors in historic New Paltz, not in the city. Marci's brother, Mike, who drove a tractor-trailer for a living because the family farm equipment had to be sold to pay taxes, was going to drive them.

Big Dan, older and wiser about new-fangled things like car washes and leery of city beltways which had him "going in circles," put Marci's brother "on commission" to drive his latest new Buick for five of them, including her mother. Mike, knowing the commission would certainly be worth more than even Teamster pay, would probably have said yes just for the fun of it. He always liked teasing Big Dan and Big Dan was always ready for the bait.

When Marci met them in New Paltz, she could tell by her mother's expression it had been an exhausting trip for her. Big Dan, she whispered, is even worse as a back seat driver. But Mike had given as good as he got. There were lots of twists and turns through the Pocono Mountains and the Catskills so Big Dan ordered everyone to buckle up and hold on because Mike was used to getting heavy freight there on time. When they got off the Pennsylvania's I-80 and headed up Rt. 209 into New York State, Mike told him they were now going onto what the truckers called the "Ho Chi Minh" trail. Naturally, Big Dan saw many Viet Cong enemies lurking along the road which he had to loudly announce to Carolina Rose.

Because they had not been to New Paltz before, they were urged to take the public tour of all the old Huguenot homes of the early patentees who, during the French Revolution fled the persecution of Protestants by Louis XIV, currying Catholic favor. The tour went well as the guides were used to tourists with bad as well as good manners.

It was when the closed reunion at the DuBois home was held that eyebrows were raised. There had been questioning glances when Big Dan heartily approved of the fact the original DuBois home had been more than a fort to protect the settlers. The big stone house, with its original portholes still visible, had also served as a tavern. Marci's mother was the first to cringe when Big Dan nudged Carolina Rose, declaring that his poker games and drinking was something that had been inherited.

However, when the president of the DuBois Family Association began reading from the Orange County History and Genealogy book about the capture of Catherine DuBois in 1660, Big Dan made a comment that clearly separated him from the rest of the reverent ancestors.

It was right after the Indians were about to burn, torture and kill Catherine and her friends. Big Dan, along with all the others, had been totally absorbed as the association director read how the Indians had been gathering wood and piling it in heaps equal to the number of prisoners while other Indians were sharpening stakes. "This band of Christian women," he declared, "bowed their heads and prayed to the Giver of All Good, that He would, in His infinite mercy, either restore them to their homes or impart strength for the terrible ordeal they beheld awaiting them." In a very solemn voice, he read on: "Then their pent-up feelings broke forth in song; and with swelling hearts, yet with voices unbroken, those captives led by Catherine, sang Marot's beautiful French hymn with great emotion." The director then concluded the reading by reverently declaring: "This was the first Christian song heard on the banks of the Shawangunk Kill. The savages were so charmed with the music they did not execute Catherine and her friends."

Perhaps it was the president's abrupt summary from his solemn presentation but whatever it was, Big Dan, said, "Bullshit, no Indian would give a damn about a Christian song." Even these well-established blue bloods could not maintain their decorum as they stared him down. Big Dan didn't smooth things over by adding that Carolina Rose certainly didn't charm anyone at home with her singing ability, but he allowed as to how the Indians would have had their hands full trying to keep her quiet.

Still, Big Dan and Carolina Rose could not be denied their heritage and a contribution to restoring the bar in the old inn was accepted by the committee.

The third visit by the group to New York came only two years later, with Marci's brother still in tow as Big Dan's chauffeur. It was to Albany's new downtown performing arts center built by Governor Nelson Rockefeller. Big Dan and Carolina Rose had met the dancer from New York who had bought the old Kuykendall home which had been abandoned along the river. They had read a review in the Baltimore Sun that the dance troupe performances were risqué and not suitable for youth, even when accompanied by their parents.

This, of course, had piqued Big Dan's interest, so Marci had gotten her third call. Since she lived near Albany, it would not "put her out" and it would be a good trip for her mother, too. Marci, who for years had been friendly with the new owners of the old house, Jeremiah and his poet friend, Jonah, did not mince words when she asked them for seven front row seats in the Egg Theater. "You've met Big Dan and Carolina Rose," is all she had to say.

Jeremiah and Jonah were delighted. This was a chance to introduce the two to interpretative dancing. The louder they were the better. Both of them had grown to dislike polite and emotionally-restrained audiences. They told Big Dan the dance, called "Birth." was about "beginnings," and that the rest was in the eyes of the viewer. The curtains opened with all of the dancers prostrate and curled up on the stage floor. One after the other they rose to flute music, and as Big Dan, intent on showing some culture, said they sure knew how to make different shapes with all that leaping and collapsing when they went apart and came together and went apart again. Both he and Carolina Rose had clapped loud and long at each "formation."

When asked later what his interpretation of the whole thing was, Big Dan didn't miss a beat. "I always wondered how those seeds got out of their shells and turned into plants," he declared with artistic fervor. Jeremiah and Jonah were thrilled. They renamed their dance, "Dan's Garden."

Marci's mother and the others were at a loss for words. They were still aghast at watching all the dancers, who had performed in skin-color leotards, with barely concealed private parts. Big Dan had not missed that either. He had nudged Marci's brother, telling him those dancers had more muscles than truck drivers.

On the way home from Albany, Big Dan wanted to stop at New Paltz. "Wait until I tell those Huguenots," he roared, "that those famous New York dancers named a garden after me."

Kline and Bill

The hollows and hillsides of the Potomac River valley were at one time populated with several hundred people who worked their small patches. To supplement their meager incomes, they hired themselves out to farmers in the fertile flats who became overwhelmed with fields of corn, wheat, barley and oats. The Industrial Age and big Agri-business changed everything. Only a handful of people lived in the mountains and the family farms were disappearing in the valley.

Bill Kuykendall, a still struggling farmer, lamenting the loss of available labor, noted that about the only people left on the hillsides and hollows were those who didn't want to work or only worked long enough to get by.

However, one of these 'who worked long enough to get by' turned out to be Bill's best worker. His name was Kline. Kline was not only the strongest person Bill had ever seen in all his years but he was also capable of operating equipment. Bill's problem was keeping him sober. Kline's idea of "getting by" was buying whiskey as soon as he was paid on Saturday night and spending it all at the Moose Club bar until he ran out of money.

When Kline was sober, he was an amazing field hand. He could lift two 70-pound bales, one in each hand, and have a wagon loaded faster than Bill had ever done, even in his youth.

When grain was being threshed, it was Kline who was assigned to constantly feed the thresher sheaves of wheat brought in from the fields. Those driving the wagons would get little rest because just as soon as they could get lined up to be unloaded, Kline was ready for them. Those in the field knew Kline was on the job when the wagons quickly returned. Kline was like the machine he was feeding. The man simply needed no rest. He reveled in his strength and endurance. He never wore a hat or shirt because it felt good getting a tan and, besides, the ladies liked it. He took delight in telling Bill to buy faster machines.

It was the same routine when they were filling the silo. Kline became the point man unloading the wagons of corn. Sometimes the corn cutter, operated by a running belt from the power-takeoff on Bill's big John Deere tractor, would not be able to keep up with Kline. Too much corn would choke the machine, sometimes shutting it down. But it would not be a purposeful act by Kline. He would immediately jump down from the loaded wagon and pull out the corn stalks jamming the cutter. He would curse the machine.

Bill Kuykendall's laugh could be heard above the sounds of the equipment when Kline challenged the tractor, thresher and cutter to keep up with him.

Bill not only admired Kline but also enjoyed working with him. During Bill's prime years, there was no one Bill couldn't outwork. Unlike Kline, who was short and stocky, Bill was tall and slender. But both carried plenty of muscle under their work overalls. Bill had ceded his endurance to Kline and Kline knew it. He also knew that Bill would never ask a man to do something he would not do himself. Kline knew there were many people, including his brothers who had left to get factory and office jobs, who now declared Bill must be as crazy as he was. "Why didn't Bill sell out to commercial developers and take life easy?" they would ask.

But Kline would merely laugh as hard at them as Bill did when Kline accepted his challenges to outdo his equipment. "You'll wake up, one day," he would say, "and smell the land. Then you'll know."

When threshing season came and the few valley farmers left went together to rent a costly threshing machine to harvest their wheat and barley, sharing the work and the cost of the machine time, Bill would insist to the other farmers that Kline would be the best man to replace him in pitching the shocks into the thresher because he was so fast and would save all of them money. This was a feat other farmers had always asked Bill to perform for them because he was the best among them. Yet, even though Kline fed the thresher for Bill, Bill continued to do that job for the other farmers who refused to hire Kline because of his scandalous weekend behavior.

During this time off, Kline would go hunting or fishing to make a little money for his Saturday nights at the Moose Club. He was known to amuse himself picking up black racer snakes which sometimes grew up to six feet in length, wrapping them around himself or using them as a whiplash as if he were driving a team or horses. But it was the rattlesnakes that he most enjoyed, using the rattles to get the attention of the Moose Club ladies.

When farm work resumed, Kline would entertain Bill with his stories of battling the big rattlers in the woods and along the river while asking Bill about his speed in feeding a threshing machine that looked like a dragon and was called a dragon by Kline. "You know, Bill," he would say, "the way to get that beast to choke up and quit blowing straw out of its metal snout is simple. You've got to pitch at least three shocks into its mouth at the same time as quick as you can to get it to go belly up. That's how you tame it." Then he would ask, "Can you do that?"

Bill would laugh and say "No, but are you sure you don't do that just so you can rest while it is being un-jammed. I don't need the rest . . . maybe you do." Their banter would continue throughout the day.

Few could understand Bill working himself to death to keep his small farm anymore than they could understand Kline's rationale for spending everything he made on booze as soon as he got paid.

Everyone knew that when Saturday night came and the pay was handed out, Bill would wait until the next day for a call from the sheriff detailing his farmhand's condition. The sheriff would tell him how long he thought it would be before Kline would be sober enough for work. Bill was always hopeful he could bail him out on Sunday night and have him for a whole day on Monday. But usually it was well into Monday before the sheriff deemed him fit for release.

Bill would take the bail money out of Kline's pay which cost him over a day's work. But that did not deter Kline. He regaled the entire work crew with his drinking exploits, particularly the women he met in the club. They often ended up in jail with him for disturbing the peace.

Some would question if dealing with such a drunk no matter how hard he worked was really worth it and wondered how the two of them could get along since Bill spent much of his Sunday in church while Kline was in jail.

But they had never seen Bill and Kline set off in the morning before sunrise knowing just what kind of day it was going to be because they finished work in the dark the night before and had studied the skies. Even if there were no stars to be seen or a ring around the moon, they would look forward to a change of pace. Sure it was nice to know clear night skies would bring a cloudless bright morning sun promising a hot day for making hay. But a cloudy, dark night often meant they could look forward to a rainy day which not only uncurled and refreshed the parched corn but it was nice to feel the cool rain wash off a sweat they could still work up hoeing the corn.

When Bill was criticized at church for hiring the scandalous drunk, he made no excuses or attempts to explain, he merely challenged his critics to match a work effort by Kline. Kline, of course, loved this attention and Bill, being honest with himself, had come to vicariously enjoy Kline's strength and ability to enjoy life to the fullest extent.

Even when Kline turned over the tractor by going too fast off a mountain road by kicking it out of gear to speed it up, Bill forgave him. Kline was the first to say "take the cost of the repairs out of my pay, it was a helluva ride!" He came up out of the cloud of dust with the steering wheel in his hand, whirling it around like a pistol. He was also the one that grabbed a log along the road to pry the tractor upright again.

This time it was Tuesday morning before Bill could retrieve him from the sheriff. Bill did notice some bruises had appeared but Kline said it was nothing. He was now identifying himself as John Deere, garnering even more attention from the Moose Club ladies.

Only once did Kline ever bring booze on the job and that was to run a test on his boss. He knew Bill was a total teetotaler so he would have to pick the right time to trick him into drinking it. He picked a very hot day when they were making hay and it was then he managed to pour a whole bottle of vodka in the water jug, drinking enough himself to make room for it. Kline knew that when Bill did take a drink, he usually emptied the jug.

When the sweat was pouring off Bill and he finally took the time to refresh himself, Kline was ecstatic. But Bill was on to him, knowing that Kline had too often been staring at the water jug and yet not going to it. So he upturned the jug as he usually did but this time he let the water flow down his neck which was usually dripping with sweat. Kline did not notice this.

For the next few hours, Kline carefully watched Bill with growing admiration. He was beside himself with awe of someone who could drink that much and show no signs of unsteadiness or even slacking off.

When they had a couple of hours of work left, Bill sent his daughter after more water, chastising her for not going to the house to get the water the last time. "That stuff from the creek was sour from all the leaves in it," he said. Looking at Kline, he added, "and bad water is not good for you."

Still Kline did not know Bill had been on to him and just stared at him in awe.

So when word went around the Moose Club now that Bill Kuykendall could handle liquor better than anybody Kline knew, Bill decided to let the truth stay hidden. It was a harmless white lie and besides, he liked having the reputation of being best at something now that he had to relinquish to Kline his reputation of "being able to outwork any man."

Like Kline, he could smell the land, and he had his own reward.

Equal Opportunity

When Bill Kuykendall recognized the black worker in the stock sale pit with a familiar nod and what seemed to be a grateful gaze, the buyers and sellers looked at Bill questioningly.

It was 1961 and while there were protests being led by a preacher named Martin Luther King in the deep South, it had not changed anything here in the patchwork farms along the foothills of the Appalachians in West Virginia. Every Wednesday farmers would come from miles around to sell their calves, cattle, hogs and sheep. They would come in their own three quarter-ton to three-ton trucks with home-built racks to carry as many as 12 animals or they would rent professional cattle trucks from the stock sale which could carry about 30 steers.

Bill owned a medium size farm in the South Branch valley of the Potomac River where he was able to raise some 200 cattle and about 300 hogs each year. He could be seen at the sale every Wednesday, sometimes buying lean cattle to fatten, but mostly selling what he had raised or fattened. He owned a new three-ton truck and had pushed the limit up to 15 steers, certainly overloaded but of little concern to the sheriff since Bill traveled on an old country road that still had not been paved. Besides, the sheriff had been born on one of the small hillside farms that lined the narrow dry hollow road and knew Bill.

Bill could have taken the paved road on the other side of the mountain to get to the sale which would have been easier. But he had business along that nine mile long dirt road. His first stop was at Widow Smith's. Her husband had been killed in the war. She now eked out a living by raising chickens and pasturing several milk cows and goats. When Bill picked up the eggs, milk and butter she had for sale he was rewarded with a custard cream pie His next stop would be at the old Spurling place where he would be met by an old couple who scoured the area for walnuts, butternuts and hickory nuts. While they cracked most of these out and sold them by the pound, they did sell unshelled nuts by the bushel, too. But as soon as that buyer spent hours cracking them out, they were soon back to buying them as kernels marveling at how they were able to get them out as halves instead of bits and pieces. Bill's reward for the pickup was a nine-inch pan of chocolate fudge laced with hickory nuts. He also had bags of fudge for sale.

Further up the road was another war widow who had a small cherry and apple orchard and several large Hampshire sows. As an ardent follower of market prices, Bill would advise her what weeks would be best for selling the pigs so he would know to bring along a crate for them. And, of course, there was always room in the truck cab for the cherry or apple pies, one of which had his name on it.

On the way home, Bill would stop by with the money their goods had earned at the restaurant counter or from auctions made while new herds were being run in and out of the auction pit. Sometimes Bill would buy things they needed like sugar or chocolate which he knew was cheaper than what they could get from the store in town. This would be carefully deducted from their proceeds.

Many of the larger cattle sellers at the stock market were amused by Bill who seemed to be everywhere all at once. While they had to admit he came to the sale with some of the best looking Hereford cattle they had ever seen, it was the host of people who met him when he drove in to unload his truck that amused them. Over the years, Bill had become known for bringing some of the best goodies ever made to the market so there were many people who wanted to see what he had brought this Wednesday before it went up for sale. If the price they offered was right, they succeeded.

So when Bill was giving a nod to the black hired hand herding another batch of cattle into the arena below, the buyers and sellers wondered what the connection was in this case. There were lots of black hands working the yards at the stock sale hauling the manure out and spreading fresh straw in the holding pens. In fact, they lived in shacks behind the stockyard and occasionally you would see their kids toting straw bales or cleaning out the water troughs. They had seen Bill talking to this one many times during the unloading hours so mostly they chalked it up to his eccentricity. But this public display of familiarity was something that just wasn't done.

What they didn't know was that the black pit worker, whose name was Dick and Bill were what they both laughingly called each other, "silent business partners." Dick was just as good as Bill at spotting healthy, well-bred cattle. So when Bill was buying lean cattle to fatten he would get a nod from Dick in the arena that he was bringing in a good lot. These would not be cattle that had been purged from huge herds and put on pasture because they were not gaining weight and were probably ill. The lean ones Bill wanted were those raised by hillside farmers who were selling them from their small herds because they didn't have enough land to raise corn crops for silage. These lean heifers were well-behaved and one could tell some had even been pets because a child in the back of the auction might be sobbing out its name.

But in this case, it was Bill nodding to Dick that he wanted him to bring in his fat cattle for sale next. They had given each other a glancing look at the past three lots of cattle that had been in the arena. They had been a mixture of half-breeds of various shapes and sizes. Bill had noticed the big buyers from Armour and Swift had been getting exasperated as they didn't like to hang around the sale anymore than they had to. They were restless because they knew the steers they had just seen would not pass for the meat they were sent to buy for hotel steaks. Their company had inspectors and they paid their buyers to be discerning in what they bought.

So when Dick opened the gate for the new lot to come in, the timing was right. With Dick's deft directions and a partially opened gate, Bill's 15 evenly matched Hereford steers came in one after the other like models on a runway. With the added help of Dick, they circled the arena showing off their straight backs and meaty limbs. The Armour and Swift buyers took note and started bidding. By the time they were finished, Bill had gotten an amazing nine cents more per pound than any cattle sold that day.

After the sale, when Dick was helping Bill load up the lean cattle he had bought, Bill gave him two crates of sweet corn, a bushel of tomatoes and potatoes, a side of salted pork and told him he could expect a half of a beef after butchering time. Dick shook his head and said, "Too Much." But Bill showed him his notepad where he kept an accounting of his business transactions. "When I bought a load of Herefords in last week, I know what they weighed on my scales at home. You were able to add an average of three pounds more on each by watering them down. They were not only heavier but their red and white hides were spotless, making them even more appetizing to those Armour and Swift buyers." Bill went on to note that they both knew that the thick hides of cattle can carry a lot of water and he knew that it took some quick maneuvering and timing for Dick to be to do that right before the cattle hit the scales coming into the auction. "So Dick, you earned it. I got the best price I ever got over the best market price. Now tell me what you could use from the farm next week and we'll do it again."

Rattler

When she was twelve, Annie shot her best friend's dog, Rattler. She rode her brother's bike right up to Bob's house, got off the bike, and yelled, "Here Rattler! Here Rattler!" Just as it had done many times before, Rattler jumped off its cushion on the front porch and ran toward her, wagging its tail happily. Bob said Rattler was only about ten feet from her when she dropped the dog with one shot from her brother's 22-rifle. Bob's parents, who were sitting in the porch swing and saw the whole thing, were stunned.

They had done everything they could to help Annie, who was the youngest of ten children. Life was particularly hard for Annie and her sisters and brothers because their parents were tenants on a nearby farm, nd they simply could not earn enough to put food on the table for the kids, much less look after them. Worse, Annie's father was not reliable and had a drinking problem. When he did find work, the job never lasted long. Even when Bob's parents sent food back with Annie for her family, they seldom got a thank you. Why if it had not been for them, Annie wouldn't even be in school. They had quietly reported the family to the truant officer who had forced Annie's father to send her to school. Annie and their son, Bob, were the same age. They had become the best of friends. Annie had even stayed over at their house many times. For Annie to do something like shooting the little beagle that everyone loved was simply unheard of. They were dumbfounded. This kind of behavior was not normal, especially for little girls.

Annie was sent to a reform school for girls for a year. She was released simply because she had not done anything wrong since she was there. If questioned, all she would say was that she was minding her own business and would give them no trouble.

When she came back home, everything was different for Annie. The kids her age were no longer friendly. She was put into the seventh grade in their one-room school. Bob was now a grade ahead of her. Everyone was avoiding her. Occasionally she would feel Bob's stare. At times, she saw pity, which made her flinch. The others simply looked at her with curiosity but they didn't approach her. When the softball teams were being picked with each captain taking turns naming the person they wanted until a team was full, her name was never mentioned. They simply played around her, letting her stand in the ball field. Even the teacher didn't ask her for answers in class. She just handed Annie her assignments and silently picked up her homework the next day. It was like Annie had never existed, didn't exist now. So she kept to herself, pushed away memories of when she had been one of the most popular kids in school, and concentrated on growing up so she could move away.

But they talked about her behind her back and she could feel it. She would turn around and see the fingers pointed at her. She had given up trying to explain why she did it. But that didn't keep them from trying to figure it out.

They would talk about when they first knew her, how she and Bob did everything together. They road their bikes to school together. They shared the double seat in the two-room school together for six years. They used to pull up the ventilator grill under their seat and drop down into the half-basement where they would crawl out and laugh when the other kids came out at recess. Often they were the team captains taking turns naming who they wanted on their team.

After school and on weekends they were inseparable. Everyone had enjoyed the joke on them when the two had gone hunting for the first time and a half hour later rushed home to show their first kill. But it was not a turkey. It was a buzzard. They admitted they did not notice it was circling when they shot it out of the sky. Bob's father gave them credit for shooting a buzzard out of the sky as that was actually more difficult than killing a slower moving turkey on the ground or a few feet above it trying to get away.

Then there was the time the county had put a bounty on foxes to prevent the spread of rabies. Everyone was amazed that they were paying $5 for every fox brought in, a sum that was equal to many a hired hand's daily wage. Annie and Bob were among the first to show up with two foxes. They were baby foxes and it had taken the whole weekend for them to dig the kits up out of their dens. The county officials had not been amused. They did not want to pay for baby foxes. But when Bob's dad pointed out they had not been specific in the announcement they had to give Annie and Bob the reward.

No one really knew when the feud between Annie and Bob started. The teacher felt that it was just puberty showing; she had seen it before. Boys and girls would realize their differences in the sixth grade. While Bob could quickly find others boys to befriend, Annie, because of her tomboy ways, had more difficulty. She did not invite people to her home, knowing they wouldn't come anyway because their parents were talking about two of her older brothers who were in trouble with the law for having stolen a car and one of her older sisters was pregnant and no one knew who the father was.

Maybe it started when Annie decided to create a rock garden with wildflowers along the side of the road by their house. It was drawing attention and the admiration of those driving by, some of whom stopped and asked Annie if she could find some wildflowers for them to plant. One day Bob and his new friend rode by on their bikes and decided to pick Annie a bouquet of all the lady slippers which were in full bloom. They left them at the door with a note "for Cinderella." Annie had been furious, knowing the slippers might not come up the next year because they had not been allowed to seed. She waited for revenge and got it when his dad was filling the silo while Bob and his friend were in it. They were leading the pipe around to scatter the ensilage which was blown up from the cutter through the pipes, continuing down into the silo.

Annie knew their hens often laid eggs under the hen house instead of in it and if not found in time, they would become rotten. She walked up to the cutter when the men were throwing corn into it and dropped her bundle of eggs into it. Soon there were shrieks from the boys as they raced out of the silo pinching their noses and spitting, hoping to rid themselves of the smell. Annie had disappeared but when they arrived at school that Monday, they found the note she had left on the double desk Bob now shared with his new friend. It read, "Hope you liked your scrambled eggs."

It was not long after that people saw that the rock garden by Annie's house was completely destroyed.

Things began to escalate. Bob found the remains of a skunk in his lunch pail. The tires on Annie's bike were punctured so badly she couldn't patch them up enough to ride it anymore. Now she had to walk to school. The teacher made each sit on the opposite end of the classroom. Both were banned from playing ball as it became a weapon in their hands. The other kids took sides with most of the tenant kids siding with Annie and the farmers' kids, siding with Bob. "I didn't want this kind of class warfare," moaned the teacher, trying to keep things under control.

Then life changed drastically for Annie. She went one retaliation too far. Everyone knew she had about 20 cats she cared for on the farm where her father worked. With the feud now into its second month, she had begun spending all of her spare time with the cats at the barn. They were good mousers and perhaps this is what led her father to decide he needed to eliminate some of them. The mouse population was way down and there was no extra money to feed the cats. Unbeknownst to Annie, he had asked Bob's dad if his son would come down and get rid of the cats. Bob not only shot all 20 of them but he tied them together and dragged them behind his bike as he went by Annie walking to school.

A few hours later, everyone would be questioning the sanity of Annie as she dropped Rattler in his tracks.

Life had changed drastically for Annie from that moment on. No one understood the difference between 20 cats and one beagle. No one spoke to her. She spent the seventh grade by herself in silence. She did not return for the eighth grade.

Rumor had it that she was in Baltimore. She sent a gift to her sister's bastard child. Bob and the other valley kids grew up and had kids of their own.

When they had a 25th reunion of their grade school, the conversation did turn to Annie with everyone wondering what had become of her. "She was hard as nails. You can be sure she is giving it harder than she is getting it." After awhile their talk ran to admiration. Life in the valley had not only become hard for small farmers, but it was also dull. All of them were struggling just to eke out a living. They wished they were as tough as Annie.

When Annie drove up in a fancy sports car, they couldn't believe it. She looked great. She even had a big dog with her, a rottweiler. But there was a huge scar across her face; it looked like she had been sliced by a knife. They had to know. "I'll bet he's got a bigger scar than you have. Is he still alive. How are you?"

Annie looked at the older but same friendly faces she had known up to sixth grade. Bob even said, "Welcome back." Annie was only confused for a moment. She was not going to tell them that at 15 she had to sell her body to feed herself, that she had been raped and left for dead after being knifed by the john when she didn't turn over all the money. She now ran her own escort service and hated every moment of it even though it was profitable.

Annie looked at the friendly faces she thought she would never see again and simply said, "I'm coming home. The guy that did this to me is no longer alive, thanks to some help from my friend here." She petted her dog. One day she might even tell them his name was Rattler.

Sarah

She had been old so long most people had forgotten her last name. Everyone knew of Old Sarah, but, if questioned closely, they would realize they did not know her.

Sarah wanted it that way. She had kept to herself ever since her five sons and one daughter left her, either off to war or just off. She raised them by herself after the Depression. Her husband just disappeared during those hard times, saying he would find work somewhere and send money. She never heard from him.

She and her five sons and daughter practically lived on mashed potatoes and gravy, much of which was given to her by the valley farmers and their tenants who were having their own financial problems. Sarah was able to supplement their diet with greens she collected around the farmer's fences. She served them fresh in the summer and canned during the winters.

Sarah was proud. She did not want to answer questions about her sons, daughter or her husband. The only close friend she had was Bill Kuykendall, and he didn't ask questions. She could hold her head high with him. Ever since she cured a cattle ailment that stumped the local veterinarian, Bill came to her for her mixtures of herbs, weeds, flowers, ground-up seeds, shells and even horns from his own cattle. Her round oak table was loaded with vials of her potions. She even took some herself if she felt she had the same symptoms of the animals she cured. Bill's best compliment to her was when he sat down to share a cup of her special alfalfa and dandelion head tea.

Bill never asked about her sons or daughter because she told him not to. The daughter had been sent to a reform school for killing a dog. When she got out she left and was believed to be in Baltimore. Bill knew that two of the sons had died in World War II. Old Sarah had gotten a check from the government for both of them but not the one still missing in action.

The last time Bill saw the other two sons, he knew they

were heading for trouble. One was just 16 when he stole a car. The police tracked him down at Bill's farm. He was helping Bill bale hay. When he saw them coming through the field, he ran. Bill was furious when the state trooper shot him in the leg. Yes, the trooper had yelled, "Halt or I'll shoot." But he kept running. Bill had told the young trooper there was no place for him to run to and that he, Bill, would turn him in after they had finished loading the wagon. But the trooper still shot Sarah's oldest. When he got out of the hospital and jail, he disappeared.

The middle brother was caught robbing a grocery store. Bill knew that it wasn't just the money he needed. He had taken a lot of groceries, too. He remembered when Sarah threw him out with the money and the groceries.

Sarah had been alone for nearly 30 years now. Bill thought that maybe she had even forgotten them or had quit hoping that one day they would show up to make amends. He had asked the police to let him know if they ever heard anything and maybe once a year he would check back with them. Sarah put stones in the graveyard for the two who died in the war and the one missing in action and never found. But he noticed that she never visited the graveyard even though it was near several hickory trees where she gathered the nuts each fall. She even used the hulls, grinding them up for an elixir she mixed up for foot and mouth disease in cattle.

The only person she ever invited in her house was Bill. Whenever people saw her gathering her ingredients, they might wave when they saw her in the woods or in pasture fields and along the river. If the basket was filled and she was on her way home, she might return the greeting. Otherwise, she was too busy combing the area for new growth or finds.

If people wondered how she could survive, those living nearby would point out she chopped her own firewood, adding that she was still probably eating potatoes and gravy and canned greens like she had during the Depression years.

Because Sarah's children had been so physically strong, the only amazement that might be expressed by the older people, who still remembered them in the valley, was a look at their own children who had been fed better, but yet did not possess such strength and endurance. "Maybe there was something in all those weeds she gathers up," they would joke to Bill, who seldom hired the local veterinarian that they did. He swore by Old Sarah's cures and would point out that his hogs and cattle were doing quite well, a fact that would end the conversation because it was true. When Bill walked into the auction, the buyers from Armour and Swift immediately took their seats in the arena.

Otherwise, Sarah was hardly noticed in the valley, her presence hunched over with her old burlap sack going up and down the fields and woods had just become part of the landscape.

However, the year electricity came through as a result of the Rural Electrification Act, things changed. Everyone had heard about television. Many had seen the sets at big stores in towns near them. Some even had relatives in those towns with electricity. Visits to those town relatives became more frequent when their country cousins spotted the antennas on their houses.

But when they saw a Montgomery Ward truck going into old Sarah's place and the huge antenna sticking out of her silver maple tree, the valley people were stunned. They had heard that even if one could afford a TV there wouldn't be much of a reception because the closest broadcasting station was in Pennsylvania, and they were surrounded by mountains. But Sarah lived in the middle of the valley, its widest part, and Montgomery Ward had put up a 50 foot tower.

Now everyone was waving at Sarah, but nothing else changed for her. There were no invitations. So the valley people began pestering Bill about her TV set. They realized that his truck sat at least an hour longer each week than usual at her house when he was picking up his concoctions. Bill had found something just as enjoyable as her alfalfa, dandelion head tea. The show, Bonanza, was on and both of them were big Cartwright family fans.

Bill, knowing she liked her privacy, just told them the reception was very poor and it was hard to hear with all that static.

Fortunately, broadcast technology began to improve, another closer broadcasting station went on line, and a few other people in the valley who lived near the mountains where they could more easily erect a tower and antenna began to buy TV sets. So the curiosity, or maybe even envy, thought Bill, died down.

However, when the valley people looked across the valley at Sarah's place one day, they were amazed when they saw the antenna coming down. Bill merely told them she had decided she did not like TV. He didn't want them to know what happened. Bill had long been protecting her pride for her. He knew she would not want people knowing she was losing it. For the past several years he had noticed that her house was in total disarray. He had even learned to sit on the hard plank chair to watch TV because the stuffed chairs and sofa were alive with bedbugs.

While Sarah wasn't as sharp mentally as she used to be, she still had her potions neatly lined up on the round oak table.

It was near the end of one of the Bonanza shows that it happened. An outlaw shot Hoss Cartwright. Old Sarah was furious. She threw her shoe at Red Twilight, who shot Hoss in the back. That was the end of the TV set.

Sarah said she didn't want another TV, that she wanted to remember Hoss the way he was.

Old Sarah died two years later. But it wasn't Bill who found her. Her long lost daughter, Annie, came home from Baltimore. Bill had been mightily relieved when she showed up shortly after the TV incident. She took care of Old Sarah, who taught her everything she knew, and now it was Annie combing the valley for herbs. She was starting a nature food business in town.

Hampshire It Is

Of all the world's black and white animals, be it a zebra or panda, my grandmother would stand in her barnyard and declare that the most composed of all is the Hampshire hog.

She called these belted swine, milling around the long skirt she always wore, her Tuxedo pigs. "With their white front legs and shoulders they are as dressed up as any Victorian I have ever seen—certainly just as smart in their white shirts and black pants and shiny heeled shoes ready for a debutante's ball."

Despite much guffawing from her son, my father, who would point out the Hampshire hogs were better known in most circles for their taste as meat and not their dress, grandmother would persist in her opinion.

"Just look at their ears," she would declare, "and notice how erect they are, certainly not floppy like those on most white and red hogs. These Hampshire's are very aware of themselves," she would add, pointing out they were English in demeanor as well as culture.

My father had given up correcting her. While it was true they bore their name from Hampshire, England, just as their Hampshire County in West Virginia did, their lineage actually traced to Scotland. First there was a man named McGee who began breeding from a wild black and white boar he found in the woods and then a fellow named McKay introduced them into Hampshire, England, where they were given the name of the shire.

But grandmother would pay no heed to her son. She even refused to acknowledge that my father got the information from the Hampshire Swine Association which oversaw the registering of pure-bred Hampshire hogs. About the only concession she would make, being proud of the English side of her family, was that even if the Hampshire had been a wild Scottish boar at one time, it had been so totally refined by the English that this connection no longer deserved to be on its family tree.

"It's not just the ears, either, that makes them stand out," she would add. "Look at their long, equine-like noses. No stubs there. There is no sagging in their backs either. I tell you, they are English."

My father would laugh, especially when she handed out the best ears of corn to Jane Eyre and then gave the smaller ones to David Copperfield, Winston Churchill and Lady Churchill, Lord Byron, Henry VIII, Anne Boleyn, Chamberlain and Cromwell. Grandmother even had a Captain Hornblower who, much to her distaste, spent a lot of his time in the water trough instead of alongside it.

Jane Eyre was her favorite sow. Jane never failed to produce a full litter, one for each teat. Others, like Queen Victoria, were unpredictable, sometimes bearing more than they could care for, resulting in runts that had to be put with other sows if they would take them. However, they often ended up in grandmother's kitchen until they grew enough to be on their own. My father, mimicking some of his mother's idiosyncrasies, called them "disgruntled subjects" which did not amuse her.

But he had to hand it to her. The runts, which had managed to survive in spite of being shunted aside at the teats by the stronger siblings and sometimes mashed by the mother adjusting herself for the feeding frenzy, thrived under her care. Those looking at them when he took them to market would never know they had a difficult start. Many times he had been told at the sale, "You should not have castrated that one; it would have made a great breeding boar."

Only once did a Hampshire go to market from the Kuykendall farm that did not have grandmother's 'Tuxedo look.' That was Sir Walter Raleigh who had been given his name by grandmother because he seemed gracious and—"okay, maybe a bit timid," she admitted to her son, "because he let Henry VIII, Cromwell and Lord Byron crowd him out at the trough."

Perhaps it was this humble trait that caused Sir Walter to be run over by the tractor when he was about a year old. He was just a pudgy mass of black and white skin when my sister at age ten decided she could save him. We had just come back from fishing along the river and when she saw the pig was still barely alive, she ordered me to fetch the bamboo poles we had been using and to take off the fishing line. With our grandmother's big darning needle, she started stitching the pig back together while I kept the entrails from falling out.

Amazingly, the pig survived and eventually went to market

tipping the scales at just over 500 pounds. However, on one side it was lumpy and badly scarred and, according to my grandmother he, indeed, looked like a cross between a zebra and a panda. Sir Walter Raleigh's tuxedo suit was in need of alteration. The "sleeves" of the "shirt" were offset several inches from the "vest" and an extra belt of white went down the middle of the hog. The needle holes had expanded as the hog grew and the scars bore no hair but just vertical and horizontal patches of white skin.

If Sir Walter were seen in profile from his good side, you would never know he had, as my Grandmother said, "Suffered this indignity to his composure." She would go out of her way "to not make him feel uncomfortable by staring at his bad side."

Tom

It was his ninth birthday when Mike's mother yelled for him from the kitchen window. She had been watching for his father to come down the road from the upper farm. He was late for supper. But this time it was not the irritation of having to warm up the food which she said was never as good that caused her stress. It was her disgust when she saw a car had stopped long enough to throw out what looked like a cat. Even though this was not unusual—probably as many dogs also found their way to our door—she never failed to deplore the riff-raff who would do this to any animal.

Mike, the youngest in their family of one girl and three boys, was the one she now picked to take care of strays. She could tell he would be the tallest of them all because he had already outgrown jeans worn by his middle brother and was now fitting into hand-me-downs from his 15-year old brother. She also knew that his heart was as big as his size. He never failed to flinch from this duty, knowing that his mother was ordering him out the door to get the animal so she could call the game warden and have it euthanized. He hated to see the animals put down as his father would call it. Mercy killing, his mother would declare, denouncing the driver for having none. Sometimes the cats Mike gathered up were de-clawed, resulting in her condemning the ignorance of those who must not know or care that the de-clawed cat had no chance of surviving on its own. It would make her even madder when Mike returned with a female cat with sore nipples, often thin and wretched in spirit as well as nursing condition. Mike's mother would calm down enough to hope the kittens had been given to someone who would care for them.

Her orders to retrieve the cat this time included the usual question she always answered herself. "Why do they always seem to have to throw the animals out at the deer crossing sign?" It was in plain view half way up the valley road before it disappeared into a turn leading to the next farm. They have no shame, she would say, explaining that they could throw the animals out at the turn where no one could see them. Then she would wonder if they actually thought people were stupid enough to think they were stopping for a deer crossing. The kind of person that throws out an animal was likely to be spotlighting and shooting defenseless deer at night, too.

By this time, Mike was on his way reluctantly going up the road to retrieve the animal. The reason he always remembered this particular day—his birthday—was also that was the day when he met Tom. He was relieved to see it was a cat because his father had allowed some of them to survive if they looked like they could earn their keep by keeping the barn and granaries free of mice, rats and even snakes. This was a black cat and different from the ones he had collected before. It was half-grown and solid black, except his tail had a white tip at the end.

His green eyes studied Tom with interest—not wariness or fear or anguish. His rib cage was protruding from the muddy, matted hair. He let Mike pick him up but he kept his eyes directly on Mike.

Mike could see that he was not castrated and knew that his mother would immediately send him to the game warden to have him euthanized. Because most people were economically challenged, she seldom chastised people for not neutering—except those that had spent the money having their cats de-clawed but not neutered.

Mike smoothed out the tangled hair on the young tomcat and tried to figure out how to get it into the barn collection. He cleaned it up the best he could. His father would get rid of all the tomcats when his cat collection grew to the point of vastly outnumbering their prey. Mike was also fully aware of how the newborn baby males seemed to mysteriously disappear. His mother had assigned this "bag and river" duty to his father. She handled the road drop-offs to keep the game warden busy as well as aware of the drop-off situation. She had a pair of binoculars and was often able to make out the license number of the vehicles before they could leave.

As Mike was what he would as an adult call bonding with the green-eyed tom with the white tip on his tail next to the deer-crossing sign, his late-for-supper father came along in his truck and stopped to pick Mike up. Mike pointed out the young cat had a lot of energy and was completely black except for the unusual white tip on his tail.

He enthusiastically spun Tom around as he brushed him off,

so his father could see his penetrating green eyes as they got into the truck to go to supper. When his father turned into the barnyard instead of parking in front of the house, Mike knew young Tom was going to become a barn cat and that nothing would be said to his mother—now warming up the dinner—about its reproductive capabilities.

"Let's name him Tom because that is what his job will be," Mike's father said. Pointing to the pure-bred Angus bull in the barnyard, he added, "He's going to be as busy as our bull has been and we'll see if he does as well in having offspring that looks like him."

Mike's father went on to explain that they could produce a breed of cats that were all black with white tips on their tails like Tom had. He told Mike he was old enough now to know that would mean selective breeding and that the offspring of those which did not have white tips on their tails would have to be shown painless mercy in the river.

"By the time you are 14, you should be an A student in genetics and be the only one I know who has 20 black cats with white tips on their tails," he declared. Then he laughed to himself as he added that after all that inbreeding they would become English aristocrats, adding the hope that in becoming so, they would still have the ability to earn their own keep unlike British royalty.

The experiment worked. When Mike was fourteen, he had fully established himself as having something no one else had. He had always been shunned by the other valley kids for being too tall and awkward for his age, and genetically speaking, his height and foot size would not stop growing if his father's genes were dominant, so he did not think things would be getting any better.

But Tom's prowess as a tomcat to be contended with and admired soon gave Mike status. Tom had not even confined himself to their barnyard. His markings in the offspring of other cats up and down the valley did not go unnoticed. Mike soon became the proud owner of Tom.

But most of all Mike had a companion like no other. Tom also gave Mike his full attention. From that first meal of pot roast beef Mike sneaked out of the house to fill out Tom's rib cage, Tom became Mike's. Tom seemed to know that Mike enjoyed watching him eat whatever treat Mike had for him. Mike's lap was the only one he ever tolerated. Those green eyes never failed to keep an eye on Mike as Tom expressed his satisfaction with great purring when Mike stroked him from head to the white tip of his tail.

Before school and after school, Mike looked in on Tom at the barn. He seemed to be asleep a lot in the mornings. His father, who had marveled at how few neighbors had actually seen Tom in their barns, said Tom was also a night prowler so Mike should not be surprised that he slept so much.

Then there were those times when Tom would disappear for two or three days which really had Mike worried, prompting Mike at one time to try to follow him to see where he went. This resulted in Mike getting lost in the woods and not finding his way out until the next morning, causing great alarm with his mother as well as father. A search party had been formed and was about to head out again in the morning when Mike came out by the stream near his house with Tom. Mike knew to follow it. To this day Mike still wonders what business Tom had over a mile back into the mountains but that's how far he got before getting lost. Fortunately Tom found him and he was good company that night and Mike was not afraid.

Today, as Mike looks at the pictures he took with his Brownie box camera during his growing up years, he laughs at how many there are of Tom. There are at least 30 pictures of Tom with his latest look-alikes in the barn: Tom eating, Tom sleeping, Tom on the porch swing, Tom waiting for his shot of milk when his mother was milking the cow, Tom observing the Angus cattle, Tom looking out of the hay mow, Tom sitting on the tractor, and his favorite—Tom sitting in a snow throne chair he had built for him with a Burger King crown on his head. He even had one of Tom with a copper snake he had partially killed and deposited on their front porch, an act that caused his mother—who on his tenth birthday had started allowing him to bring Tom in the house to play—to immediately rescind that grant.

Mike estimated Tom was about 16 when he died, a long life for a cat. He had many scars from battles with other male cats in the valley trying to protect their domains. He had lost all but a few hairs on his head. It was badly scarred and scabby. Tom's father said it was cancer because no matter how much Mike doused his head with sulfur, the running sores remained. His mother finally allowed him into the basement when he became too weak to gather food. He had lost his teeth and one of the saddest things Mike said he ever saw was the look in his green eyes when he caught a mouse and could not eat it. The mouse, no worse for the bath he got in Tom's mouth, simply jumped out at the first opportunity.

Tom had sired about six generations of look-alikes and when he died one of his perfect sons was allowed to live and took over the job. Mike's father called him King Richard. Later when Mike was off to high school, his father stopped the successful genetics experiment explaining it should not go on any longer because such constant inbreeding and incest would result in physical as well as mental retardation. Mike, of course, knew they often exchanged bulls to insure their pure-bred line was healthy and agreed to it without protesting.

But some thirty years later, Mike, with his own family now, smiles when he visits his parents and notices there are still black cats with white tips on their tails in the valley. Of course, he always stops by a stone marker under a pear tree near the barn for Tom. Carved on it is Tom's name and a cutout of a tail with a white tip on it.

Blue Hole

All the old timers said the Blue Hole in the South Branch of the Potomac River had been a meeting place for farm and mountain kids to swim ever since their ancestors had settled the area back in the 1740s. Only my grandmother would challenge this by picking up a smooth, flat rock and skipping it across the river eddy we called the Blue Hole where it would sink in its whirling waters. The deep whirlpool, formed by a curving river driving itself into a mountain waterfall at that point, was framed by limestone cliffs on each side. "That Blue Hole is full of good Seneca skipping rocks," my grandmother would declare as she gathered more stones. Her parents had taught her how to identify Indian artifacts. She would challenge everyone to climb the cliffs to find a smooth outcropping with a fish carved in it by the Indians. "It points to this blue hole and eddy where the fish are plentiful," she would say.

She had been saying it for three generations.

When she was a little girl, huge grapevines grew on the sycamore trees among the limestone rocks. As kids, they would cut and swing out on nature's ropes, giving their best rendition of Tarzan yells as they dropped some 20 feet into the Blue Hole. The mountain kids had learned how best to cut the vines from their parents who made a living by cutting cherry, maple, walnut and other hard woods and floating them down river to a furniture factory where the north branch met the south branch. The Tarzan yells, along with some imagined Jane and Cheetah calls of the wild, were a contribution from the valley kids who had mail service. My grandmother still had her collection of Tarzan and Jane comic books.

But years later when she was taking her own kids to the blue hole to meet the mountain kids, they no longer had grapevines to swing out on. When the railroad came through, the banks were cut back and the sycamore trees with all their hanging vines were cut.

Because most of the hard wood trees were gone, the mountain

people were planting apple, cherry and peach trees to make a living now. The railroad made it possible to get the fruit to market.

Valley farmers were able to increase their profits by turning over some of their corn and pasture fields along the river into tomato, bean and sugar corn produce fields. The train stopped at four different places in the valley to pick up the mountain fruit and valley vegetables. A trestle bridge was built over the mountain waterfall for the train to cross. My parents and the other valley and mountain kids now jumped from 15 feet from it into the Blue Hole. They used the platform holding the huge tank that the train piped water to from the mountain waterfall for its steam engine. But safety was always a concern, and each summer the eddy and blue hole was tested. Everyone would hold hands, form a line and walk up and down the river to find the deep places that had washed out from the winter's high water.

Even when she was in her 80s and our generation was old enough to go swimming in the Blue Hole, my grandmother still set the rules for swimming at the Blue Hole. She was still able to able to skip rocks. Now she was pointing out where huge chunks of the limestone cliffs used to be and how there once was a old carving of a fish pointing to the Blue Hole. She invited everyone to look at her collection of Indian artifacts she had found in the area, stone axes, arrow heads, pottery shards, pestles and mortars, beads, and her favorite, a fishbone made into a comb.

While she did not like the railroad, she did credit it for exposing the mouth of a limestone cave. In it, my great grandmother spotted an old dugout canoe which she immediately claimed and gave to a museum in Washington, DC.

But it was during her last days, when she saw the effects of agri-business, that tears would well up in her eyes as she watched us wade into the Blue Hole. It is so shallow now it has given up its whirls, just sitting there with no expression. Irrigation systems to increase produce production and a chicken processing plant at the headwaters of the South Fork of the South Branch have changed the river. While the processing plant was forced by the government to separate the feathers before dumping the waste into the river, there are no controls on waste water runoff from the processing plant or the hundreds of automated chicken houses. No one fishes the eddy anymore because what fish are left are not safe to eat. The water contains antibiotics fed to the chickens, blood, manure and chemicals from fertilizers. There is so much brown scum on the rocks, kids today wear big tread tennis shoes to keep from slipping to get to the blue hole, now turned a brownish green.

I remember my grandmother's last trip with us when she insisted she be helped to the mountain waterfall where she washed the scum off her skipping rock. She said the Senecas would "want it that way" as the rock skipped through a clump of algae on top of what once was a clear, blue swirling hole.

When my grandmother died at 82, she left me a skipping rock. She also left me her Indian collection. In it was the carved fish which she had recovered when they blasted out the mountainside to get the railroad through. With it was a note which read: "Hopefully, the day will come when you can put this fish back where it was so it can point to the return of the Blue Hole."

Madman Millard

When Tom Millard put up a tent along the mouth of the South Branch of the Potomac River where it comes out of a seven-mile gorge, people were alarmed.

It wasn't just because he had a habit of setting himself up on land wherever he felt like it. People were used to getting the sheriff and having him moved off their property.

What worried the valley people was that Tom was becoming dangerous. He drove an old beat-up 1936 pickup truck, the one that had a hole in the rail behind the cab to insert a shovel or pitch fork. Tom carried his shotgun in it. Several farmers swore they saw a bullet hitting the dirt in front of them when they were plowing or cultivating.

On the single road in and out of the valley, Tom was a menace. Every land owner in the valley had learned to let him have the center of the road. He would aim his pickup right at them and if they did not pull over to make room for him, they knew he would not hesitate to hit them. It had happened twice to one farmer, Henry Van Meter. He had not pulled over and Tom dented the side of his truck. Van Meter was able to pound the dents out since there was no use suing Tom because, as the sheriff said, Tom had no insurance and in the 1960s you didn't have to. There was nothing the sheriff could do until Tom hurt someone and then he could put him in jail for awhile.

As the largest land owner in the valley, Van Meter seemed to have the most trouble with Tom. Once he was driving a team of horses pulling a wagon loaded with hay to his lower farm. Tom managed to sideswipe his wagon with his pickup, dislodging several bales of hay which sent nearly the whole load tumbling over the high road bank into the river.

One of the startled horses, breaking out of his harness, had to be retrieved. Van Meter began calling Tom, "Madman Millard."

All the farmers and other land owners got used to watching

the road for Madman Millard and avoiding him if possible. Tom Millard didn't bother those who rented houses or trailers along the river. It was just the farmers and those who owned land that were his targets.

Tom's mind was back in the early 1700s, when his ancestors had been one of the first white Europeans to find the South Branch Valley—"the whole valley"—he would shout out to those who questioned him. Even though his ancestors had stayed on the land some 20 years before they fled during the French and Indian Wars, Madman Millard felt the valley belonged to him as a descendant. Others could point out their ancestors were there at the same time but they were not chicken like Tom's ancestors and had built forts to protect themselves from the Senecas, Shawnees and Susquehannas. This would send Tom into a rage.

Moreover, some of them, like Van Meter, who challenged Tom on whose ancestors were first, had gotten a tomahawk grant from the Indians before the English claimed the area for themselves. Tomahawk grants, which were gashes cut in trees to mark four corners, "Meant nothing," according to Tom, who pointed out that there were three tribes who thought the land was theirs to hunt. Tom figured the tribe that supposedly sold the land to Van Meter was probably only given a steel axe for it by Van Meter who used it to make the notches in the tree.

Van Meter, as well as other heirs to the land, could also point to English documents proving the land was theirs. In 1747, when the English granted Lord Fairfax over 500,000 acres of the northern neck of Virginia, the surveyors came through and found Dutchmen like Van Meter were already settled there. The English, interested in opening up the territory west of the Appalachians and into Ohio, needed settlers and let the Dutch stay on the land, charging a rental fee which all had to pay. Some left for the west rather than pay and others stayed and paid the rent. After the Revolutionary War, the land was officially deeded to those occupying it. Some of the sheepskin documents even had the signature of George Washington on them. He was just 16 year-old when he explored the area as a young intern to Fairfax's surveyor, Genn.

But Tom refused to listen to what happened after his ancestors fled the valley during the French and Indian Wars. He just felt his ancestors were the first white men there—therefore the land was theirs and now his.

For years, Tom put up a shack anywhere he liked. He made his living trapping and selling animal skins. He lived on deer meat and other wild animals and was often accused of stealing tomatoes, cabbage and watermelons.

With the law on their side, the farmers made sure the sheriff moved him off their farms. Otherwise, they just ignored Tom and let him have the road when he wanted it. They didn't mind his trapping and killing animals since they were even greater garden pests than Tom was.

Farmer Van Meter, even though he shied away from going on the road again with his horses, did not give up in his attempts to "straighten out" Tom. One day Tom came up behind him when he was on his tractor pulling a manure spreader. Van Meter knew Tom would try to pass him and edge him off the road. Just when Tom was right behind him at a fast speed, he turned on the spreader. Tom's pickup swung wildly in the manure greased road, but he still managed to get around the spreader and went past Van Meter skidding and cursing.

Van Meter was laughing as hard as Tom had laughed at him when he was reloading his hay. But when Van Meter rounded the turn up ahead, he quickly realized why Tom had not crowded him off the road while passing him. The tires of his tractor blew out when he crossed the strings of barbed wire Tom had strung across the road. Tom was just ahead shaking his fist and yelling at him to return his land.

The sheriff always tried to catch Madman Millard in the act of destroying property and running the farmers off the road but Tom knew his unmarked car. He also knew those who did not own land and gave them a friendly wave. He never gave the sheriff any trouble when he was told he was trespassing and had to move his shack off the land he could not prove was his. Tom just did as told, taking his animal skins with him, and setting up somewhere else until a complaint was filed.

When Tom put up a tent on the new state park at the mouth of the gorge at the southern end of the valley, the sheriff could not do much about it. The river access sign stated that campers were allowed.

Nothing could be done unless Tom harmed someone. Now that Tom was camped along the river, he became a menace to the farmers who allowed their cattle, pigs and other stock to drink from it. He felt free to trap and shoot at these "trespassers" in the public river.

Those renting trailers along the river banks began to get alarmed when they saw Tom paddling down the river in a dugout canoe, which he claimed he found in a cave in the gorge where some damn Indian had left it.

Tom had even taken to carrying a bow and arrow and wearing just a loin cloth. Kids playing in the river would race to their camps when they saw the angry, fully bearded and sun-burned Madman Millard aiming his oars at them as he floated down the river.

This behavior continued for two years before Tom met his comeuppance. An Angus bull drinking from the river had not appreciated it when Tom put an arrow into his side

The bull charged Tom, turning him over in his canoe, and then trampling him into the river rocks, breaking many bones. The campers notified the sheriff who brought the emergency squad with him. Tom would no longer be a threat to the valley. He would spend the rest of his life in the county home recuperating from his severe injuries.

The bull, which carried the brand "VM," was retrieved by the owner who declared—after getting the arrow out—that this was one bull that would live a long, long happy life and never see a stock sale.

Grilled Chicken

When the ambitious state trooper, Charles E. Carter, checked the grocery store receipts he found in George Culpeppers's garbage cans, he knew he had him this time. There it was—three receipts showing the purchase of 200 pounds of sugar in just a week's time.

Now all he had to do was visit the A&P and Shaw's Grocery to find the cashiers who could verify the purchases of such large quantities of sugar.

Trooper Carter was still fuming from his rejection by the FBI agent when he told him George Culpepper couldn't possibly need all that corn he was buying for his chickens.

Culpepper had a 50-acre farm and raised some 1000 chickens a year. It had been obvious to Trooper Carter that the land was hardly fit for goats. There was no way he could raise enough corn for all those chickens. So he had checked around to find out Culpepper has been buying corn from neighbors—enough corn to feed each chicken 30 pounds a day.

But when Trooper Carter reported this to the FBI agent in charge of Bureau of Tobacco and Alcohol regulations for the area, he had been told to stick to highway matters, that Culpepper had a large family, and that maybe they ate a lot of cornbread. The agent also noted that his check of the neighbors showed that there had been a mistake made in bushels sold, so there was no proof of the misuse of corn. The agent also reminded the suspicious trooper that making moonshine was not his business anyway; it was a federal violation, not a matter for state police.

Trooper Charles E. Carter was not one to back down, particularly when his judgment was questioned. He knew the rumors that Culpepper had expanded his shine business throughout the eastern panhandle of West Virginia. He had also seen the new porch Culpepper had added to his house and found out he had paid cash for a brand new Dodge Ram truck with a V-8 engine.

"Well," said Trooper Carter to himself, clutching the grocery receipts and signed verifications of the purchase by Culpepper he had gotten from the cashiers, "I have him now. Chickens might eat corn and even some of that cornbread. But they sure don't chow down on sugar."

He sent the evidence special delivery to the FBI agent and a copy to the state captain of the police force. He included a report he had heard from deer hunters who had described the deep hollow where two mountain streams met and formed a perfect little waterfall making it even easier for Culpepper to make his shine without manual power. The hollow was naturally foggy, giving cover to fires he made to mush and ferment the corn. Trooper Carter could lead the federal agent to it. All they needed was a search warrant.

Trooper Carter was eager to add to his commendations. He had already been cited by the captain for his dedication to keeping the highway free of reckless drivers and drunks, which had resulted in fines that set a record for that county. Now he was confident his diligence in getting rid of an illegal bootlegger would surely result in him becoming a sergeant.

His first clue that things were not going as he had hoped and planned was when a letter came back from the FBI agent denying his request to accompany them on a search of the still back in the mountains where George Culpepper made his brew. The agent again reminded the young trooper he was out of line in his investigation, that it was a federal matter and that he, the proper agent, would take care of it.

Before Trooper Carter could send his suspicions that the FBI agent might already be too familiar with Culpepper to his state captain, he got a framed citation award for dedicated service and a letter came from the State Captain.

Trooper Charles E. Carter was being "promoted" to serve in Logan County. The captain, in citing Trooper Carter's distinguished and dedicated record, ended the letter by noting that this new assignment would be "an even greater challenge because of the recent illegal riots of union coal miners protesting working conditions—a duty that would require an officer with the high standards and dedication to service that Trooper Carter had often displayed."

Yet, there was no mention of a pay raise or becoming a sergeant and Trooper Carter was no fool—Logan County was like being sent to Siberia. Just how powerful was this FBI agent? What should he do?

He could send his suspicions to the Attorney General, Robert Kennedy, or even to President Kennedy. But, considering how their family fortune was made, that might not be such a good idea.

Instead, Trooper Charles E. Carter bought some cornbread and sent it to the FBI agent just to let him know he knew and would not forget. He even mailed it from his new address in Logan County, the town of Justice.

Civil Strife

Ever since they were formed, the Hampshire County Chapter of the Daughters of the Confederacy in West Virginia celebrates Memorial Day by draping the huge Confederate statue at the entrance to the graveyard with a 30 foot long boa made of blue cedar, arborvitae and mountain laurel laced with dogwood sprays.

Each year, a descendant of Rebel John Gray from Hanging Rocks shows up at the steps of the county courthouse to read from Gray's diary and to pass around his Cavalry sword and bible. Lieutenant Gray had been one of Stonewall Jackson's major scouts whose job was to monitor Yankee movement and report whatever he could find out from observations from those who had interacted with the enemy soldiers. According to family lore, he had gone through 25 horses during his four years of service, some shot out from under him and others just wore out.

The names of the 79 Confederates who saw action, over half of whom died in battle, are always solemnly read, followed by a prayer. After a respectful rebel yell by the men who attend the event, the Daughters of the Confederacy and their retinue quietly disperse to the graveyard for the final part of the ceremony at the Confederate statue where the wreath is placed.

Because a book has been published about Lieutenant John Gray, "Rebel from Hanging Rocks," a John Gray descendant has always been chosen to lead the group and serve as president of the association.

Only one descendant of the other veterans has ever complained about not doing the honors at the cemetery. This complaint came from the great, great granddaughter of Captain George Ashby, Abigal.

She protested her ancestor had done more for the south than Lieutenant Gray. "Captain Ashby," she proudly said, "saw more action as a battle commander than someone sneaking around as a spy. Moreover," Abigal added, "Captain Ashby died for the cause instead of staying alive like Lieutenant Gray." But her protests had been shunted aside when it was noted Captain Ashby was not buried in the Confederate cemetery, but rather at home in the family graveyard. There was no reason to honor him at the cemetery. Besides, his name was read at the courthouse steps. This brought on an unladylike response from Abigal Ashby which, in turn, did not sit well with the entire blueblood society. The Daughters of the Confederacy prided themselves on good manners and even after a century, referred to the Civil War as "the recent unpleasantness."

No one disputed the fact that it was very "unpleasant" during the Civil War, especially for Hampshire County and its county seat, the town of Romney. Romney is just a few miles below the Mason-Dixon Line and as you enter the town, a historical marker informs you that during the Civil War, it changed hands more times than any other site. Its only challenger is Winchester, VA which is still trying to document their claim that they changed hands more than the 56 times.

The Frederick County Chapter of the Daughters of the Confederacy in Winchester also notes that Winchester was a city, not a town, as Romney still is. They proudly point out that they restored Stonewall Jackson's headquarters in Winchester while the one in Romney is currently a funeral home.

The Winchester ladies also never fail to point out Winchester had seen a lot more action and the only reason Romney changed hands so many times was because of the railroad; otherwise it was of no significance. Stonewall had even tried to resign from the Confederacy while he was headquartered in Romney, noting in his diary that Romney was a "dreary mud-hole."

The Romney ladies argued that Winchester would not have survived if it were not for their Confederates. Romney Rebels had easy access to disrupt the Baltimore and Ohio Railroad, which served the Yankees with supplies. That railroad was crucial to winning. So, the Romney ladies declared, it was the Hampshire County Confederates who had to run the Yankees out of town 56 times to protect cities like Winchester in Frederick County.

It was not until 1864 that West Virginia became a state. Adding more insult, the Winchester ladies would retort by reminding the Romney ladies that it was not just the Civil War that broke them up; it was always known the House of Burgess and tidewater Virginias considered anyone west of the Appalachians poor mountain relatives at best.

Even though there were Northern sympathizers in

Hampshire County and an adjoining county was even named Grant after the war, the South Branch Valley of the Potomac River was mostly Confederate because many of the farmers, even the smaller ones, owned slaves. Both the Grays and Ashby's had slaves. Their argument today—while always being politically correct in deploring slavery—was not about the war itself but who conducted it with the most "honor."

As a result, the Hampshire County Chapter of the Daughters of the Confederacy in Romney not only had their hands full defending themselves from the proud Frederick County Winchester, Va. ladies, but they also had to deal with dissension in their own ranks due to Abigal, the great, great granddaughter of Captain Ashby. She persisted in declaring that Captain Ashby was a braver soldier and more of a victim of Yankee dirty tricks than was Lieutenant Gray.

Historical records show that a desperate Lincoln, in trying to do all he could to stop the war, had approved several Pennsylvania regiments having their scouts don confederate uniforms so they could easily invade the homes of officers. The West Point code of honor had been in effect to the point that the Yankees—even though disguised as Confederates—were only to confiscate horses, interrupt supplies going to the Rebels and take Confederate officers on leave as prisoners. Five officers had been taken from Hampshire County valley homes when they were on leave. However, as the Romney Daughters of the Confederates, now being led by Sue Ellen Gray, pointed out, Captain Ashby had been a fool. He refused to give up his horses or be taken captive. Getting shot was his fault.

Everyone knew it was best to feed the Yanks and have something available for them to take so you could survive to fight another day. Today, there are 14 homes on the historic tour list where people can see stairwells with hidden spaces underneath to hide sympathizers. The step caps still lift to reveal storage boxes to hide jewelry and other small valuables while the underneath side of some staircases feature a hidden door. Those who had stone houses – as Captain Ashby did - were often not as cooperative with the occupying Yanks as those with older homes built of chestnut and walnut logs. When word spread the Yankees were in the valley, huge meals were prepared for the Yankee soldiers to discourage any burning such as had occurred when Sheridan went through the Shenandoah Valley and Sherman marched through Georgia.

"Today the old Ashby place is not on the annual tour," Abigal Ashby protests, "because the Gray descendants still run the Sons and Daughters of the Confederacy." Thus, they continue to deny the Ashby's their due. She could always be counted on to write a letter to the editor that Captain Ashby had been the real hero, albeit a dead one. Sue Ellen Gray would counter with the argument that Captain Ashby was proven a fool because Pennsylvania regiment records showed that he had been given a choice of capture or to run. He chose to run and the Yanks waited until he was 50 rods away before they shot at him. Sue Ellen Gray would then note that Captain Ashby, who was short and stout, was not only stubborn but a good target . . . that he should have chosen to stay alive to fight another day.

Even if Captain Ashby had taken the chance to escape, the disgruntled great, great granddaughter of Captain Ashby argued, he had not died a coward and, worse, it was murder. She reminded Sue Ellen Gray that her famous rebel born at Hanging Rocks, on a farm only half the size of the Ashby one, successfully hid in a well when the Yankees came looking for him. She called the Gray family cowards because they were feeding the Yankees to divert attention from searching the well. Abigal Ashby ended one of her letters to the editor adding that Lieutenant Gray was slightly built and maybe could have dodged the bullet if he had been brave enough to try outrunning the Yanks.

Still, the Hampshire County Daughters of the Confederacy in Romney led by Sue Ellen Gray, persevered in their theory of southern hospitality being a better strategy if you are going to survive to win another day. The only one dumber than Captain Ashby, they would add, was Captain Isaac Kuykendall who had been captured. When the Yanks tried to take his gold pocket watch, he dropped it on the ground and stomped it to bits. He, too, was buried in a family graveyard.

The fact many families did have relatives fighting on both sides was ignored as one of the reasons the town may have changed hands so many times. Many did not own slaves and did not approve of it. One of these was Isaac Kuykendall's brother, John, who fought on the Yankee side. He was buried in an unmarked grave in the black cemetery just below the Confederate one.

Still, the Memorial Day ceremony honoring the confederates always seemed to keep its decorum as a solemn tribute to the dead despite the protests of the great, great granddaughter of Captain Ashby. In fact, one of the lowest attendances came at the 125th anniversary of the war's end. Some people had not only stopped attending but others were even criticizing it, reporting that the

Civil War was a black mark in history and should be forgotten, not memorialized.

But there were always those who would not forget, including the gun collectors society. One of their members recalled how an ancestor of his, along with all the other troops in McNeil's Rangers, had played a trick on the Yankees during their formal surrender at Appottomax. Instead of handing over their current rifles, they had substituted the revolutionary war firearms they had inherited. The gun collectors were now mourning the loss of these antiques which would have been a nice legacy of being heir to even more valuable 18th century weapons.

Still it seemed the Hampshire County Daughters of the Confederacy in Romney would give up their solemn ceremony on Memorial Day as attendance each year dwindled. By the time the nation was celebrating the year 2000, it seemed the annual event might just stop after some 135 years. Even the 90-year-old widow of a confederate soldier, who had been 16 years old when she married an 80-year old former Confederate soldier, was dead. Only a handful of descendants and historians were attending the event.

But 2000 was also a year when the town, no longer a nearby hub of railroads or a breadbasket of the south, was struggling to survive. Tourism and entertainment seemed to be a feasible new direction for struggling small towns and cities across the nation and Romney was no different. When a federal grant was offered for a Civil War Museum, the deal was snapped up. Romney would again be on the map and the rusty historical markers noting Romney's record of changing hands were refurbished.

So maybe it was this renewed notoriety—as the Northern defenders called it—that caused the tiny confederate contingent conducting the ceremony in the new millennium to be so rudely interrupted by a huge crowd. News of the museum opening had been well publicized, including the Memorial Day Confederate ceremony. As the traditional garland was about to be put on the Confederate statue, the sounds and rebel yells of some 50 Harley Davidson riders, brandishing the southern flag on their cycles, invaded the cemetery.

It became a stand-off as the Confederate well-mannered blue bloods looked in horror at the cyclists who tried to mingle with them. Later, people would describe it as cultural warfare. There were supporters of the leather-clad, eagle crested riders who said they had every right to be there. The daughters, aghast at the revelry, said the riders were misinterpreting the ceremony;

the point was to honor the dead, not to create another unpleasant war.

When the riders had ended their Dixie song with a chorus of "The South Will Rise Again," Sue Ellen Gray, who had led the ceremony for 30 years, was later hailed for conducting herself in a very civil manner despite the rowdy crowd. When the wreath was placed on the statue and raucous rebel yells drowned out the traditional prayer, Sue Ellen Gray walked over to the riders with Lieutenant Gray's sword and the Bible he had carried with him in her hands. She read a note which she said he had written that said, "He who lives by the sword, dies by the sword."

No one questioned this except Abigal Ashby who was now attending the event because the newspaper no longer carried her letters. She announced that after the war and the threat of a disfranchisement amendment was going to be added to the West Virginia constitution against those who supported the south—Lieutenant Gray had said he was thinking of going to South America instead of staying and fighting this injustice. "So much for waiting for another day to cross swords with the Yanks," she fumed. At this point, Sue Ellen Gray lost some of her decorum and suggested that the cyclists visit the Ashby farm where they would be most welcomed.

Today, with the Civil War Museum now drawing a crowd, attendance is not only growing at the Memorial Day Ceremony but civil war re-enactments have become a part of the Hampshire County Heritage Weekend.

Fortunately for historians, the national re-enactors that come with troops represented by Stonewall Jackson and General Grant do not allow local rivalries to prevail. The south wins one day and the north the next day. However, the staff of the new Civil War Museum has its hands full trying to contain those who would relive or rewrite history and those who need a thorough education as to what it was all about. From the day the museum opened, the staff knew it had quite a challenge when the bikers showed up with a southern license plate with a handmade banner stating, "The South Will Rise Again"

While displays and lectures are frequently held at the museum to give both sides to the story, it is probably the re-enactments that might do the best job of informing people just how unpleasant things really were during the Civil War. After the banks of the South Branch of the Potomac River were littered with hundreds of union and confederate re-enactors "dying," the crowd was astonished to hear that some 500,000 had died during that civil strife.

One group discussed how they could not believe that Yankees cared so much about slaves that they were willing to die for them. Another group said they could not believe that southerners cared so much about having slaves or leaving the union that they would die for the cause.

But maybe the best comment was from a young history student who said that once the killing begins, you can not stop hate. Hate feeds on itself and the reason becomes revenge.

Figuring It Out

Dried remains of their tomato fight were still strewn throughout the garden as eight-year-old Dickie and his big sister, Gina, gathered those that ripened during the week. While Gina was only a year older than her stocky brother, she could easily out pick him because her long, slender hands could cup even the largest tomatoes quickly and efficiently. But in the past year, her little brother caught up to her in height and had asserted himself by hitting her with an especially rotten tomato the week before.

This led to a prolonged battle. Gina finally won, but the ruined tomatoes had not gone unnoticed by their parents. Gina and same were grounded to the potato patch after school that week which was harder, back-bending work. Following the plow which left foot deep trenches was tough enough. But getting the big "bakers" as their mother called them back to the basket was worse. Both slept well that week and vowed they had learned the lesson of not wasting good vegetables. In their prayers before bed, they even had to add thanks for the tomatoes that help put clothes on their back and shoes on their feet.

The tomato lesson was still on their mind when they saw the bright red convertible come through the field and park along the elevated bank road. The levee, which had been built and partially paid for by the federal government, had kept the last three floods out of their produce gardens. Dredging of the river at the same time resulted in the river running deep like it had generations ago. The fishing was great. On weekends, their parents made extra money charging campers for a site which included Porta Johns and picnic tables.

When the couple in the red convertible arrived Friday evening for the weekend, Dickie and Gina stood back marveling at its sleekness. They had asked the young couple how much it cost, a question which had brought a verbal reprimand from their dad and an amused look from the driver. The driver added to Dickie and Gina's fascination of the sporty car by revving the engine. The wheels spun wildly in the dirt road, leaving them in a cloud of dust, an added bonus received with glee by Gina and Dickie, but not by their parents.

With the tomatoes now picked, Dickie and Gina eyed the convertible which had been parked on the road along the top of the levee all morning. Now that their father was with the hired hands pulling sweet corn at the end of the field, they figured they had time to take a closer look. A big sycamore tree which was shading the car blocked the view from the field. They wouldn't be seen. Besides, it would take the corn crew at least an hour to pick their way up the field.

"Got to see if it has a stick shift," Dickie said as he led the way. He was holding it over Gina that their dad let him move the pickup truck ahead when they loaded the tomato baskets.

As they crept down the river side of the levee towards the convertible, they heard a heavy moan in the willow brushes and reeds below them.

"Someone's hurt," they said almost at the same time. Dickie signaled a halt instantly when they saw it was the couple from the convertible. They were naked. Instantly, they shushed each other and hid behind a willow shrub where they could look down into the moving grasses and branches.

The moans were even louder now, and the woman shrieked as she dug her fingers into the man's back.

"Wow, this is some fight" declared Dickie.

Gina, with a worried look on her face, said, "I think he is really hurting her. And he is bigger too."

"Yeah, he sure has her pinned down."

"We better get Dad here."

"No, I don't think she's hurt. If she was she'd be screaming."

"You're right. She sounds more like a cow with a weaned calf".

"Look at that. He's milking her."

"We better get out of here."

"No, wait. Look. He's turning her over. She's not moaning now. She looks sleepy."

"Whoa. Would you look at that? He is sticking his thing in her rear end. We have got to get her some help."

"She's not screaming. She's moaning again."

"You're right. He looks like that bull that gets up on the cows. Now he's groaning."

"He looks like Granddad when he can't go to the bathroom."

"He is really shoving her. Look, she's got her head caught between the willows. She's yelling. But she's not hurt I tell you. She's grunting, too, like pigs being fed."

Their view was nearly obstructed by the whip lashing of the tall grass and reeds below. They looked all around to see if anyone else could hear or see what was going on. But all was quiet, the sun as hot as ever, relieved only by the slight summer breeze. The sound of the tractor starting up at the far end of the corn field was only a murmur.

All of a sudden the groaning, grunting and thrashing below stopped as the couple separated and lay motionless on their backs.

Gina whispered, "Do you think she's dead?"

"Maybe both of them are," Dickie declared. "The sweat is pouring off of them."

"They're still not moving. What should we do? We can't go down there. They're naked."

"Yeah, and they're bigger than us."

"Maybe we can throw something to see if they move."

"I know. I'll throw Wilbur down there. That ought to wake them up."

Dickie took the long, slim green snake he had found in the tomato patch out of his pocket and unwound it. Gina grimaced. She hated snakes but put up a good front of not letting her brother know. She even found Wilbur in her bed and managed to throw it back at Dickie, who had enjoyed her distress immensely. Gina was waiting for the day when he would tire of Wilbur. Their dad said it was harmless and that some folks believed if it bit you, you would die laughing.

As Wilbur boomeranged through the air, Gina and Dickie ducked tightly behind the shrub. It was only a second when a piercing scream sliced through the air. Wilbur had landed on the woman's stomach. She had jumped up so quickly Wilbur had fallen off onto the guy who was now flailing him off. Dickie and Gina watched as both headed straight to their tent, capsizing the picnic table in the process.

Dickie was the first to speak as they, startled and scared, stared at each other. "Wow. They sure aren't dead."

"We got to get out of here. I'll bet dad heard that scream."

"No, the breeze is blowing the wrong way. I think we're safe."

"Duck, now. He's coming out of the tent with a baseball bat."

"Oh my gosh, he looks like he's going back there to go after Wilbur."

The woman was standing behind him half-dressed. She was yelling at him. It was then they heard the bad word they had learned in school and were puzzling over. When the man had laughed at the woman, she had gone back into the tent and yelled, "F . . . You."

"I've got to save Wilbur," whispered a panicked Dickie to Gina. "Quick, you go draw him away while I circle around and get Wilbur."

Gina slid down the field side of the levee bank as Dickie started belly crawling down the side of the levee into the willow and reed patch.

When Dickie was only about three car lengths away from the man, he spotted Wilbur who had scurried off into the reeds which were beginning to turn brown. Dickie knew Wilbur would be spotted soon if he didn't get to the green grass where he wouldn't stand out. The man was getting closer. It was then the horn from the convertible began its piercing sound. There was no let up. The man cursed, turned around and went up the levee hill toward the car to see what was going on. Immediately, Dickie was able to dash forward, grab Wilbur and rush back to the tomato patch.

Dickie had just gotten back when the horn had stopped blowing. He heard some cursing that his dad would not approve of. He hoped his dad had not heard the horn going off, but he could still hear the tractor. That might have drowned out the sound of the horn.

But he was more concerned about his sister. She must be the one who blew the horn. What if she didn't get away in time?

Then he saw her come out of the edge of the cornfield into the tomato patch. There was no one behind her. She crept up to the baskets of tomatoes they had picked.

"That was really close," she breathed.

"What was that cussing about . . . did he hit you?"

"No, he never saw me."

"He sure sounded mad."

"He was. He fell in the cow piles I put beside the car door."

"What did you do that for?"

"Well, I jammed a stick between the car seat and the horn so it would constantly blow and I didn't want him to know I did it. I figured he would blame the cows."

"A cow could never do that. He'll come looking for us."

"No, he won't. Dad says those city people don't know

anything about cows. He'll think the cows did it. He was cussing the cows for leaving all that shit there. He fell in it."

"What about the woman?"

"She saw him. She was laughing when he jumped into the river to clean himself off. He yelled that Dicke thing back to her, that bad word, "F . . . You.""

"We've got to find out what that means. Then maybe we'll find out why they were fighting when they were naked."

"I still don't think they were fighting. Something else was going on. You were right. He did look and act like that bull."

"But Dad told us that the reason the bull was doing that was because it had an itch just like the cow did and that's how they scratched it."

"Okay, but why is it always in the Dicke place for both of them," reasoned Gina.

"Yeah, and why does everybody tell you that F . . . is not a nice word. I can't even play with our second cousin anymore because I used that word in front of his mother. And the older kids laugh at us when we ask."

"Look they are driving away now and here comes Dad. They are stopping to talk to him."

Dickie and Gina immediately went to work picking tomatoes as fast as they could. It was not long before their father came up to the patch with the pickup truck. He expressed amazement at all the ripe tomatoes they had found.

A look between them also assured the other he was not mad. So things must be okay. Gina ventured a comment. "We saw you talking to the couple in the red convertible. Are they having a good time fishing?

"Guess not," their father said. "They were in a hurry to leave. I think they must have had a fight."

Dickie and Gina looked at each other. This didn't make any sense but they were not about to say what they had heard the couple yell to each other.

Later, when it was obvious they had escaped being seen by the couple as well as their father, Dickie declared, as he fed Wilbur some ants, "We've got to figure this out. We can do it. Next weekend is a three day holiday. There will be a whole bunch of campers here then."

"Right!" declared Gina. "I'll bet that bad word is a city word. If we have to, we'll ask someone from Baltimore or Washington who usually come for Labor Day weekend."

Lucy's Pears

As long as anyone could remember, the old pear tree bore the name of the oldest person in the valley. Several took offense when the tree was named after them, but not Lucy. At 94, she had already surpassed the oldest person who ever held that honor.

The ancient Anjou pear tree was gnarly and each year the huge hole in its trunk got a little bigger. Lucy still had the old sepia print she had found of her parents posing in front of it when they were married in 1901. The tree, like today, was still refusing to give up its prime location by the walk to the front porch. Even back then the hole in the trunk was big enough to store a broom to sweep the walk and porch. On the back of the print, her mother had written the date, their names and below, "Aunt Anjou Charlotte, 91." There had been seven other people who had died in their early 90s and had the tree named after them.

Lucy's great grandson, Jacob, had taken a picture of her with the tree, carefully labeling it, "Great grandmother Lucy, age ___, 19 ___, the best of the best and oldest yet." He assured Lucy, he would fill in the age and date when it came and keep it with the old sepia photo of her grandparents.

Lucy smiled as she tapped her cane against the tree, a cane Jacob had fashioned out of one of its fallen branches. It might be gnarled but it was sturdy. While the struggling pear tree had given up it efforts to push aside the flagstones by its side, it was still holding its own against an upstart squatter Maple which each year stole more of its sunshine. Both were now providing shade for the porch.

People walking by always commented on the tree's ability to survive, marveling at how there still had to be enough life in the old trunk somewhere to nourish the tree even though its hollow trunk had opened up so much now you could get inside the tree from three open holes. "Lucy" still blossomed and produced some pears, albeit very small ones, and in the fall the auburn maple took a backseat to the Anjou's bright yellow foliage.

The tree had survived another winter. It was spring now as Lucy once again used its hollow trunk holes as a place to store the old hickory broom her mother had gotten from the Amish. The Amish make them by partially pulling back strips on a long straight branch of a hickory tree or its sapling and binding the strips into a bundle with a piece of leather. These brooms are tough and used by the Amish to sweep dirt paths between their buildings

Lucy was using the broom to sweep the flagstone walk. Because the hollows in the trunk were now so large, she had fastened the broom high inside the trunk to keep it dry.

As the holes in the tree trunk became even wider and deeper, she began storing limbs and twigs falling onto the lawn from the upstart maples and ancient locust trees around the old farmhouse. Jacob, now 17, would be by later with the riding lawn mower. Clearing the lawn of debris made mowing a lot more fun and certainly easier for him because he did not have to stop and get off the mower to clear the obstacles. It had been Jacob's idea that Lucy stow the sticks in the tree. He had worried about her falling going up the steps to the back porch to put the kindling in the wood box. That was his job, he declared, when he handed her the cane he made out of a branch of locust she had pulled out of the yard.

"Oh the things we have seen," Lucy said to the tree as she looked down the valley of the south branch of the Potomac River in Hampshire County, West Virginia. She smiled at the black and white stone pig at the head of the driveway that her granddaughter had put there years ago. She had done it to remind everyone of the days when Lucy had raised some of the finest Hampshire hogs in the county. Her granddaughter had always been amused when she came back from college to find Lucy using an old baby bottle to nurse the runts in the kitchen. Queen Victoria was one of her favorite sows, but Victoria was forever having more piglets than she did teats to feed them. Lucy would gather up the smallest before they died or were smashed by a tired Queen rearranging her underside for the coming onslaught.

The trip to the tree had become a ritual for Lucy and even though she had to be helped off the porch's steps by Jacob now, she would have it no other way. She would be of help, maybe even to the tree.

It might take her most of the morning to clear the yard of the few branches that came down each week. But it was a chore she looked forward to. She imagined she was feeding the tree, pleased to see that it accumulated water in the bottom from the lawn sprinkler which might be helping it in its fight with the encroaching maple tree. It had been a very dry summer.

Lucy decided to count her blessings, too. As she added each stick, she decided she would give it a name, too.

First, came the first Jacob. She picked up a branch from the oldest locust surrounding the house. There had been many Jacobs in her family but the oldest one from the valley was one of the settlers who had been captured in 1757 by the Indians and presumed dead. He had escaped four years later and returned to find that his wife had remarried and had two other children. He then went back to the Indians and was reputed to have ended up as a translator for Pontiac who rebelled against the northern settlement of the French and Indian War by staging another uprising.

Lore also had it that he had married one of Pontiac's daughters and that his Indian name was on the document ceding Chicago to the white men. He must have been a nice guy, thought Lucy, remembering, with a laugh, that his namesake today, her great grandson had declared that must have been the first divorce in Virginia because he had left papers which were now in the county courthouse leaving the farm to his wife and her new husband.

There had been a Jacob even before they got to the valley in the 1740s. The first ancestors had come over from Holland and settled along the Delaware River. He had been named a brother by the Leni Lenape Indians who were forced out of that area when it became heavily settled by the Europeans. It was this tribe that had told him about the valley in the mountains along the south branch of the Potomac River. Her great grandson had not minded carrying the name of Jacob, noting that maybe both Jacob's life with the Indians had been easier than what their brothers in both valleys had been doing then—clearing rocks and trees to make the fields.

Lucy spotted a windblown pile of twigs and leaves near the old family fort which had been built during the French and Indian War and was now being used to store the lawn equipment. Before electricity had come in, it had been used to pack meat in salt to preserve it.

As Lucy gathered up a bundle of branches under her free arm at the fort, she thought of her husband now dead for nearly 60 years. Farming had been prosperous for the entire family then. He was one of the first to have a car in the valley. Ironically, he had died in it when it slid off the icy mountain road. They had only been married five years. Lucy had been able to pay two hired hands and their families from the farm's proceeds during those early years.

The depression had not been as bad for farmers as it had been for the rest of the country. They still had the ability to raise food. It still saddened her to remember taking some of it to those like the Kline family who were trying to get by on gravy and potatoes. She had gotten the Model A Ford repaired and learned to drive it herself.

Then FDR had come along with the New Deal and things got better. Even though the hard-working farmers renamed the WPA, the "We Piddle Around Crew," Lucy knew it was a deal that had saved the country. She often compared the New Deal benefits to that of the GI bill after World War II that allowed so many children of the tenant and hillside farmers to go to college.

When World War II came, her son had been drafted. Farming was still prosperous then and he had even managed to build a new split-level house by the road for his growing family. But when he came back from the war with severe wounds, life seemed to drain out of him. He died in 1950. When his wife died a few years later with what they called consumption, known today as tuberculosis, Lucy was left with four grandchildren whom she raised.

But that was years ago when she could still do a full day's work, thought Lucy as she struggled to bend over to get another branch.

She recalled how the cattle herd had been taken over by her cousin and how she had invested in incubators to raise lots of chickens, something the four young grandchildren could help with until they were old enough to get back in the cattle business. The fields were also rented to their cousin who supplied her chickens with grain, corn and straw for bedding. She was able to see that the three daughters got a college education. They had become teachers and one of them had married a local man. They were living in the house by the road now with their family.

Lucy had been delighted when her grandson Bill and his wife showed an interest in farming, They continued to live in the old house with her. It had started out as a log cabin but during the past 250 years it had become a huge L-shaped house with three chimneys and fireplaces on each floor. There had been plenty of room for her grandson's three children when they came along.

Jacob was the oldest, the one now heading towards Lucy with the mower. She watched him, looked at the tree and hoped that she would be around to see five generations.

Lucy picked up a limb from the intruding maple tree and placed it in the pear tree. She rued the day farming had become so hard. She looked at all the house and camping trailers along the road and by the river. She thought of Willful who owned most of the land in the valley now. He also owned a bank. He had parlayed both to make money as one family farmer after another had to sell, sometimes because there were too many people to inherit the land or the property had become more valuable for commercial use, resulting in higher taxes. Many farms also failed because they couldn't compete against the big western farmers who had the advantage of three crops a year and could more easily pay the astronomical prices for farm equipment.

For about ten years, the farmers in the valley shared the cost of equipment but it wasn't enough. Only three farms were left in the valley that used to have fifteen working farms.

Willful used his bank and lack of concern for the environment to buy the land, strip the hillsides of timber, and sell it off in parcels making him a rich man, albeit a very unpopular one. He used much of the middle of the fertile valley as pasture for his vast cattle herds which did compete with the west. No longer could you look down into the valley from the mountaintops and see perfect rows of checked corn from any angle or ripening wheat fields hiding fawns of the same color. Instead, one saw the river lots sold by Willful now packed with trailers and roads going through the pastures to get to them.

Wilfull had learned to be a corporate bottom line farmer. If a cow had trouble giving birth, so be it. He was not going to hire someone to watch the herd during spring birthing. The hired man would cost him more than the cow dying in birth with the calf. He fed cattle as cheap as he could by even hauling chicken manure from the huge Pilgrim's Pride chicken plants in the next county. The locals did not eat beef from his cattle, fearing they were full of antibiotics from the chicken manure or the fast-growing hormones he injected into his cattle to get them to market faster. He could care less as his market was the masses in the cities.

The mountainsides, which were also sold by Willful after harvesting the timber, were now lined with trophy houses built by retired Washington, DC people. The newcomers were now complaining about the unsightly view of trailers and the smell of cow manure although they liked looking at the cows, it was said.

Lucy saw her great grandson coming with the mower. She asked him not to mow down the new locust sprout coming up near the edge of the lawn. It would make a fine tree someday, she said, so he got off and used some of her sticks to protect it. He laughed when she said she was going to call it Jacob.

Lucy went back to the tree with another stick from the locust. She loved her great grandson. In addition to eleven grandchildren and now three great grandchildren, Jacob was the one that was showing interest in keeping the farm, no matter what it took. And it was taking a lot. Jacob would have to struggle to keep the farm going. But all of them, Lucy, her grandson and his wife, and great grandson Jacob and his two sisters, were finding ways to make a living on the farm.

Rather than sell their river or roadside land to Willful for development, they had rented spaces along the river to campers. While they could no longer afford hired hands, the homes they used to live in were now used as rental property.

A growing population had created a market for produce such as tomatoes, green beans, cabbage, peppers, onion, potatoes and sweet corn. With equipment, planting the vegetables was not labor intensive. But harvesting it was. Despite offering a reduced price if you picked your own, there were not enough takers. Some of the vegetables went to waste because they could not get it picked. When one of the campers, on a retired military pension, was looking for extra money he suggested he could pick enough to fill his pickup truck and take it back to his home where he could sell it to neighbors. Other campers soon joined in, some for home grown food and, to the amazement of Lucy; some said they were doing it for exercise. They had found a wider market for their produce without transportation costs.

When a big Wal-Mart store came into the next county, they had been amazed to see people paying several dollars for plastic and dried flowers in baskets. They began raising the type of flowers that you harvested when they were dried. People preferred these over the plastic ones and soon they had another growing business Even the campers became involved in combing their local graveyards for discarded baskets, spray painting them and filling them with dried flowers. The local funeral parlors also began selling as many of these as the florists were real flowers.

Another big project became painting pumpkins and selling them. You could get four times as much if one were painted. This job was particularly sought out by Jacob's younger sisters who spent hours doing it. After supper each night, the entire family could be found on the front porch following the sketches in the kid's elementary school art book showing how to make frowns, scowls, smiles, smirks, and just about every emotion you could dream up. Lucy particularly liked doing the smiling ones, adding a winked eye.

While Wal-Mart could buy regular pumpkins in huge quantities picked by immigrants and undersell them, Jacob had been delighted when he outsold them with his painted pumpkins on a lot beside the entrance to their big box store. Ironically, Wal-Mart was located on a former cornfield sold to them by Willful which had once been owned by their cousin who had to sell.

With her health beginning to fail, Lucy had been assigned the front porch to watch her great grandchildren as they did their chores, to direct the campers to the river, and to sell freshly picked produce, dried flowers, Indian corn, gourds and pumpkins to those who drove by.

Hunting was also big business now and it was amazing what people would pay to shoot something. Her grandson even helped the Department of Natural Resources stock the woodlands with bear for the hunters.

But it was her great grandson's idea that had been the most fun of all their profitable ventures. Jacob had taken a computer course in school and came up with the idea to use it to create a maze in their corn field. The first one was the design of their county which was celebrating its formation 250 years ago. A local pilot had taken a picture of it which had made its way through all the state newspapers, free of charge. Even school children from the bordering counties were bussed in to enjoy their Halloween venture through his hidden ghost maze.

This past year Jacob had quickly picked up on the idea of using the new quarters which were issued by the federal government with designs to extol the virtues of each state. Despite the complexity of the West Virginia quarter with the New River suspension bridge in a mountain setting and other state symbols, he used his computer to figure out the dimensions of the artwork in a two-acre field by the cattle barn. He cut out the sections as plotted. An aerial picture of it now hangs in the state treasurer's office. Again, he received free publicity and has now been hired to design corn mazes in other states.

So many people came, Lucy could hardly handle the crowd and collect all the fees from her front porch rocker. Jacob joked that maybe he would quit raising cattle as these ventures were far more profitable.

Never had Lucy had so much company and enjoyed life so much. She loved answering questions about the valley, its history, its people. She asked questions, too. Soon she was just like the telephone operator for the valley had been fifty years ago. She knew everyone and everything that was happening. People stopped by just to visit with her.

But Lucy still made time to clear the yard of sticks and debris and sweep the walk. She smiled as Jacob made the last round with the mower. She looked at the pear tree and said, "Things are still looking up for us," she said. She noted it had enough pears to make at least four quarts of jelly.

Whatever Happened to the Darby Brothers?

My brother Mike never liked using the telephone, so when I got a call, it would require some action. He was calling from Ohio to tell me, in New York, that Luther Darby had died, and he couldn't go to the funeral, but if I could, I should go.

I didn't think twice about it. While I have missed the funerals of many relatives in West Virginia, Luther's was one I felt compelled to attend, not just because it was sad, but I was also curious as to what had happened to him and his brother Henry. The last I had heard, Luther was still in jail. Both Mike and I felt very few people would show up. Mike was amazed there was even going to be a formal funeral. We had both been shocked to find out what the county had done with the body of Kline, one of Luther's friends.

The rules were that the county would bury you if no one else did. If the officials knew where you came from, the graveyard in that area must take the body. Kline was buried at St. Luke's Presbyterian graveyard which overlooked the hollow where both he and Luther were born. Kline had given up early in life, drinking himself to death in his 40s. The grave was marked by a whitewashed wood slat cross. Mike and I believed the story that the county had run out of adult size coffins and broke his legs to get him in the children's size. For years, the mound of dirt in front of the cross showed that the grave was only four feet long and he had been at least six feet tall. Fortunately, the mound finally settled in on Kline.

To my amazement, Luther's funeral was going to be at the fancy Presbyterian church in town and he would be buried there. I immediately ordered a huge bouquet of daisies to be sent to the church.

As I drove home to attend the funeral, memories rushed through my head like so many petals being pulled off the daises.

The last time I saw Luther was when he dropped by the house to see Mike. He told us about Kline, and how he was now pushing up dandelions. Luther was not as smart as his older brother, Henry, but his misuse of expressions always had a certain irony, as they reflected reality to him.

I can still see us sitting there in the living room during that visit. Neither Mike nor I corrected him. We knew what he went through in our two-room country school. We had quite a time reminiscing about our childhood during that visit. Luther was in Mike's class and I was two years older. The first through fourth grade was in one room and the fourth through eighth grade in the other room. There was a Morning Glory stove in each room for heat and at recess we brought coal in from the shed and carried water in from the spring by the river. Outdoor johns were moved each year to a new spot. Each desk had a fold-down seat in front for the next seat. Everyone knew our teacher, Miss Maple, was becoming mentally unbalanced and a replacement was being sought. In the meantime, everyone hoped Mr. Riley, who taught the higher grades, could control things if they got out of hand. He often had to.

Because Luther had dark hair and was short and stocky while Henry was tall, thin and blond, there had been the usual speculation as to who their fathers might be. But the Darby brothers were close. Henry was four years older, and when he heard the bump on the classroom wall, he knew his brother was in trouble and he got Mr. Riley to intercede.

Miss Maple was especially hard on Luther. It was true that Luther smelled and often had lice. She sat him in the back away from the rest of us. We also had the dunce's high chair which he often occupied. Each grade would be called to the front of the class for their lesson while the others were expected to draw or read, depending on which Miss Maple thought we were capable of. All of us knew she favored the valley kids over the mountain kids, but my brother had befriended Luther and to Miss Maple this was an action she had to stop.

The day she caught Luther moving up to share his double-seat desk, she didn't use the ruler to whack him, she used the coal shovel. Luther managed to break free to get to the wall to signal Henry. Luther said he was "plenty sore" before Mr. Riley could get there. After that he began inserting his big, flat geography book in his pants. Miss Maple did not see that well and none of us told her. Luther would take his lickings with the appropriate amount of painful cries. Mike and I laughed with him as he feigned pain.

When Mike recalled how Luther had gotten the best of Miss Maple one day, I understood why Luther had always sought

Mike out as his friend. They were in the third grade and by this time I was over in Mr. Riley's room. They were learning about gravity and Miss Maple had declared there were absolutely no exceptions to the rule that whatever went up had to come down. The kids were amazed when Luther challenged her. She ordered him to the front of the class to explain himself which he did by standing on his head and eating an apple. Miss Maple was so mad she tore the collar off his shirt when she yanked him back to his chair. After that, Luther said, he loved school. "He said everyone except those stuck up cousins of yours seemed to like me."

As we reminisced that day in the living room, I joined both of them in laughing about those good old times we had at recess playing ball and doing the chores. But there were some memories I chose not to bring up. I remember how Miss Maple would read our report cards out loud to the class. The blue cards merely required her to check whether we were satisfactory or unsatisfactory. Luther led the list of the hollow kids who were mostly unsatisfactory. Not only were the courses to be checked off but so were health habits. While Mike and Luther were laughing I remembered and regretted now how embarrassed I had been when Miss Maple had checked me one year for not using my handkerchief. She had said I must be getting too friendly with Luther.

If Luther remembered that, he wasn't saying anything. He and Mike were deep into truck driving stories. Mike had gone to a tractor trailer driving school and was all over the country now driving for McLean. Luther was driving a truck for the local Hercules Powder company and, seeing my expression, explained the procedures they used to assure the dynamite was safe to carry.

Seeing as how I was living in New York now, Luther felt compelled to tell me he had been there, too. At that he and Mike talked about their first trips there. Both had used the Holland tunnel to get to Canal Street where most of the distribution centers were located. In Mike's case, he had a load of cigarettes from Virginia and was more worried about high-jackers than trying to find his way into the big city. New York State was taxing cigarettes so high it had become worthwhile for mobsters to jump the trucks at stops and relieve the drivers of their loads. They could even sell them legally because they were stamped. McLean had designated certain gas stations as safe for refueling so he hadn't been too worried about being high-jacked there.

"But coming out of the tunnel the first time was terrifying,"

Mike said, "because I didn't realize that all those black guys who jumped up on the truck were just doing it to get tips to clean the windshield as I waited to get through the tolls. When I realized this, I told one of them I would buy him a huge meal if he would show me where the warehouse was. I only took one man with me even though they all wanted to go, but I figured I still had to be careful."

Luther, agreeing that was a smart move, allowed as how he never got out of the tunnel the first time he went into the city. "You all remember old man Galosh and his peach orchard, don't you all," he said. "My first job was driving for him. I know you know him Marci because Henry said he picked peaches with you there one summer. Anyhow, you all might remember how cheap he was and he would only give me enough money to buy gas to get to New York and back and enough for two meals. He didn't spend nothing on his apple trucks neither. Well that damn broken-down truck gave it up right in the middle of that there long Holland tunnel. Traffic was probably backed up half way down the Jersey turnpike and when the rickety racks of that old truck broke, peach crates were all over the place. Next thing I knowed I was in jail, and they wouldn't let me call. They traced the truck to old man Galosh and that was the end of my job. I even had to hitchhike home. But it was worth it to see him have to fix his trucks up."

With the mention of Henry, I felt able to join their conversation wholeheartedly and began telling Luther how Henry had one-upped old man Galosh at his peach orchard. All of us under 14 were given the job of "ground-hogging" which was to pick up the new-fallen peaches and those on branches low to the ground. Because it was a perishable crop, we worked from sunup to sundown. It was also very hot. We had to make sure we didn't step on the bees going after over-ripe peaches on the ground. The only relief was getting the sack full of peaches and heading to the wagon with it where we could get some water. We had noticed the small church in the middle of the orchard where old man Galosh would go to pray. He was very religious.

One day it hit Henry how we could get some rest and cool off even if it meant listening to a sermon. When it was really hot and the bees were biting, he let out a cuss word. Old man Galosh would march us into that church and give us a talk on using the Lord's name in vain. The rest of us then took turns finding a reason to swear and thus getting a reprieve in the cool church.

"Sounds like Henry, that's fer sure," laughed Luther. "He always was the smart one." At that point, Mike and I looked at each other and decided we should tell Luther about the time Henry got stuck in the silo. We were filling the silos for the winter with feed for the cows. The men were in the field cutting the corn and Daddy and two other men were driving the horses and loaded wagons up to the silage cutter where the corn was thrown off into the cutter and blown up through the pipe down through the linked pipes into the silo. We kids would take turns going into the silo to lead the pipes around so the silage would be scattered evenly. When it got deep, we would take one of the pipe links off and continue walking in circles around the inside of the silo with the pipe to keep it even.

One day Henry decided to take life easy and he took off two links thinking the silage could scatter itself from that height. While he was having a cigarette he did not realize his feet were getting buried by the incoming silage. When he tried to move, he couldn't. Three loads of silage was dumped on him. When Henry did not come out to go back to the fields with us, our father went in to find him and said it was a good thing he had six feet of stupidity going for him. He had found Henry up to his ears in corn.

Chuckled Luther, "Now that was one time he outsmarted himself." Luther told us that he had not heard from Henry in years. "He went into the service and I just hope he is o.k."

This memory also triggered my curiosity as I found myself now heading into the funeral home. I wonder, too, about Henry. Did whoever is holding the funeral know how to contact him about his brother's death. I was surprised to count eight cars in the lot.

The first person I met was Henry. I had no trouble recognizing him although it had been 50 years since we "ground-hogged" together. He was as bald as I was gray but there was no mistaking that laid-back, lanky form that unfolded itself to get up to greet me. "So we meet again. And in church, too. I take it we have learned more than four letter words to get in here."

There were several kids and adults gathered around him as he thanked Mike and me for the daisies. I explained Mike's deep regrets for not being able to attend. "I know about your brother," he said, "Luther said he was the best friend he ever had."

Then he introduced me to the group. Luther had a daughter. I forgot Mike had mentioned that he had gotten married when he got out of jail. She had just graduated from high school and said she was going to West Virginia University that fall. I couldn't help it. I gave her a big hug even though I didn't know her. "I know you went there, too," she told me with a big grin. "Dad told me."

Then I met Luther's wife. She was as shy as Luther had been in the first three grades. I gave her a hug. She then introduced me to her family, two of whom I recognized as Kline's youngest brothers. They had worked for my father who they said was the hardest working man they had ever met, adding that everyone else was expected to do the same. "But he never asked us to do anything he wouldn't do," they declared with affection.

It wasn't hard to realize the rest of the group was Henry's family. They were as smartly dressed as Henry was in his navy blue suit with a well-matched tie. They were living at Cape Canaveral now. Then I found out what had happened to Henry. He had joined the Navy and, after taking courses to get his high school equivalency degree, he had gone to school at night to get another degree in engineering. He ended up with NASA and was now retired.

Later, after the ceremony for Luther, Henry and I were standing alone over the big basket of daisies. The florist had certainly responded when I asked them to get the biggest basket they could find. The daisies also looked a little odd among the traditional roses, carnations and lilies. Henry had understood their meaning.

We talked about what had happened to Luther. Old man Galosh's small orchard had long been gone. The huge Byrd orchards of Virginia had expanded into West Virginia and had taken it over, along with other small orchards. Byrd was known for hiring gypsies, displaced people released from mental institutions, as well as Jamaicans he brought in to work his orchards. Luther was driving an apple truck for him. One day he came upon a rape scene. It turned out Luther knew the men as well as the woman. When the woman's scream attracted attention the two men fled and the police found Luther leaning over the body. They arrested him and, according to my brother who had talked to Luther, they made no attempt to believe him about the other two men. At the trial they denied raping and stabbing her in the orchard. They even said they had not been there. Luther told Mike he was trying to stop the bleeding and that a passerby had called the police. She died as the police were arriving. So, it was Luther's word against the two other local guys.

Luther went to jail for 15 years, a sentence many thought too light, but the judge had been suspicious. The reputations of the other two men were no better than Luther's. And Luther had not run. But, it was two against one, so Luther lost.

The first thing Mike did when he heard about it was to visit Luther in jail and tell him he knew he didn't do it. Henry had read about it in the newspapers and also knew his brother was not capable of rape, much less murder. He had done everything he could to try to get a new trial, but to no avail. Luther was let out a few years early because of good behavior and simply accepted the discrimination he had always known.

Henry, unlike his brother, was not as forgiving of local prejudices. He decided he wanted nothing to do with Hampshire County ever again. He confined his contacts with Luther to Christmas cards. Once Luther made a trip to the Cape to tell Henry he was going to get married to one of Henry's old girl friends and asked if he would mind.

The burial ceremony was just as impressive as the eulogy written by Henry and given by the new Presbyterian minister at the fancy town church. Ironically, I noticed Luther's grave site was next to the Maple plot. Henry and I smiled knowingly to each other.

What Is THAT?

The four lane interstate highway plowed through the Appalachian Mountains shoving aside the hillside farms as if they were just a gigantic potato row. The fill on both sides was bulldozed into the hollows as the super highway furrowed a straight shot through the begrudging but yielding mountains. There were a couple of small West Virginia towns tucked into the narrow hollow valleys. The highway pillar architects called for stilts of steel to step over them.

Looking up from one of these small towns through two sets of 180-foot-high pillars towering over them was a gathering of business people from the five stores plus the minister from the church and the postmaster. One set of the span footings had filled the lots behind the hardware store and the diner. The other set was on the far side of the creek running along the narrow road through town. It now framed the oldest building standing in town, the 1796 Baptist Church.

The group, now coming out of the diner after having attended church, no longer had to shade their eyes to look up. It used to be the only sun they had seen in the past from their narrow hollow was the high noon one. Now the bridge span had blocked that out.

The hardware store owner, Jeb Welton, who was the oldest of them all and took pride in never letting his shoulders stoop like others had from hard work, was still munching on an extra corn dog he had ordered, when their comments were drowned out by an overhead tractor trailer. When it quieted down, Jeb, wiping the mustard off his overalls, said it for everyone: "Jesus Christ, it is almost like we aren't even here."

They didn't know how long they would be either. The huge highway through the mountains had exits every 15 miles or so and their hamlet had not been big enough to warrant one. The gas station had already gone under now that people were using the turnpike instead of the county road. The locals had to drive 20 miles to get gas now. The hardware and grocery store and the diner were struggling after a boost in business while the interstate was being built. The hillside farmers had not made much money in eminent domain proceedings because the land needed from them had been bought up by a corporate farmer before anybody knew about it. It was said he not only had connections with Washington but he was so powerful he had managed to get them to change plans so the highway would go through there. He already owned a bank and the businesses surrounding the major exit.

It took nearly ten years for the interstate to complete its invasion through the Appalachians down into Virginia with the Blue Ridge Mountains giving it the greatest challenge. During those times, the added business from the construction workers had been good for the town and hillside farmers. But now that the interstate had opened, they not only lost the construction business but all the out-of-town traffic that used to use their county road.

"The only local person who seems to take it all in stride," said Jeb Welton, as they walked past his hardware store, "is that nut up on the mountainside." He had taken to affectionately calling John Bolt a nut not just because of his name association and purchasing habits but because of his odd behavior.

Bolt was never unfriendly but he was never friendly either. He kept to himself and was only in town if he had something to go there for such as gas, a package from the post office or groceries or something from the hardware store. He had never been in the diner or the church.

All they knew about his past was that he had been in World War II and had bought the ridge with his pension. Jeb had found out Bolt had been an aircraft mechanic. He figured that he sure must have been a good one because he had never seen anybody do so much with whatever he bought. "He's the only person I know who ever wore out a screwdriver," he declared.

Jeb was the only one in town who had ever been in Bolt's house. Out of curiosity, he had gone up there to deliver some welding equipment and while Bolt had not been impolite, he had not asked Jeb to sit down either. Jeb had taken a quick glance at everything, including an old photo of John Bolt with a group of pilots. That's how he knew John Bolt had been a mechanic.

Jeb had told the story many times. There were about 20 pilots in the picture and they, " . . . surrounded Bolt and looked like they were real pleased with him." Bolt had painted some rivets purple and these were located under many of the pilots. Bolt had told him which ones were shot down and which ones were captured but he would not say their names. "Too painful," he said. He told Jeb life was easier if you didn't get too involved and that was why he didn't. He told Jeb he would pick up his own things in town in the future.

During all this time, the towns-people had watched his house on the ledge take on its unusual but always useful additions. Every car that had lost a hubcap on the jackknife curves of the county road was now serving as siding for his house. You could not even see the wood frame anymore. If a car had been wrecked and abandoned, parts of it showed up in his house such as license plates which were used as shingles. He had both full and bucket car seats inside his house and three rumble seats from old Model A Fords sat on his front porch. His collection of hood ornaments was used for things like door and faucet handles. Because he lived on a rocky ledge, he had filled hundreds of tires with dirt to form planters for his garden.

Stocking the store for the hillside farmers to make sure they could get a plowshare, fencing and farm tools had become routine for Jeb. But when Bolt arrived, it was a whole different matter and Jeb was proud of his growing knowledge about ozone, welding equipment, generator parts, and whatever else Bolt came up with for him to order.

The older ones among them still remembered the night that Bolt's place lit up. For years they had been trying to get the utility company to bring electric lights to their hamlet, to no avail. There just wasn't enough of them to make it worth their while. But that didn't stop Bolt. In fact, he had electricity fifteen years before it finally came through for them. Bolt made his own wind generator plant, redesigning some old propellers he brought back with him from the war.

They had counted at least five different wrecks in the structure supporting the propeller blades which was made up of what used to be tailpipes, under frames, axles, steering columns, fenders, hoods and running boards.

It was when the postmaster announced that their county road had gotten a name that the group got to thinking maybe there was a future for them after all.

The interstate architects, who had turned over the highway signage jobs to a sub-contractor were not surprised when they saw that the Exit 20 sign now read, "What is THAT?" They had already chuckled over Clifford's Hollow, the Trough, Hardy's

Homestead, Bean's Settlement, Blue's Gap and Lost River. They knew immediately where "What Is THAT?" was.

Everyone had been talking about coming across the new $2 billion bridge to come face to face with a house and gardens on the mountain ledge that was like none other they had ever seen. The architects were used to seeing high-end McMansion homes being built on scenic mountain ridges along major highways they had created. But, this only happened when the interstates were near major cities and within commuting distances. Or, they would see vacation trophy homes with huge plate glass windows reflecting the lake country below.

But "What is THAT?" had been there from the beginning and had gotten even more bizarre each year as construction went on.

John Bolt adapted to change. He could no longer count on recycling wrecks from the ravines below the jackknife turns of the old county road. But, as Jeb declared, Bolt did one helluva job using leftover interstate construction material. You could spot different lengths of pipe and tubes used in the spans now recreated like a giant octopus from the nearby waterfall reaching out to different tire piles in his garden. He had first used this spring fed stream above him to provide running water into his house which also gravity fed several of his tire piles. He had only needed a few tailpipes for that. But now he had enough piping to irrigate all of his garden from the waterfall. In fact, the huge tires he had used from front end loaders and other construction equipment were large enough to accommodate fruit trees.

The construction workers, grateful for the mechanical help he had given them, even helped him get some of the heavier scrap metal up to the ridge for him. John Bolt was now building himself a new house out of concrete forms, steel beams and some massive steel plates that were left over from the bridge floor span. Parts of heavy equipment were neatly stacked as inventory.

Those days of spotting the parts of an old blue Studebaker, a green Hornet, a black Model T or the fins from a red DeSoto had been something just for those traveling the old county road to behold. For miles on the new interstate now, you could also see remnants of the yellow Caterpillars, black Ingersoll-Rand, green John Deere equipment and red Internationals.

Yes, there were some that called "What Is THAT?" a giant eyesore but, even so, it was obvious they were intrigued. So far the only collisions on the new interstate had been by rubberneckers crossing the lane in front of another car to get a closer view of Bolt's place.

People were starting to get off the exit which was 12 miles away and make the drive on the rough county road to get a closer look at Bolt's place.

Bolt had told Jeb they were pestering him to death, wanting to buy the old license plates, the hubcabs and even his door handle hood ornaments. They wanted to see how his wind generator worked and how he built his irrigation system. They wanted stuff from his garden. They saw a lamp he had made out of a traffic cone and wanted him to make one for them.

Jeb and his little group thought this was hilarious. Then it hit them. Tourism. Of course, that was the way to survive. They would get people to get off that blanket of steel going over them to come down into their new "What is THAT" town, even if they had to offer skydiving lessons like they did at New River in their new souvenir shop and entertainment businesses.

Paw Paw

Marci took a deep, anxious breath as she left Maryland and crossed the Potomac River bridge on Interstate 81. She took the third exit for West Virginia's Potomac Highlands. Like the setting sun, she had an appointment with these mountains; a date with destiny she felt compelled to keep. Could she find her? What would she say if she did? Was Megan even alive? The 25-year-old memory in the back of her mind had moved up to the front of her conscience.

She knew the year it had happened. It was in 1972, the year of the Northeast Blackout and a huge gas shortage. She had taken these back roads home in the hopes of saving gas with the extra 50 miles she would save not being on Interstate 81. She was familiar with these roads because in her pre-teen days she used to go with her father who used to buy calves from the hillside farmers who eked out a living with a few cows they could barely afford to feed during the winter. She clutched the $50 bill her father had given her—only to be used in an emergency he had said. She should have used it in 1972.

She had never taken this shortcut after 1972 because she didn't want to be reminded about something she should have done and didn't do. It has been on her conscience all these years and now she decided to confront it. She would try to make amends. Memories came rushing back to her as she came around a sharp bend in the road after crossing Paw Paw Creek.

There they were in her memory: Two girls and a boy were standing in front of a huge red Cadillac blocking the road. Marci hit the brakes and swerved the wheel hard to the right. Her car careened into the ditch. Marci felt it begin to turn over. The last thing she remembered before her head slammed against the window was releasing the brake so the car would right itself.

Her car had landed upright in a heavy thicket of paw paws, young sprouts shooting up after a telephone line had been installed. The paw paw patch was so supple the branches didn't even snap under the force or weight of the car, but formed a cushion under and around her car. A huge shagbark oak tree was dead ahead. The paw paws had saved her from hitting it. She leaned back against the soft leather bucket seats, waiting for the pain to go away.

She began to blink her eyes slowly in case they began hurting, too. The glistening red hood of her T-Bird came into focus. It seemed to hatch itself right out of a huge green nest of leaves. She concentrated on the shield shaped leaves protecting the tiny paw paw buds. "Paw Paws," she said. The 'poor man's magnolia' is what her mother called them because they made a poor showing against their Magnolia kin further south. But the leaves are pretty, she thought. Then the aging paw paws deep in the woods seemed to stare at her with stern opal eyes, just like the ledges overhead. Marci began blinking faster to make things real. She imagined her father's old 49-truck coming out of the dark woods. It was green too, but friendly.

Then she remembered what had happened, the kids in the road. "Are you all alright" she yelled as she peered into the dust from the road that was now enveloping her, too.

Marci yanked open the door, jumped over the ditch and ran towards the Cadillac which she could barely make out in the whirling dust. "Are you okay? she screamed.

The little boy ran toward her. He was crying. He was covered with dust. Marci picked him up. As the dust continued to reclaim their ruts, she saw the two girls still at the front of the car. The little girl was hugging the big girl. She ran toward them with the boy in her arms.

"Are you okay? she yelled again, this time in a thank-God-you-are alive voice. Then she demanded: "You are okay, aren't you?"

The smaller girl, who looked about eight or nine, extended her hand and said, "Hi. I'm Megan. This is Sally Mae and you've got Jim Boy. Thanks for stopping. We sure can use some help."

Without realizing it, Marci found herself calmly responding to an offer to shake hands. Then she remembered. Question after question gushed out, "What are you doing here?. I nearly killed you. Where are your parents? Don't ever stand in front of a car in the middle of the road? What is this car doing here? Where are your parents? Do you live near here? Who are you?"

When Marci ran out of breath, she realized she hadn't given them a chance to answer. She also knew that only one of them would be able to answer her.

The older girl, Sally Mae, had square-cropped blonde hair

that looked like it really had been shaped by a four quart saucepan. She had one large pink curler doing battle with a cowlick right behind her bangs. Her sunburned face hid some of her freckles and you could tell she had a problem with pimples. She was large but not fat; she just had large bones and a stout figure. Even though her bust was well developed, Marci figured she couldn't be more than fourteen, maybe fifteen.

The girl she knew who would have the answers was small and thin, maybe ten or eleven. Megan's hair was so black and shiny you could nearly see yourself in it despite the dust. Her skin was flawless. Her eyes were lime green, like the youngest of the paw paws along the road. She moved like a ferret.

They were both in pinafores made from those color calico cotton bags used by Southern Farms to sell seed corn by the 100 pounds. Marci briefly wondered if the bags had come from her father years ago.

Marci put Jim Boy down. He looked like he was about five. He was pudgy and he still had baby fat around his arms and legs. He was no longer crying, but he wasn't looking any better for it. His skin color was yellowish. His eyes were a deep blue. But they were vacant, completely vacant.

Marci had recognized the look in his eyes. His big sister had it too. They were retarded. She turned her attention to Megan.

"O.K. Megan. Let me start over. What are you doing here in the middle of the road with this huge car?"

But before Megan could speak her big sister Sally Mae lurched out of her grasp. She tugged at Marci's jacket and stammered, "Meg ast her . . . it'ens her falt . . . it'ens her."

"It's nobody's fault!" Marci said, trying to calm the sharpness she heard in her voice. She knew her dislike for tattlers should not apply in this case, and she had been disarmed by Megan's taking command of a ridiculous situation. So, she patted Sally Mae on the back and changed her tone of voice. "We just have to do something about getting you home, that's all. Where is the driver?"

"I am the driver," Megan declared, flinching at the pity she now spotted in Marci's look and handling of Sally Mae. "And we're not going home! All we need from you is some gas."

For the first time Marci laughed. She didn't know if it was from relief or the absurdity of it all. But she did know she liked this little spitfire so she fired back: "Sure you're the driver. You'd have to stand on the seat just to see out of the window of that gas guzzler you've got there."

The irony was that the price of luxury cars had dropped because of the scarcity and cost of gas. Now the poor could afford them, too. And the foolish, too, thought Marci remembering what her friends said about her buying the T-Bird. Marci decided she would have to take a count in the executive parking lot and see if it was full of Japanese compacts. Then reality jolted her back to the situation at hand.

"O.k. Miss Megan," Marci proclaimed. "Tell me where I can find the driver? Then I'll go get you some gas. First, we need a drive . . . one that can see over the windshield." Marci felt more comfortable using humor to negotiate with Megan.

Marci's laugh was picked up by Sally Mae.

"Me . . . Me . . . Me," she stammered. "I 16, I is. I drive. Meg na big nof to poosh gas. She sit on me lap . . . . She steer. I poosh gas. I poosh brake. I good . . . I good . . . tel her Meg . . . I good . . . you sa I good . . . you sa I good . . . ," protested Sally Mae as she went back to Meg's side and tugged at her pinafore pocket. ". . . doncha Meg . . . doncha Meg . . . . Sa I good . . . " Getting no immediate response she began to cry.

"Yes, Sally Mae, you are the best. You are even better than." and before Megan could stop herself " . . . pop."

Marci jumped on it. "Where is your father?"

"We're orphans!. All we want from you is gas. Are you going to get us some or do we have to wait for someone else?"

Marci could tell by the look on Megan's face she would do just that so she decided to take another approach. "O.K., but the first thing we've got to do is get this car out of the road so someone doesn't hit it - or you - like I almost did. You wait here. I'll get my bird out and push it out of the road with it. Then we'll go get the gas.

Marci was relieved to find there really was no damage to the T-Bird. The growth of paw paws had taken a beating and there were only a few scratches on the bumper. In a few minutes she was out of the thicket and onto the road. With Megan's help directing her forward she was able to ease up to the Cadillac and push it out of the road. She had to hand it to little Miss Megan. It was Megan, not her, who remembered to put the big Cadillac in neutral before she pushed it.

"O.K. everyone, hop in, we're going for gas," Marci said after Megan answered that yes, the car was far enough off the road.

But Marci knew from Megan's expression that wasn't going to happen. "We're staying here with the car!" she declared.

Marci didn't like leaving them. The crimson sky had lost its glow on the horizon. But after all, she rationalized, she had found them that way. Besides, once she got to the gas station she would find out what was going on and get some help. There was no way they wouldn't know who they were. Marci had noticed that Megan glanced at her license plate when she was checking out the one on the Cadillac.

"O.K. Megan," Marci agreed, "but I'll be right back. Make sure everybody stays out of the road. It will be dark sooner than you think. I should only be gone a few minutes. There used to be a Sunoco station up near Ice Mountain. Is it still there," she asked, as she automatically checked the road for traffic despite the fact she hadn't seen a soul on it for at least an hour. It was then she spotted the pothole again. It was the same one her father had complained about. The car stalled when she hit it. It still hadn't been fixed.

But it was the stricken look on Megan's face that made her forget the irony of that. Megan had lost her spitfire composure. She yelled: "Don't go to the Sunoco Station, go to the Esso!"

Then seeing the confused look on Marci's face, she had pleaded: "Go to the Esso. It's on the right side further down the road. We got credit there. Tell them Sally Mae sent you. You won't have to pay. Ask for the ten-gallon can."

As Marci sped down the road, she couldn't figure out Megan. She wanted to know more and then again she didn't want to. She wanted to be home showing her father her new car. Making it easier for her was the proud Megan. She didn't want to tell.

She wanted to get this situation handled as quickly as possible. It really was getting dark. You couldn't even tell where the sun had gone home.

The Sunoco Station was just ahead and it was open. Marci didn't even hesitate to pull in. If Megan didn't like this place, then they must know her parents. She would find out what was going on and get somebody to help so she could go home.

The old man met her as she was coming in the door. "Ya lost missy. We don't get many cars with New York plates in here, specially not in one of them dere Thunderbirds. Where did ya git that car?"

"It's mine. My name is Marci. You might remember my father. Years ago he used to come through here buying skinny cattle every fall to fatten up for the winter."

"The one with the 49 Ford truck.."

"Yes, that's him. I'm his daughter. But that's not why I'm here. There are three kids stranded up the road with a huge red Cadillac. Do you know them? Their parents, are they . . . ."

But before Marci could finish, the old man interrupted with " . . . are nothin but trash and them kids are jus as onery. Doncha fool with 'em missy. Their ole man can git pretty mean when he's drunk and dat is most of the time. Ya jus drive on and git yerself home . . . ."

Marci remembered the pinafores. Her mother had made them for her and her sisters. She must care. "But what about their mother. Can I call her from here?".

"Dat ma is even worse than he is, if ya know whut I mean. Jus ya git on and don't ya pay no mind to it. She'll find 'em on her way home. She always does."

Seeing that Marci still was not convinced, he continued: "Doncha worry non about it. Jus git. Dey kin sleep in de car till she finds 'em. If 'ens she's whar she usually is, if 'ens ya know whut I mean, she'll have to go home dat way ventually and find em."

"But somebody has got to help them now," Marci protested. "They are out of gas and it is almost dark. Do you realize that that little Megan steers the car and Sally Mae . . . . "

The old man's cackle stopped Marci in mid sentence. She had not liked the way he had leered at her when she walked in the door. And she had not appreciated his wink with the "if 'ens ya know whut I mean" comment. She was sorry she had not gone to the Esso Station.

"So it's da little tart with da car dis time," he said. "If 'ens she's got Sally Mae then she must have the other retard, too. She usually don't run with de others. Dere's at least ten of 'em young 'uns and dey all got different pappys, if 'ens ya know whut I mean."

Then the old man launched into a discussion of the entire 'brood' as he called them, betting with himself as to the likely father of each. "Wouldn't sprise me a'tal if dat Jim Boy isn't his brother's son. He's da oldest and he is as mean and dumb as his ole man. But dat little Megan is a corker. She's no good, but ya got to hand it to her. She's a sly little thing. Tough as shagbark, too. But ya jus wait . . . "

"Look," demanded Marci, disgusted and impatient, "where's the phone book? I'll call Miss Megan's mother?

The leer on the old man's weathered and tobacco stained face returned. "No need fer a phone book, missy. No need a'tal." The old man grinned, and spat on the floor, as he unwrapped another plug of tobacco. "No phone here either."

"What about the Esso Station up the road?" Marci demanded. "I'll bet they have a phone," she declared, ignoring his sneer. "Megan told me to go there for gas, that they had credit there, too," she said as haughtily as she could.

The old man's face broke into hundreds of wrinkles as he began jeering, cackling and making hissing sounds which Marci knew were now aimed at her, too. He began slapping the cash register as he doubled over, time and again, with laughter. Then he began wheezing and coughing up spit so hard Marci thought he would have a seizure. She found herself dodging the phlegm as she pushed a chair toward him. He managed to calm himself down long enough to clear his throat of a huge knot of snot that he cupped in his hand.

When he saw Marci's look of disgust, he didn't bother concealing it, but wiped it across his pants leg and began cackling all over again - enjoying the confused look on Marci's face.

"Credit! Ha! 'Credit.' Is dat whut she calls it. Dat's a good one. Credit. Dammed if dat don't beat all." He began cackling again seeing Marcy's confusion.

"Well, My High and Mighty Missy", he went on, enjoying himself. "I suggest ya wait outside de station while dat little Miss Megan, as ya call her, sends Sally Mae in to pay de bill. Sally Mae learned it from her mother, if'ens ya know whut I mean. And dat little tart learned how to use Sally Mae to pay for the gas from her drunken pappy, if'ens ya know whut I mean."

Marci nearly ran into the gas pumps as she drove off. She had contained her fury at the old man long enough to buy a ten-gallon can of gas.

Marci was also furious with herself. She realized she hadn't done Megan any favors, that was for sure. "Now everyone would hear about the credit they had at Esso ..that poor Sally Mae . . . and Jim Boy, too . . . hopefully you are so retarded you don't even know what is happening."

It was not a nice thought, but Marci wished it was so anyway. It was Megan that really concerned her. How was she going to survive it all?

When Marci pulled up, Megan jumped down from the hood of the Cadillac with a broad smile. Sally Mae lunged out of the back door of the car with Jim Boy in tow. He was struggling with a huge yellow stuffed Big Bird, the one from Sesame Street. It dwarfed him.

Marci's smile disappeared instantly when she saw the Sunoco

label on the can, her green eyes took on the deep opal of the old paw paws behind the shagbark oak.

"Sorry Megan," said Marci. "I know you said go to Esso and I should have. I don't like that old man there either. But it was getting dark and I just ran in real quick and bought this can. Consider it a present from me."

Not getting a response, Marci rambled on, trying to retrieve Megan's trust. "We'll just put the gas in now Megan. No one even needs to know you took the car. We'll get you home before anyone knows. Okay?"

Sally Mae whimpered loudly. "Meg . . . Meg . . . She mak us'ns go home . . . Ya promised. Ya promised. We go to fair. Ya say we go to fair. I want to ride roun . . . roun . . . me go roun . . . and roun . . . ."

Megan turned to quiet Sally Mae. "It's okay, Sally Mae. We're going to the fair like I said" She reached into her pocket and came up with two peppermints. "Here, have a peppermint and give one to Jim Boy, too."

Marci recognized the pink zig zag trim on Megan's pocket. Her mother had decorated their pinafore pockets with those elasticized stripes too. 'They will keep things from falling out of your pockets, too,' she had said. She had even put her sister's pocket on the left side because she was left-handed.

Megan turned her attention back to Marci. "We're meeting mom at the fair," she said determinedly. "It's not far from here." From her pocket this time came one of those squeezable lips change pouches from which she counted out six quarters. "I can pay you for two gallons of that gas."

"Forget it Megan," declared Marci quickly, amazed at how quickly she came up with the sum. The old man had gleefully announced to her that gas had gone up to 75 cents when she was paying him. It had been about 35 cents a gallon just a year ago. "I don't want any gas money. It's too high anyway. All of us should be driving compact cars. I just want to make sure you are okay before I go home."

Marci also knew the rides were a quarter. On the way to get the gas she had seen a sign for the fair. It was about 20 miles. In that car, it would take about two gallons so maybe Megan was meeting her mother at the fair.

"Are you sure your mother is at the fair? Will she be able to drive you home after you get there. You can't drive this car in the dark like that. In fact, you shouldn't be driving it at all. You do know that don't you? You really should go home."

Sally Mae started to whimper again, but before Marci could make out what she was trying to say, Megan replied, "No one is at home. I told you. Mom's at the fair. We're meeting her there. Now can we get the gas in. Please!" She shoved the quarters at Marci.

"No, Megan," declared Marci, noting that ledges above were taking on a sinister look as evening shadows swept across them "I will not, absolutely not, take your money." Then as casual as she could sound, she added: "I used to go to the fair with my brother and sister, too. I even had a sister like you that used to buy me rides."

Seeing Megan's face relax," Marci added. "You can spend that on your sister and brother—okay?"

Marci felt the full warmth of Megan's sunny smile. For the first time Megan looked directly at her. Marci blushed. She wanted so much to be liked by this kid.

Marci picked up the can of gas and headed for the Cadillac. "As Frank Sinatra should have said, we're going to do it your way." She gave Megan a playful tap on the shoulder. "You're a good kid, you know that. Don't let anybody make you do something you don't want to."

Then, feeling helpless and realizing Megan was as vulnerable as the young paw paws under the power lines and the ledges, she added, "Even if somebody forces you to do something you don't want to do, always remember that you are a good person. You're a good person no matter what. Okay, is that a deal?" Marci held out her hand like her father always did with the hillside farmers.

Megan shook her hand and grinned as Marci, trying to keep up a good front, did a little skip with the gas can. Sally Mae and Jim Boy felt the good mood, too. They began laughing and running after Marci as she then made an elaborate dance over to the Cadillac.

But Marci's reverie didn't last long. As soon as she saw the unleaded gas only label on the tank she realized they had another problem. She had not gotten a funnel when she ran out of the station with the can. She once had that problem trying to fill her new car at an old station still using leaded gas. The new cans did not have the long narrow snouts to force the valve open.

One thing was for sure, she decided. She was not going to go back to that old man. She would make do. She tried jamming a stick down the narrow inlet to hold the valve open. But very little gas was getting in. Then she remembered the Liefraumilch wine she was sneaking home for her grandmother.

The county they lived in did not allow liquor stores. So when her father went to Hardy county, he would get her some Mogen David wine for her fruit cakes. He had shared his suspicion with Marci that not all of it was making it into her cakes.

So when Marci had gotten the job in New York, her grandmother had suggested that maybe the wines one could purchase there might be even better. Like her father, Marci had allowed as to how the cakes were getting even better with each new wine she tried.

The Liefraumilch came in a slender bottle with a long narrow neck which Marci realized could serve as a funnel. Marci congratulated herself for thinking of it as she ran to her car to get it. She laughed at herself for briefly thinking about drinking it, but then she remembered she wouldn't have to throw it out either because she had a thermos full of coffee which was cold anyway. She could pour it in there.

She was just about to uncork the Liefraumilch when Megan, coming out from the back of the Cadillac, yelled. She was waving a hose.

"Brilliant! Just what we need," Marci declared. "Absolutely brilliant, she happily announced as she took the hose from Megan. "Now we can get this show on the road."

Sally Mae began jumping up and down with delight and then ran in a circle saying . . . roun an roun an roun. . . . . Marci laughed when she realized that Sally Mae was forming nearly a perfect circle as she imagined her trip on the merry-go-around. Or maybe it was the swings. Or the ferris wheel. They had those, too.

Marci jammed one end of the hose down the gas can, placed her mouth on the other end and sucked. She had seen her father do it effortlessly many times to fill the tractor. But nothing happened. So she took a deep breath and sucked hard. It worked. But she had forgotten the last rule of lowering the tube fast into the inlet. She choked on a mouthful of gas that fizzled out before she could get it to inlet. Then she realized it was too short. She was going to have to hold the can up to the inlet and suck the gas out at the same time.

But before she got into position, Sally Mae was tugging at her shirt. She was holding several longer tubes. "Da-Da . . . he mak gas go car to car." Marci laughed. She couldn't help it despite the look on Megan's face which was warning Sally Mae to say no more.

"Look Megan," Marci explained as she smiled and squeezed Megan's arm, "I don't judge people by their parents. You are a very smart little girl and that is all that is important. Always remember how smart you are and when you grow up you just drive yourself out of here." Megan looked at Marci's car.

For a fleeting moment Marci thought of just driving off with her. "One day," said Marci, "you can drive back here with a car just like that one and get Sally Mae and Jim Boy.

This time it was Megan who blushed. She looked away from Marci towards Sally Mae.

"And Sally Mae," added Marci, following Megan's eyes. "It looks like you have been holding out on me. That was real smart. You and Megan are a real team. I am going to follow you all to the fair to make sure you get there."

Marci could tell that Sally Mae was not understanding much, but she spoke directly to her slowly and directly anyway for Megan's benefit. She knew a lecture was not something Megan would appreciate anymore than she did.

"Sally Mae. Mind you, I do not approve of your driving the car that way. You could get into trouble with the state police. Sometimes they do drive in this area. I know because my father and I used to come through here a lot. You should ask your mother to take you or get you a ride to the fair. If you do something nice for her, I bet she'll help you. Or maybe when your father feels alright and is in a good mood."

Feeling Megan's derisive shrug, Marci decided that approach was not feasible so she searched for another solution. "You must never hitchhike with a man you don't know. A man or woman together would be o.k. Or better yet a couple of women. But hitchhiking is never a good idea because you never know if they will be mean or not. If I was in your position and I really had to get somewhere, I think I would wait until a neighbor I know that is safe is going. First I would ask them to take me to where I want to go. If they say they can't, then I would get on their road and hitchhike when they came by. They would probably pick me up. It would be worth a try."

Again feeling Megan's negative reaction to the neighbors, Marci went on: "Okay, so they might feel sorry for me. That's okay. One day I will be in a position to feel sorry for them. How about that Sally Mae? And, something else, too. If somebody does something really wrong to you, get a neighbor you trust to call the police. They will help you." Marci could see out of the corner of her eye that Megan was mulling over the suggestions.

Turning her attention to the long hose, she gaily announced. "Well team, here goes. Let's see if I can get it right this time."

Even Jim Boy picked up on the renewed gaiety. He began clapping his hands as Marci successfully transferred the gas into the Cadillac.

"You know Megan, Marci said. "I could go for a piece of peppermint after the taste of that gas.

Marci knew she had made a friend. Megan even unwrapped the piece of hardtack for her. She was beaming with satisfaction.

"Thank you for the gas. It is a big help. Then, tentatively, she asked, "Will you ever be coming through here again with your father?

Marci's heart sank. She knew her parents would point out that they already had parents and you shouldn't get involved because you could make matter worse. She remembered the time people in the valley had gotten upset over a moonshiner who had moved in. They told the police but nothing happened. The shiner threatened to beat his wife and children for telling. So they had begged the valley people not to say anything for their sake. Marci could hear her folks now saying," . . . how sad it was . . . there are hundreds of poor kids like them . . . there is nothing you can really do . . . you can't solve the world's problems alone . . . the government today makes it difficult to get involved in other people's problems . . . the police can't do anything until someone is hurt . . . ."

Marci knew that social services in this area were non-existent. There still might be a 4-H club agent in this area, but then Megan wasn't a farm kid.

She thought of the new $50 bill her father had given her for emergencies.

She rationalized that it would probably be taken away from Megan or that if she used it to run away, she could face a fate worse than she already had.

Marci put on her best smile and said, "I wish we were going through here. I am afraid those days are gone for both of us. He doesn't buy skinny heifers anymore from the hollow farms here. I have a job in New York and I don't get down here much."

Marci could see that Megan was fighting off a look of disappointment and replacing it with a look of indifference. Marci tried to soft-pedal the reality with a casual comment. "But when I do come down this way, I will drive through here and maybe I will see you. Right now, I will follow you to the fair to make sure you get there."

Megan ignored her comment as she signaled Sally Mae and Jim Boy to get into the car. "You don't have to follow us to the fair. We can get there," she said stiffly. She motioned to Sally Mae and Jim Boy to get in the car.

"But Megan," protested Marci, "I want to follow you to

make sure you get there okay. Besides, I'm going that way anyway, okay."

Then, trying to sound more light-hearted as they got in the car, Marci added. "I hope they still have a Ferris wheel there. I used to really like those."

Sally Mae answered for them, as she sat upright behind the steering wheel to make room for Megan. "Meg . . . Meg . . . she like Ferris wheel when it go up up . . . me . . . I like swi . . . swing . . . swings. Jim likes to gr . . . gr . . . gr . . . in the little cars. We put him in the little cars."

Megan climbed up on Sally Mae's lap. She gave the horn a quick tap and said, without looking at Marci again, "It is getting dark. I bet they are turning on the Ferris wheel lights now."

Megan turned the ignition, it caught and Marci could hear her repeat directions to Sally Mae for pushing the gas on the right and the brakes on the left.

Marci followed them until they came to the turnoff for the fair. The taste of the gas mixed with peppermint and Megan's paw paw eyes stayed with Marci as she drove on to connect with U.S. Route 50.

Marci came out of this 1972 reverie when she realized she was now on top of Ice Mountain and it was 1997. When she came to the bottom of Ice Mountain she felt she was on time. The road was there. She followed the creek. The curve ahead . . . that was it. That was the one she had gone too fast around and had so little time to keep from hitting them. The paws paws were still there . . . stubby, oversized stumps and limbs from battling the telephone company line brush cutters. Marci stepped on the gas as she rounded the curve. Maybe that would bring her back, them back.

She stopped and got out. Everything was quiet. No birds, no wind, the creek was so low you couldn't hear it and there had been no traffic for miles. Even the stony faced ledges just sat up there without saying anything. The shagbark oak was gone. The veneer and then the clear-cutters had been through the whole area. She had noticed how thin and scraggily the forest was ten miles back.

But the paw paws were not giving up under the old telephone line. She wondered which generation she was looking at now. She sat there for awhile. Just listening. Nothing.

She got back into the car and decided to find other things that looked familiar. When she drove by the Sunoco station and saw that it had been turned in to a flea market, she cheered. She tried to imitate the old man's cackle and gave a V sign for Megan.

When she got to the spot where she thought the Esso station must be, there was a brand new building there, a large sign on the door read: Paw Paw Community Center. Marci pulled in. She had found a place for the worn out $50 bill. She asked the teenager at the desk if she had ever heard of three children she met 25 years ago, Megan, Sally Mae and Jim Boy.

The teenager, called out for her mother. "Her name is Megan."

Marci was speechless when Megan came around the corner. It was her. There was no mistaking that look in her eyes as she sized Marci up.

Marci couldn't think of a thing to say. She felt relief she had survived. But she still felt guilty. She should have done something to help back then. She was retiring soon and would be moving back to the valley where she was born. Maybe she could still do something.

Megan said, "May I help you?"

For a moment Marci felt relief. Megan didn't recognize her. But Marci had to get rid of the guilt. Marci handed her the $50 and told her she should have given it to her 25 years ago. They discussed what happened in 1972. Marci asked if she needed volunteers . . . that she needed to clear her conscience for not doing something.

Megan told her it was Sally Mae who had helped all of them when she told a cop who stopped by there what she was doing. It was not long after that, she grinned, that Esso put all of them into a home and even paid for Megan's social services degree at the University.

Marci asked about the old Sunoco Station, now a flea market, with that disgusting "If you know what I mean" old man in it. "He's dead and Sunoco now has a brand new station just down the road. Jim-Boy works there," grinned Megan.

Megan told her that Sally Mae was now in a half-way home in Winchester and very happy. In fact, she was on her way now to pick her up for the Hampshire County Fair. "She still likes the merry-go-round better than the Ferris wheel. And I still carry my bag of peppermints for her. Maybe you'd like to go with us."

Dick Van Meter

"Look out! He's coming this way."

Marci Kuykendall did not even have to look down the street as she got out of the car. She could tell by her sister Decker's voice that it was Dick Van Meter. She quickly joined Decker as they went the other way which would mean they would have to go around the entire block to get to the store now. But it was worth it to avoid Dick.

Last time she had seen him was when she stopped at Richard's fruit market coming into town. It had been an eight hour drive to get home and she was looking forward to just off-the-vine-ripe tomatoes. These were so delicious she was not going to fry them, just slice them and eat. She saw the fresh sweet corn sign and was pleased to find out it was the white corn called Silver Queen, the ears might be smaller but they were tastier than the yellow corn.

When she went in to pay Richard, there was Dick, sitting in Richard's chair while Richard bent over to get to the cash drawer to make change. Marci knew the locals had learned to tolerate Dick's ways even though it was disgusting to her how he lorded over them with his ideas of past grandeur. The Van Meter family still had the most land in the valley even though they did nor farm it anymore. Dick had given up farming to live on his inheritance and rented his portion of the farm which amounted to about 500 acres.

Marci and Decker's ancestors had been among the first settlers along with the Van Meters so there had been many marriages between them. Marci recalled how her father always said it was too bad the Kuykendall men were prone to die early while the Van Meter women lived into their nineties. Often the land would be turned over to the Van Meters.

As a result, there was little Kuykendall land left in the valley and very few Kuykendalls. Many had gone west. The Van Meters had held onto about half of the land and sold the rest to commercial developers. Marci and her sister had managed to buy the original log cabin their ancestor had built along with ten acres from one of the original 1200 acre farms. The log cabin had been added to over ten generations and was now an L-shaped two-story house with a chimney on each point. Beside it was the family fort which had been built during the French and Indian wars.

"So when are you going to get that graveyard off my land," declared Dick. "I am tired of you not paying rent. And I'm tired of paying someone to keep it up."

Richard gave Marci a questioning but amused look. He had not heard this one before. The locals always described Dick as being tighter than the bark on a tree. He was even known to take leftover food off the plates of those leaving the local diner before the waitress could clean up. People were still talking about his being caught taking a load of wood saying it was free because it was on along the road and everyone owned the roadways. But charging rent for a graveyard was a new one for Dick.

Marci explained to Richard, speaking loudly and decisively to make sure Dick Van Meter got the point again, that the graveyard had been there when the Kuykendalls settled the land and that the law was that it would stay there forever. She went on to explain the graveyard was registered as a legal burial site by the county and had checked that in the history of the United States, there was no such thing as rentals on graveyards.

But Marci knew what was coming next. Dick would go back to all the work he did keeping the graveyard "up."

She had first heard this when she was in the bank line cashing a check and she had not noticed he was behind her. It must have been the cash in her hand, she thought, that triggered him into his miserly instincts. Dick went on at great length about how the fence around the graveyard was always breaking down and he was no longer going to cut all the weeds out of the plot. Worse, those awful thistles were seeding and spreading into his pasture field. His renter was complaining.

Other people got back in the line to hear how this conversation would go. They knew that Marci and Dick were first cousins. They also knew she was a lot like her mother who did not tolerate fools. Marci peppered Dick with comments of, " I know your renter. He could supply the world with thistle seed because he never takes care of his own land much less that of what he rents," and "You tell me you can't see the tombstones because of the weeds in there and I'm telling you can't see the graveyard for all the thistles you have in your rented field." As for those fences, Marci added, those cows must find something in the plot to eat other than thistles because they are always breaking the fence down every time we repair it. I should charge you for cow damage."

Dick protested that her mother, who was a Van Meter, never would have allowed those thistles to grow. He added that the nearby Van Meter graveyard, surrounded by a nice Victorian iron fence, was well-kept up and not a disgrace to the Van Meter ancestors. He noted that he would never even have allowed her mother to put Kuykendall stones in there if she had not been a Van Meter originally.

Marci knew it was true that her mother had added two headstones to the graveyard which had been found face down as fill in for a flagstone walk. Decker had been the one who took them down to the Kuykendall graveyard and placed them near the other hand-cut river stones.

Marci agreed that the graveyard had been a mess since her mother died. "So tell me when you cleaned it out. I'm down here a lot each summer and I would have noticed and I must say that it sure doesn't look like a very good job was done."

Dick, remembering his family once had a good reputation as farmers, added that he was not able to do it all himself so he had hired someone to do it and paid him. Hearing this, Marci had demanded that he give her the name of the person who he had hired so she could pay him herself. She knew she had him there because he would not be able to come up with a name. She also knew if she humored Dick with $5 or $10 it would be a mistake because he would he would raise the rent each time she saw him.

At that point, Dick had left the bank, grumbling but never in a subdued manner. After all he was the oldest of the living Van Meters now and he had demanded nearly everyone address him as "Mr. Van Meter," making an exception only to those he felt were his equal which were few.

But here a summer later, Marci was back for another visit to the home place again, having another round with Dick Van Meter, this time at Richard's fruit stand.

Time had taken a new turn in Dick's reasoning. Now he was saying that her mother had put the entire graveyard down there, not just the two stones from the flagstone walk. "I only let her do it," he declared, "because she was a Van Meter."

He went on about how he was going to pull the stones out and dump them at their house. Her mother had found the two stones upside down in the flagstone walk leading to the Kuykendall fort. "Those stones should be put back at the fort where everyone can walk all over you Kuykendall's," he yelled for effect. Then he went on to downgrade the fence they had put up last summer. Marci sarcastically retorted that the barbed wire was needed to keep the cows from leaning over into the graveyard in their insatiable appetite for more thistles.

Then Marci, remembering how she had spent several hours in 102 degree heat on a visit a month ago to rid the graveyard of thistles to pacify Dick, asked him if he had looked at the graveyard recently . . . that she had, indeed, been cleaning it out ever since their conversation in the bank.

Maybe it was the mention of the bank that reminded Dick but he was quick to demand. "If you don't pay rent or get that graveyard off Van Meter property, I will move it myself. You Kuykendalls should be ashamed of yourselves, the way you treat your dead. It's a good thing we Van Meters got most of the land."

Richard, whose ancestors had worked on both Kuykendall and Van Meter farms, was the only one laughing when he heard Marci explode, "Now you look here Dick Van Meter. Unfortunately, both my grandmothers and great grandmothers were Van Meters. I'm ashamed to say it but I have more Van Meter blood in me than you have. One day I may become the idiot you are. You leave that graveyard alone or you'll have both my Van Meter sides on your back."

Washington Seen

We just stood there looking at each other in the store, trying to figure out who it was from the past. We knew we had shared something, something that was better left in the past. Yet, it was not an unfriendly look we shared.

It had been some 20 years since I had been shopping in Cumberland, Maryland, where my mother used to bring me and my sisters for what was then big city shopping to find a special dress. The independent store was still there, and still expensive despite competition from big mall stores like Macy's or Marshall's. As we continued to eye each other, we realized we both were holding the same sweater at the cash register.

Then it struck us at the same time, both asking, "What are you doing here?" as we saw images of each other at the corn packing shed when we were fourteen years old. I realized the question might be insulting to Helen and quickly mumbled that she must live here and it was me that was a stranger to the store as I had not been there since my mother bought me a high school graduation dress. Helen, knowing that I would never have dreamed that she one day could afford to be shopping there, had replied that yes, indeed, she lived only five blocks from the store, adding that she was a frequent customer.

We hugged each other as we picked up where we had left off 20 years ago, two scared girls not knowing what life was about and anxious to find out. The fancy department store no longer had style shows, but it still had the corner show room which was now a small café. There was a line so Helen and I put the sweaters on the counter, telling the clerk we would be back. When we sat down, we almost simultaneously said, "You are looking good." Then we laughed, knowing we would have never been so formal with each other back in the sugar corn packing shed.

Helen and I had been the only girls working in the shed that summer and happened to both be "going on 16." It had been our first real-paying job with social security deductions and we had naturally lined up with each other as the foreman explained we would have to be at work at 6 a.m. every morning, we had 30 minutes for lunch and we could go home at 8 p.m. that night. There were about 20 boys our age plus several old men deemed too old to pick the corn in the hot fields. The shed had just been modernized with a refrigeration system to keep the corn fresh as it came in from the fields. The corn was dumped in the huge tank of cold water and a conveyer belt brought it up to the station where all the workers teamed up, one on each side of a crate, to pack in five dozen ears. In the old days this job was performed right at the edge of the hot fields so Helen and I soon learned not to complain about our hands getting cold and stiff as we packed corn. We also knew this job paid better than cleaning and cooking for the boss so we quickly joined the others in commenting how nice it was to be working in a cool shed instead of outside in the hot sun like the adults were.

But despite our becoming fast friends that summer, both of us knew our lives were quite different and we would not likely meet again unless it was back at the corn shed for another summer. My parents were farmers. My dad had gotten pneumonia that year and money was hard to come by as he had to hire an extra man to do the work he couldn't. So, despite the objections of my mother, my dad sent me to work in the corn shed which my mother had declared was no place for a young girl. Helen, on the other hand, came from a migrant worker family which eked out a living following seasonal perishable crops. Ever since she could remember, Helen had picked peaches, apples, beans, even cotton. Unlike me, Helen had never been to school but had learned to read and write from her mother who had had some schooling before marrying her father. He was working the fields now and I had not liked him when I met him. He looked at me with a look I didn't understand then. After that the foreman had told me not to go near him.

During the lunch break, Helen and I would cook some of the corn to go with what people had brought in their lunch buckets. Helen would serve her father and I had noticed she would become very timid when he came in at lunch and at the end of the day. While it was hard work and one could explain getting bruised if the conveyor built got too close or one of the heavy crates fell on you when the conveyor belts moved forward, I had noticed Helen had more than the usual cuts and sores from the thin, papery shucks covering the corn ears and the sharp, stalky ends. But Helen would only look down if questioned and say that she was the one in the family that never seemed to do anything right and that her father was upset with her because of it.

It had not made a lot of sense to me and it still didn't when Helen and I decided to sneak on one of the big refrigerated tractor-trailers that came in to take the corn to Pittsburgh, Washington, Baltimore and New York. Neither of us had ever been to a big city and we decided on Washington since that was where the Capitol was. Knowing my mother's dislike for the people who worked in the shed, I made up a story about staying with the foreman's family which my mother approved of. I was with Helen when she told her father she was going to stay with me that night which seemed strange because he was not mad, just sounded so surprised. He had to know we were best friends even though I had stayed away from him.

When the Washington truck driver was overseeing the loading of the corn crates into his tractor trailer that evening, we sneaked into the upper bed loft in the back of the cab. We figured that if we kept quiet by taking a nap, he would not discover us until it was too late for him to turn back. He was not much older than my brother and I had assured myself he would not be mad at us.

Our plan worked, especially since we were so tired from the day's work that we soon fell asleep in his upper bed loft. In fact, we didn't wake up until he was backing into the dock to unload the corn. Between the confusion of the teamsters at the dock on strike and the exasperation he felt just getting through the picket lines, he just sat there looking at us as he adjusted his rear view mirror to see what was going on in his upper loft.

After much explanation from us, he decided there was nothing he could do. He would hurry back and drop us off early the next morning at the corn shed when he left an empty trailer there to be loaded during the day. Still, he was upset and when he saw that he was going to have to unload the truck himself because the dockhands were teamsters, he told us we could earn our trip by helping him unload. In fact, he would even drive us by the Capitol Building on the way home so we could see it.

Hours later, the trailer was unloaded and we were giddy with laughter as we were mesmerized by the huge size of the distribution center, To me, it was larger than the valley I came from and, unlike Helen, I had never seen so much produce in one place but she had as she described fields of melons than went for miles in the Carolinas. One of the managers who had been sent in to make sure the center was open even gave us a tour which included a sampling of apples, oranges, bananas and strawberries. He also gave us an official sweater worn by the dockhands since the distribution center was also refrigerated.

The driver was as good as his word. He let us set up front with him in the high cab and we had a grand view of the lit-up Capitol at night. It looked just like the picture we had seen on the huge calendar that was pasted up on the big ammonia tank in the corn shed where the foreman checked off the days of work, noting who had been where.

On the way back the driver pulled over to take a quick nap and sent us to the overhead bunk to get some sleep, too. But we were too excited to get much sleep as we chattered continuously. It was when Helen rubbed one of her bruised arms and said that she had the best rest she ever had with Marci in the overhead bed that got the driver's attention. She mentioned that the driver had not come to bed with them. She wondered to me if he hit people after he played with them in bed.

The driver, who had been listening and teasing us to get some sleep, immediately changed his attitude—so much so that Helen and I felt we better not say anything more until we could figure out if he was mad. He became very serious. His full attention was on Helen as he asked some very gentle questions. It was very confusing to both of us and Helen answered as best she could so he wouldn't be mad. He had been so good to us—driving by the Capitol and not bawling us out for hiding in his truck. We arrived just as the sun was coming up and he made us swear no one would know that we had been in Washington with him. He even dropped us off about a mile below the sheds so no one would see us.

When the crew showed up for work, we came from behind a stack of empty crates, pretending that we had just arrived, too Work resumed as usual and we were elated that we had seen the Capitol and sneaked off when we could to recount our adventure together. When the Washington driver picked up the tractor trailer load of corn that evening, he made a point of coming over to Helen and I to assure himself no one knew about our trip. When my ride home came, he followed me to make me promise again never to say anything no matter what happened and said that everything was going to be alright no matter what anybody said. When I left he was still talking to Helen.

The next morning was very confusing and scary to me. Helen's father had been found in the field badly beaten up and Helen had not shown up for work. The foreman was not that concerned since the sugar corn picking season was nearly over and, besides, who knew what Helen's father had done to get himself beaten up. The foreman had never liked him. He even loaded him on the truck that the migrant workers came in on from their camp and told them not to send him back when he recovered.

I worked at the refrigerated corn shed for two more summers after that and each time asked the migrant workers if they knew Helen. But none of them did. Several times I spotted the driver who had kept our secret about hiding on his truck. I would ask him if he ever saw Helen and he would just smile and told me not to worry about Helen that he was sure she was fine and that she was a good girl.

Now, twenty years later, Helen and I were paying for our sweaters and laughing, wondering if that is what triggered our memories and how the cashmere sweaters we got on sale were very different from the heavy wool ones in the food distribution center in Washington.

My puzzlement about Helen had finally been cleared up. I found out the driver and his friend had taken Helen to a home for girls to get her away from her molesting father. The driver had checked on her for years and even helped her get a job. She was now a manager of an A&P grocery store. She and her husband now had two children.

Helen saved the best news for last as we chatted in that department store café. She said, "Why don't you come to dinner tonight. We're having an outdoor barbecue. You may recognize my husband. He owns several tractor trailers now."

I was delighted. I got the address and on the way there, I passed an open air fruit market. I already had a bottle of wine for the celebration. But it hit me that there was something much better to bring. I saw they had sweet corn. I asked if they sold it by the crate. I laughed as I heaved the heavy crate of five dozen ears into my car.

When I got there, one of Helen's kids opened the door. I asked the kid to get her parents as I needed some help unloading the car. It broke the ice. We had a wonderful evening, full of laughs and catching up on all the good things that had happened since the summer of '58.

I left in happy tears when they toasted me for having introduced them. It had been my idea to hide on that truck and go to Washington.

The Hunting Camp

For the past 40 years Jim Tot, Jr., during deer season in November and December, worked at the hunting camp up Buffalo Creek hollow in West Virginia. It was good money—better than what he made in the sweet corn fields or orchards during the summer months. For one thing the hunters had money—some of them were from out of state with big blue and white collar jobs. The work was easier, too. But, he was getting tired of it all—not of the same old big buck stories but of the kind of people that were hunting these days.

Still, he was not about to be critical of the cruder crowd because the money was coming faster than ever, particularly when he became entertainer as well as cook and dishwasher. He would keep his private opinions to himself about the changes, not that anyone these days asked for them. He knew that the gentlemen hunters from the old days probably didn't consider him one of them either, but at least they asked serious questions and seemed to value his opinion even though he was there to serve them.

When the 2007 season opened, Tot Jr., now rested from two month's of hard work picking peaches and apples, was not surprised to arrive at the camp and find that it was already a mess. Even though the season did not open until Monday, each year the number of those arriving Friday night for partying seemed to grow. Before he got to the front porch, he could smell the stench of beer cans not fully emptied. Somebody had put his trash barrel from the kitchen opposite the porch swing which he could tell had been used for target practice. Some of the cans had made it into the barrel which he was grateful for as he picked up those around it.

No, Tot, Jr. did not complain. Like his old man, who could train dogs to corner but not kill their prey, he simply said to those getting ready for the next flying Budweiser missile, "Back in the old days, they didn't allow booze to be sold in this state. Deer season was kicked off with some shine and they made a formal ritual of drinking it around the fireplace. Even when they were totally blinded they didn't feel the need for target practice. They usually slept through the first day and none was more grateful than those big bucks out there. So was I. I could spend more time cooking then cleaning."

Just in case he'd gone too far in his cajoling, Tot, Jr., feeding their feeling of superiority, missed landing a few empties into the barrel. "Yep, you're lucky I'm a better cook then shooter," he added as he picked up and handed the missed ones to Four Wheeler, an auto salesman from Ohio who was back again this year. Four Wheeler, a favorite of the other hunters for his supply of fine oil compounds to polish their guns, got his name from the big, outsized SUV he drove. He had taken out two rows of seats to haul his prey although he still liked to tie one to the front grill just to assure everyone he had bagged his limit. Hunters were now legally allowed to kill four deer because of the heavy deer population which was due to 10, 000 acres being sold by a major lumber company after they stripped it of timber leaving plenty of undergrowth for deer. The farmers were also supporting the increased kill hoping it would stop the crop damage even though they sometimes lost a steer to an overanxious and probably inebriated hunter.

Four Wheeler sunk seven out of the ten cans he threw at the barrel, eliciting cheers from the others with one saying his girl friend was not even a seven on a scale of ten. About the only thing that hasn't changed, thought Tot to himself, was that women still were not allowed in this hunting camp. Looking around at the mess, he decided that perhaps this was one of those situations where the feminists did not mind being discriminated against.

As Tot went into the cabin he complimented the group, with just a little condescension, on their ability to count. He smiled when he saw the photo of the old hunting group hanging above the fireplace. He wryly noted that the old gang not only acted with some decorum but also dressed better. Most of them were wearing the traditional red and black hunting shirts and sports slacks. Several had pipes placed in ash trays on the coffee table which he had made for the camp out of a cherry tree trunk. They looked happy as they were toasting each other with cut-glass tumblers filled with shine.

Back then the county had been dry. Tot's father had gotten his young son the job at the hunting camp which had proved fortuitous for moon shiners like him looking for a market. The out-of-state hunters, used to a celebratory libation, were particularly grateful that their hunting lodge caretaker could provide these extra services. It was a win-win for all of them and even though he was much younger than the hunters, the young Jim Tot and his father were often asked to join them after dinner for their nightcap.

Tot, Jr. shook his head as he compared the men in the photo with the men on the porch wearing t-shirts advertising everything from Disneyland to the NRA, as well as a few political ones such as John Kerry's "poodles don't hunt" and Hillary's face behind a target. Some were wearing their bright colored vests, even though they were only required in the woods. Tot winced when one of the men tossed a still lit cigarette butt off the porch. But he didn't go after it, remembering it had rained the day before and would probably cause no problem.

Wondering what happened to many of those in the photo, he recalled Bill Kuykendall's daughters who went off to college and got jobs at Union Carbide and GE. They often referred executives they met to the hunting camp and he had enjoyed talking to them. He still owned the stock they had transferred to him as a tip, which he, in his youthful immaturity at the time, had not really appreciated.

He laughed at himself and was grateful for his ignorance in that he had not been able to figure out how to cash them in or even ask for dividends as it grew. Unlike the farmers in the area, he was he was going to be able to retire with a tidy sum that would be even more than his social security.

He expressed a quiet thank you to the group in the photo. He supposed the executives today with their big pay were going on safaris instead of to West Virginia camps. Still, it had been a good time for all and he always smiled when he thought of the year that too many of them showed up from GE so Bill Kuykendall housed the extra VPs from the lamp plants in Ohio in his new Quonset hut hog house which he had just bought. Bill had not put his hogs in there yet and it was fully lined with fresh straw. Even though the brass had to bend over to get in it, they seemed to thoroughly enjoy roughing it up. The only one upset was the daughter who didn't want to go back to work after she heard about it, although her father had assured her the VPs had not known the hut was for hogs.

Then there was that time a bunch of Union Carbide executives, arriving in a new Lincoln, and either too old or not in shape to walk in the woods, were told by Bill they could drive up into his back-40 pasture where the deer were alway eating him and his steers out of clover. They had driven up from Charleston in a snowstorm and had salt all over the car. When they drove into the field, the cattle, including two large Angus and Hereford bulls, surrounded them, licking the salt off the car and leaving them cowering in the car for about an hour before Bill rescued them.

While coal was still king in West Virginia, fees from hunting were the second biggest income producer in the state. The governor had created a game department to raise and stock bear and ring-necked pheasants. A morning dove season had been added with just a few protests from aging hippies, now too old to have much effect on calls for peace, much less saving its symbol.

Out of state hunters had to pay $2500 for just a bear hunting license. The governor was still trying to promote tourism through the "wild and wonderful" and "almost heaven" programs as another way to improve the state's economy, but few people made it their vacation destination. Tot figured that those that did visit those parts where mountain tops had been removed by the coal companies might donate money to reforest, so that would be some help.

As Tot unwrapped the bear meat he had frozen from one he shot before the season started, he felt a little guilty. He rationalized it was good advertising for the season because the men would certainly enjoy using their cell phones to tell the wives and fellow workers that they were already eating bear meat.

No doubt about it. Hunting was good for the local economy as well as the farmers trying to keep their crops intact. So, Tot took extra care in making the best bear stew he could, throwing in lots of vegetables donated by the farmers. He also baked a huge potato for each man and several pans of corn bread, wondering if that was enough to sober up the porch crowd.

When he called them in to supper, there was much braggadacio about who was going to get the first bear or buck, and some falling of chairs as they struggled to the table, and great exaltation as they chowed down. After opening more beer cans to wash it all down, they demanded Tot tell them about the old days and the time the executives got penned in their car by the bulls.

It was then that Jim Tot, Jr. had an idea that would make everyone happy, and certainly his life easier. "You know," he said, "bear stew goes best with some shine. In fact, everything does. If I got you fellers some shine, you could save a lot of money on beer, and we could sit around the fireplace like the old days."

When a celebrating shot rang out from Four Wheeler's pistol into the fireplace, Jim Tot, wincing, knew his suggestion had more than met their approval. With some careful maneuvering, perhaps, he could bring back some of the good old days. He would see how things went and maybe he would even bring out the cut-glass tumblers he had hidden in the cupboard.

G.W.

People in Hampshire County said G.W. Culpepper was the meanest man who ever lived in the valley. Everyone called him G.W., including his wife and three sons, because that's what he wanted and keeping on G.W's good side was of paramount importance. Even his youngest son, Joseph, who was mentally retarded, knew enough to agree with everything G.W. said and did, or bear the consequences.

The other two Culpepper sons hadn't learned that lesson and had the scars from cuts and burns to show for it. In fact, their uncle, G.W.'s brother, Delmar, took the two boys in when it became obvious they were not safe in their own house. That left G.W.'s wife, Matilda, and Joseph, at home. By all accounts the only defense they had against G.W.'s wrath was to keep him supplied with his own moonshine which put him in too much of a stupor to do bodily harm.

G.W.'s moonshine was a mixture of wild cannabis hemp and corn, an addictive combination that kept his customers coming back. It may also have been a contributing factor to G.W.'s mean streak but as long as he continued to drink himself into a daily stupor Matilda and Joseph could be assured of a relatively peaceful environment.

Matilda's claim to fame was her corn bread, considered the best in the valley and verified by the blue ribbons she won at the Hardy County Fair ten years in a row. That may have been her second best recipe, the first being the ingredients in the hootch that kept G. W. at bay.

Delmar believed that their father's history of making moonshine and subsequent run-ins with authorities was the reason G. W. was so belligerent and vicious. Back in the days of prohibition, revenue agents raided the still, arrested their father and sent him to prison. The family was then left without resources and their pride wouldn't allow them to accept help from their neighbors or the local church.

Then a horrendous series of events occurred which would test the resolve of Job, Delmar explained. G. W's father was fatally shot while trying to escape from prison, his baby sister died of starvation, and soon after that his mother drowned herself in the nearby river. G. W. and his brother were taken in by his mother's sister, who already had her hands full raising eight of her own children. She died of consumption when G.W. was ten years old, leaving the two brothers to fend for themselves without benefit of parents or schooling. G.W. was able to put meat on the table with his father's gun. Every animal in his path became the government to him, as he lashed out to survive. Delmar, who was younger and able to make friends easier, was able to get work on nearby farms and orchards. They barely had time to get to know each other as they struggled to survive.

When G.W. married Matilda, it had been Delmar's hope she would be able to show G.W. the world was not such a cruel place. Delmar attributed Matilda's crooked arm and limp to G.W., but she would answer his questions just as she would with a neighbor—with a huge smile, a smile that made everyone cringe even more when they noticed missing teeth.

It was well known that what Matilda really feared was someone making G.W. mad because it was she and Joseph that paid the price. If any of the Culpepper's wanted to help, they would keep people away from G.W. Delmar made sure Matilda knew that if things really ever got out of hand he would step in again and rescue her and Joseph despite his brother's temper.

As for G. W., if he was unknowingly being isolated by his family, it was fine with him. He didn't like people any better than he liked his hunting dogs. He kicked and beat them when they failed to tree a coon, or bring back a pheasant, or rabbit. He raised beagles, and those who bought pups knew to buy them as young as possible, or he would make pit bulls out of them. The only animal he seemed to like was an old red rooster whose daily activity was bullying the hens.

Thanks to Delmar, his and Matilda's oldest two sons became respectable citizens in the county. When they were working apple, cherry and peach orchards—where pay was based on how many you picked and not how long you were there—they nearly doubled the average piecework pay. The valley farmers also sought them out when they were overwhelmed with spring crop planting, or cattle feeding in the winter, knowing they would get more than their money's worth.

The oldest son bought and cleared several hillsides to raise sheep, goats and a few pigs. He added to his income by driving the school bus because he lived at the end of the valley and trough road. The middle son raised chickens which was a good front for all the corn he needed. He added to his income by making moonshine. He was respected because his corn liquor was as smooth as Virginia Gentlemen and was often drank by them. He advertised his shine locally as "Not G.W.'s."

But it was Joseph, the retarded son, who many said had no chance. They would add it was perhaps fortunate he was retarded because he had to live with G.W. He would be seen for the rest of his life riding his bike to and from town every Saturday. Delmar had given him a Schwinn Aerocycle with a huge basket on front to carry groceries. The bike was the envy of all the valley kids and he never failed to keep it spotless and kept repainting it to maintain its original bright red color. He was slightly built and could have mixed in well visually with other kids riding their bikes if it had not been for the goiter on his neck that kept growing as he got older.

For some 30 years Joseph never failed to bike each Saturday to town and come back at sunset. G. W. never left the hollow and Matilda only came out when she was going to the annual county fair with her cornbread. She sent the butter she made and eggs she gathered to town with Joseph who used the money to buy groceries. Joseph's early ride down the valley and back again that evening became about the only reminder valley people had of the meanest man in their midst. His hatred had been contained by his family and his laced liquor.

Joseph had made it to the third grade in the two-room schoolhouse before Miss Maple had declared him retarded, but it was enough for him to become a friend to all young kids. So, when the valley people offered a menial job he could do such as loading hay bales, or mucking out manure, he found a way to befriend those his age mentally.

While G.W. was known to collect all the money Joseph made from the farmers, what he didn't know was that some of the farmers had made arrangements at the grocery story for Joseph to be given candy and a ticket to the Saturday afternoon matinee. On the way back home on his bike, Joseph would pass out candy to the kids. They would also hail him down to find out what the movie was about because many of them would be going that night with their parents. Joseph would often surprise everyone and gain the admiration of the children with innovations like attaching a deck of cards to the spokes of his bicycle which gave out the sound of a motorcycle. Even when his uncle Delmar died, he was able to keep up the maintenance on his bike.

The day Joseph died from what the locals called water on the brain, and the medical profession called hydrocephalus, was the beginning of the end for Matilda. At his funeral, which was probably the best attended funeral in the valley, she just hunched over the grave. She was buried the following Saturday beside him.

G.W. would continue to live for five more years. He moved the dogs and the rooster in the house with him. He became a menace to the valley now that Matilda and Joseph were not there to do his bidding, and his brother had died. He bought a pickup truck to go to town and didn't care what side of the road he was on. If he didn't like you, he would aim his truck at you to see who would turn first. That, of course, was everybody. So, he continued to get his way. His eyesight was failing, and many said his moonshine was now half insects along with cannabis.

The day they found him at the bottom of Breakneck Mountain, no one was shocked and many relieved. When he was buried beside Matilda and Joseph, there was a gasp. No one had ever bothered to understand what G.W. stood for. There it was, George Washington Culpepper. His oldest son explained it as best he could.

His granddad, who had gone to jail back in the 20s during prohibition, had named his father. He claimed that George, who had surveyed the area back in 1747 was one tough son-of-a-bitch who didn't take fools lightly. He had helped that English dandy fight the Indians, and then he had to fight the English. Now somebody was needed to fight another bunch of fools in the town that had been named after Washington. He wanted G. W. to be just as tough as George was back then.

One of the not-so-mourning funeral attendees who had been run off the road the week before, moved over to Matilda and Joseph's headstones, and added, " It certainly would have been better for them, too, had he been born back then."

At Your Service

When you do go home again, particularly after 40 years, one of the best places to catch up on what's happening is to visit the graveyard. Yes, I said graveyard.

In this case, I recently visited the church of my youth, a small Presbyterian church built just before the Civil War in what used to be Virginia but is now West Virginia. The one room, plain clapboard church pretty much looks like it did back then except for the addition of a Sunday school room, a small kitchen and a picnic shelter out back. It is located in a tiny rural farming valley along the South Branch of the Potomac River in Hampshire County. The attendance there, according to written records, has never been more than 45 people at church, held at night, and a high of 59 in the morning Sunday school in 1952 which probably included me.

Some of the plain six-over-six window panes are original and still washed once a year, so you can see out and "be seen," as my mother used to say. On the south side, you get a nearly complete view of the graveyard. Back in her day, all the men sat on that side of the church with the women on the other side, which looked out on a Buffalo Creek. That was, "Fine with her. Certainly a better way to think about the hereafter than looking at tombstones."

Men on one side, women on the other—was the practice still being maintained in my teens. I can still recall the high alto and soprano voices on the women's side during hymns and a couple of bass drones coming across the aisle where a few of the men would sing. My mother, noting only the preacher would be getting a stereo sound, wondered why he did not call for more hymns because surely he knew his sermons were too long, particularly if he looked at some of his parishioners nodding off. She felt an hour was just right on a Sunday night while the youngsters probably could use more than that at Sunday school in the mornings.

The reason the men sat on the side with the view of the graveyard, my father explained, was not because an early hell, fire, and damnation preacher may have put them there—it was because, before electricity came in, there used to be a pot belly stove on that side, which the men had to keep going. You can still see the burns on the oak plank floors from times of overheating, as well as the round patch in the ceiling where the exhaust pipe went out.

But, I was not to see any recent changes inside the church on my return visit the first week of April. The church and annex was locked. Even the picnic shelter had chains securing the tables to the floor.

Then I remembered my mother telling me that, back in the late 80s, the congregation had to start locking the church. She blamed it on newcomers like those Washington people who were building vacation homes in the mountains, or those with less money setting up RVs along the river, all influenced by the value of old artifacts from watching TV programs like "Antique Roadshow."

In the space of a week's time, farmers up and down the valley noticed the weathervanes missing off their old barns and at the church. Two oil paintings were missing along with a collection of old foot warmers in which you could insert a heated brick. The chandelier, which used to be in the original Van Meter house in the valley and thought to have been sterling silver, also vanished. No one had paid much attention to the old oil paintings other than they had always been there, and no one could remember hearing who had given them to the church.

As I looked through the windows—and there are still some of the original bubbly old panes left—the church still looked spotless and well-kept. The Sunday school and Church attendance sign was still up front between the piano and the preacher's pulpit. I was dismayed to see that church and Sunday school had been combined and services were just twice a month, with the last attendance being 18. Back in the 60s, church services had been held at night to assure that farmers had time to feed their stock. Then I realized there were only three family farms left in the valley.

This first week of April had come in with rain, fog and colder than usual weather and the weatherman had predicted that by the end of the week, the sun would come out and finally bring us a real spring. Even so, the white fluffy flowers of the service berry trees around the graveyard held more credibility than forecasters. These feathery spring sentinels were a welcome contrast to the stark mountains surrounding the church in the hollow still telling you winter has not left. At the far end of the graveyard, there were signs of the redbud about to come into bloom so spring was not far off. The bank along Buffalo Creek had a few Dutchman's britches about a week from blooming. But it was still cold and wet from nearly 10 days of drizzle and fog. In the graveyard, the contrast between then and now began to speak to me. Fifty years ago, the graveyard was about half the size of what it is today—all of it located on the hillside because people back then preserved all the flat land they could for farming. A new part had now been added to the rear of the church taking up most of an old pasture field. I walked around the church and the L-shaped annex to check it out.

In the still low-hanging fog, I thought I saw a couple pinpoint lights beaming upward through the mist, momentarily scaring me until I realized the light must be a reflection off the piles of plastic flowers. Some of these had been scattered by the winter but the lights were coming from particularly large bunches of slightly faded red, blue, pink, yellow and purple bouquets. Upon closer inspection, I found they were little hanging gardens locked into place on highly-polished headstones along with plastic Bible replicas.

But it was the laser-like lights coming from these massive headstones with carvings that got my immediate attention. I had not realized that our electronic age had also impacted this small rural graveyard. But there they were. Imbedded in the huge computerized graphics, showing countrified Thomas Kinkade scenes, were solar chips powering "eternal" lights. This digital age had also made it easy for people to express more fully their favorite poet's best wishes for the departed. Some descriptions were up to five stanzas long. I felt it would have been more interesting had they told of the person's life rather than repeat long-winded poetic homilies of being in a better place. Right above the names were etched flower wreaths surrounding glass-enclosed portraits of the departed in their best finery. Several looked much more youthful than their ages recorded on the headstones, a similarity I had noticed now that newspapers allowed people to do their own family obituaries.

Not recognizing the names of the people (I was to find out later that word had gotten out that this rural church did not charge for grave space and that the locals were about to put a ban on outsiders being buried there), I hurried up to the older hillside graves. There old memories flooded back to me of families I heard of or knew. There were lots of Dutch, Scotch-Irish, English, French and Germans with names like Van Meter, Culpepper, Kuykendall, Dubois, Decker, Ashby, Gray, Darby, Buckley, that were familiar to me, many of them relatives.

Most of the headstones had simple inscriptions of birth,

death and parentage and some were marked off as family spots with the corner stones and a family pedestal. Those in the 1800s often had a carving of a lamb atop it or praying hands in relief. Two stones showed the index finger pointing up with the inscription of "gone home" which I guess was presumptuous of some of the early Calvin purists. Because one gone home stone had fallen over and was pointing in the wrong direction I did my best to reset it and tamp it down so it would be pointing in the right direction.

Along the road that went by the graveyard was the poor section where the burial was usually conducted by the county. These grave markers were mostly simple wood crosses. To the credit of the county or maybe the people still going to the church, these crosses were kept up and looked as if they had recently been painted white. It was among this grouping (a miniature reminder of the unknown soldiers' graveyard in Washington) that I spotted a modern tombstone like the one I saw behind the church in the old pasture. It was also a recent burial. While it had no laser-like light, it did have an enclosed photo of the departed whose age was just 21 and the cause of death—a motorcycle accident. I immediately recognized the name; he was the son of Kline, who spent at least one day of every week getting sober in jail after a Saturday night of spending what he had earned working for my father. His picture clearly reflected his age. But unlike those portraits on the modern tombstone behind the church, his photograph showed him unshaven and bare-chested with tattoos of dragons and mermaids on his chest and arms.

Nearby, some 15 stones either had names scratched in them or none at all, each with a small footstone. These were the oldest ones, some of them older than the church. I remembered my mother saying it was a good thing the church was built near them because that saved the unmarked stones from being carried away. Just before she died, she lamented the fact that the state of West Virginia, not knowing any better (with the added comment of "Did they ever") had taken over the old county poor farm where many people had been buried in the early 1900s with just a river stone to mark the site. The state, not realizing it was an old graveyard, had gathered up the stones and used them in a stone wall for the new canoe and fishing access point to the river.

Anyhow, when I saw two plain rocks with the names of Hattie and Charles Buckley scratched in them and the year of 1862, I remembered the story that had passed down the generations and was even told at Sunday school during my days. It seems that one of the Buckleys had been at the Battle of Kernstown during the Civil War. It was said he left without Stonewall Jackson's permission. Some said he had smallpox, others that he had been shot in the leg and was afraid they were going to take it off while others said he came home to do some spring planting and just got sick before he could get back. But, whatever the reason, he died four days after getting home.

In those days, the body was stored until the ground was soft enough to dig a grave which was usually about the time the first flowers of the season came out—those white five-petal wisps on every branch of the service berry tree. The parishioners had helped the grieving young widow bury her husband and they had covered the grave with the white blossomed-branches of the service berry tree (Amelanchier arborea). Its common name became service berry because these were the first flowers to appear in the spring, thus used for early spring burials. The later white dogwoods were also used and also had religious significance because it was said the Romans used a dogwood tree to make the cross which they forced Jesus to carry before they nailed him to it. The four stained corners of the dogwood blossom were said to represent the nails in the feet and hands.

My mother much preferred the service berry for its "announcement that spring was coming, even for those in the grave." Moreover, she would commend the tree for its blue-black berries which ripened in June and were a favorite of the deer and birds. She would remind her audience that back in the old days, when people had time, the tiny berries from the service tree would be picked and made into preserves, even tastier than blueberries.

A minister planted several dogwood trees by the church and used them each spring to go into great detail about the crucification of Christ. My mother had them replanted behind the annex after the seminary moved him to another church. She was also probably the only one not upset when the oil painting depicting Christ on the cross with a crown of bloody thorns and a protruding bloody heart was stolen, "even it if was valuable."

But I digress. The young Confederate widow Hattie Buckley, whose husband had died just days after coming home from battle, sent her two young children back to Winchester, Virginia to live with her parents. She vowed never to leave her husband, no matter how hard life on their small hillside farm might become. Soon after her husband's burial, with the service berry tree's blossoms still on the trees and on her husband's grave, the congregation was sitting in Sunday school. When she appeared by the church windows, she looked like a white apparition coming out of the fog down through the hillside graves. The wispy flowers had stuck to her cold and wet clothing. Those looking out the windows were probably taken aback as I had been, puzzling over the strange lights coming from the modern tombstones.

They found out that Widow Buckley had spent the night atop the grave covered with service berry blossoms. She died of pneumonia shortly after and became the subject of a ghost story for the next couple of generations, including my time.

I looked at the service berry trees in full bloom, realizing they were now offspring of the originals. I broke off enough branches of the nearby trees to blanket Hattie and Charles's grave in a cover of white.

I also took several branches and put them on the graves of Kline and his son's. I was glad I could not see the graveyard full of plastic flowers and laser lights behind the church from there. I was home. Life was familiar again.

Snowball

He has been setting in the front of the Courthouse so long that he has become as familiar to local people as the aging, rusty cast-iron state historical marker declaring Romney, West Virginia had changed hands 56 times during the Civil War, the most of any town. When they had to do business inside the Greek-Revival style stone courthouse with four columns, a commanding presence on Main Street, they would nod to this lone figure greeting them with a bright, "Welcome to Romney."

But to those travelers who did not think of U.S. Route 50 as Main Street but just another slowdown to points east or west, the figure on the Victorian-style wood bench with its wrought iron gargoyles, under the Civil War sign, was a juxtaposition. He would cause them to look twice as they waited for the only traffic light in town to change.

He was black and old and scrawny but flashing a bright smile. His friendly wave and what seemed like a rebel yell of "Welcome to Romney" took them by surprise. They had already passed the historical markers for Stonewall Jackson's headquarters during the winter of 1862, now a funeral home. It was even more disconcerting for those northern tourists who were looking for Fort Mill where the Yankees had encased themselves in trenches that were still visible atop South Mountain overlooking Romney.

For those strangers who were curious enough to pull over and investigate further, they would be more aghast when the deeply wrinkled but tidily-dressed old man would introduce himself as Snowball, Sambo and the Mayor. He would explain these were the names everyone knew him by and he did not seem offended or impressed with either name. More questions would make them realize that he was retarded. If their curiosity and perhaps indignation was enough, they would go inside the court house to encounter the office of the county clerk.

Nancy was a small, petite blond who knew everyone's

business—if they were protesting an assessment on their property, making a sale, getting a fishing or hunting license or had business with the sheriff or the judge, good or bad. When she saw the visitor was a stranger, she would ape the reception they had gotten outside, "Welcome to Romney."

A stranger would soon find out that she was not only very alert but was obviously amused at their surprise of seeing the happy black man in front of a courthouse building where they thought a judge probably once ordered them hung. If she surmised they were being patronizing, they would get a more personal history lesson of the Civil War that was better than they could get at the new Civil War museum in town.

First, she would explain that his real name was Marshall, possibly named after Thurgood Marshall, of Supreme Court fame. To those who didn't seem to know who Thurgood was, she became creative and said she had been told once his real name was Jefferson Jackson Washington, IV, and that his ancestors could be traced as slaves to three presidents. Actually no one was sure what his name was or just where his family was. Nancy also liked to incorporate Marshall into the area's history. After the Civil War, she would tell them, his great grandparents had settled in Romney where they ran a blacksmith shop. JJW, Sr. had learned the business from his father who had made horseshoes and done livery work as a slave before he was freed. The farms in Hampshire County were dotted with draft horses as well as riding horses, which the county had been noted for during the Civil War. Many of them were used by Calvary officers scouting out Northern troops for Stonewall Jackson. JJW, Sr., decided to stay in the county while others continued to head west or north to look for work in big cities, particularly in Chicago. Often, seeing a stranger's confusion as they continued to stare at Snowball outside on his bench, Nancy would add, "Or maybe his great grandfather decided to stay because he figured a town that changes hands 56 times had learned to be more tolerant."

Then, noting that yes, he was retarded, she would add that just like many of the isolated rural families—and the British aristocracy for that matter," she explained, "there were few black people suitable to marry so JJW, IV had paid the price of too many in-laws with the same name."

She explained that as the years went by and automobiles replaced horses, his parents died and his sisters and brothers had to leave for better opportunities. JJW, IV was left behind.

That was 30 years ago, the visitor would learn. It was then

JJW, IV, hanging around the courthouse, met the young town clerk with the blond hair and big heart named Nancy. She gave him a job cleaning out the public restrooms in the basement of the Courthouse. When the town put in a water system and running water was now available in local shops and diners in town, there was no need to provide toilet facilities. Nancy, as town clerk, was able to convince officials that the non-used public restrooms could be turned into an apartment for Snowball and he could live there and do errands for them.

Nancy had seen enough of those homes for the retarded when her cousin had to put his son in one there years ago. She knew the conditions were deplorable and that Snowball, being black, would have an even more difficult time there. She was able to do the paperwork to convince the Social Security administrators that it would be better for the County to manage his disability checks than having the checks and Snowball sent to an institution. It took awhile and the sheriff just laughed when Nancy put her name on the application as having the Power of Attorney to place him in the county's new Institute for the Disabled in the basement of the Courthouse.

From that day on she managed his disability check. As meager as it was, he never wanted for good food, nice clothing and even a TV set when cable came in the area.

But JJW, IV preferred to watch people go by the Courthouse and sat there most every day, even when it was over 100 degrees warm or below zero in the winter. His first "Welcome to Romney," was sung out to Nancy as she came to work each morning, always checking to make sure he was properly attired and fed for his day as town crier.

As for his nickname of Snowball or Sambo, the town clerk pointed out to strangers that JJW, IV just laughed when they called him that as well as those who greeted him with "Good morning, Mr. Mayor."

She declared, "It's his nature to be happy and friendly and over time, it is amazing how he has inspired other people to be so despite their troubles. If someone tried to give him a hard time, I can promise you that the majority of the people in this county, no matter how they address him, would do battle with them. He has become a town fixture, someone and something to feel good about. He has made a better person out of all of us."

Yee-haw Jihad

His first memory was being taken out of church by his red-faced parents, his mother in tears, yet rough-handling him into her arms, and his father glaring at him with an anger that even the preacher couldn't muster in his railings against Satan.

Dickie's cat, Munchie, was dead now. People still talked about the time when Dickie was four-years-old and sneaked his cat into church under his coat.

Munchie, smelling the aroma of warm bread in the old high ceiling, one-room church with a pot-belly stove partially heating it, had slipped out from under Dickie's coat and made its way, unnoticed, under the pews, to the Eucharist offerings placed under a white linen shroud.

The preacher was catching his breath as everyone was reciting the Lord's Prayer prior to his readings from St. Paul and the Corinthians. It was when Dickie's head had been forced down by his father for the prayer that he saw Munchie go under the shroud. He remembered trying to crawl under the pews to get to his cat but his father was now clutching him tightly, forcing him back on the bench, and arching his head in a bow.

Dickie's worst fears were revealed after the preacher lowered his voice in reverence and reminded everyone to wait before they dipped Christ's body (the bread) into the wine (Christ's blood) which he had shed for them. He quoted St. Paul, "The bread that we break is a communion with the body of Christ. The fact this is only one loaf means that though there are many of us to form a single body with Christ because we all share in this loaf." He had gone on to Luke's version of the last supper before removing the shroud, "And he took the bread , gave thanks and gave it to them, saying this is my body which is given to you, do this in remembrance of Me."

It was when he reached for the shroud, now moving on its own, that Munchie jumped off the silver platter knocking what was left of the bread on the floor.

Folks said they did not know who moved faster, the preacher—who immediately declared Satan was in their midst and began whaling at the black cat with his cane which he had referred to as his staff—or Dickie, who broke out of his father's grasp and scooped up the cat, both of which were grabbed nearly as quick by his father.

The preacher and most of the congregation were irate. They calmed down somewhat when Dickie's father said it would be Munchie's last meal even though some pleaded the cat's case by saying it could not help it was born black and had Satan in him.

Life didn't get any easier for the young Dickie, who mourned the loss of his euthanized cat. Various recallings of the incident followed Dickie through the rest of his forced church and Sunday School years and through the two-week Sunday school camp held each summer.

It was at this camp and the memorization of the catechism, a perquisite to becoming a member of the church that Dickie tried to endear himself with the preacher and his avid followers. He would follow the Bible to its every letter. It was when they were studying the story of Moses and the burning bushes, that Dickie got the idea of re-enacting this Bible story for the younger students, so they would remember it and pass the tests coming up for all of them. He would be a hero. There were plenty of bushes in the pasture surrounding the church. He could use the creek just below the nearby hillside for the Red Sea. In his pocket was, Wilbur, his pet garter snake which he would use to restage Moses' miracle of turning his rod into a snake.

Everything seemed to go as planned. The Sunday School teacher just smiled at Dickie's enthusiasm as he asked to read the lesson on Moses and lead the students to the pasture. Just as Dickie had planned, the slow burning pine cone he had lit earlier under a brushy, parched bush was now igniting its dried branches. He watched the flames spread and timed his reading of the Bible story so that they arrived at the bush when it burst into full flames.

Unfortunately for Dickie, the area had not had rain for several weeks and was very dry. The bush not only quickly went up in flames but it ignited the dry grass around it which quickly spread to other bushes and then up the hillside. The whole valley soon saw the blaze and, like they had during fires from lightning or careless deer hunters, they came running to put it out.

Fortunately for Dickie, by this time his father had become disenchanted with the church. He had been caught making hay on

Sunday and although he pleaded he only did it because it was going to rain the next day and he was sure the Lord would want his cattle to have a dry meal, it didn't satisfy the preacher. What made it worse was that for the next two months the spotty rains that did come that dry summer never seemed to drop on his farm, a phenomena the preacher declared as retribution. Dickie's father, who lost his role in the church as elder, a position his father and grandfather before him had, just quite going to church. .

Dickie's mother, now intent on assuring that his younger sisters would become devout church members, decided it was o.k. for Dickie to just help his father in the fields.

But Dickie's curiosity about religion had been aroused. It was not long after his expulsion from Sunday School that he had his next misunderstanding with a group of hard-shell Baptists who had rounded up many from the valley and hillsides for a river baptism.

Dickie heard about the event from his classmate Bob who was to be baptized along with his parents. Knowing his parents would not approve, Dickie sneaked down to the river and hid himself behind the big rock where the preacher was now reading his baptismal passages from John's Gospel: "Unless a man is reborn in water and the Holy Spirit, he cannot enter the Kingdom of God."

When the preacher waded out into the river, Dickie could see that it would be over Bob's head. He knew Bob could not swim and would panic. But still Bob's parents were pushing him towards the preacher for saving while Bob, realizing he was over his head, clung to the preacher.

Dickie felt he had to do something. He knew Bob would be pushed down three times. When the terrified Bob screamed as the preacher began to push him away from him and down, Dickie dived off the rock and reached for Bob.

The Baptist minister, as strong in body as opinion, ended up baptizing them together for the required three Father, Son and Holy Ghost dips.

While Dickie later tried to explain to the shocked and reverent crowd that Bob could not swim and Bob added that it had been a big comfort to him to know that Dickie, who could swim, was next to him, the Baptist preacher and his followers were not sympathetic. But this didn't stop Dickie the next day from teaching Bob how to swim just in case there was a repeat baptism.

By this time, Dickie's disgusted father, tired of literal

translations of the Bible, made up his own explanation of his son's exuberance by telling them that the Hebrew version of the Bible said "thou shall not drown the unanointed."

But despite his father's growing indifference to religion and warning to just ignore them, Dickie was still curious. There had been much discussion in the valley about a Holy Roller preacher coming in who wanted to use the one-room schoolhouse on Sundays for his services. The school was used for elections and other community events on weekends so it was ruled that it could also be used for church services.

Dickie's parents forbid him to go when they noticed his interest after speculation this might be one of those churches that used poison snakes to determine if a parishioner was a sinner or not. Dickie couldn't imagine anyone actually putting their hand on a rattler or copperhead to make the decision, so he was determined to see how they did it.

Dickie took his sister, Gina, with him as there might be less trouble if two of them were there. He told his parents they were going on a bike ride that day.

The service has already started when they got there on their bikes. They recognized some of the pickups and cars, but figured if they went in the back they might not be seen or recognized. Dickie was wearing his dad's old sweatshirt with the hood nearly covering his face while Gina, who never wore a dress, was now camouflaged in her older sister's wraparound skirt which she had triple wrapped around her waist.

This plan ran afoul the minute the preacher spotted Gina, who had also put on some of her older sister's lipstick and rouge to appear older. "Yee, who wears the makeup of Jezebel, have sinned," he roared as he pointed to Gina. Gina, stunned, found herself being dragged to the front of the room where she turned redder than the lipstick she was wearing. Dickie, who had managed to quickly seat himself behind his double seated school desk, was pondering what to do when the preacher asked the congregation if they would pray for Gina who was to go outside, remove the offending Satanic makeup, and walk in backwards because she had sinned and was not fit to face Jesus while they prayed to save her soul. The crowd agreed, with Dickie loudly endorsing the action. Gina did as told and had no trouble backing in as she was now a fifth year student in the school and was familiar with the seating. She was grateful to spot Dickie in his usual seat who motioned for her to sit beside him although she winced when he yelled, "I guarantee on a stack of your Bibles she has repented and will not wear that stuff again.'

The service continued with the Holy Roller preacher chanting his lessons of hell, fire and damnation from the Old Testament. He elaborated mostly on Matthew's admonition to sinners of "Depart from me, ye cursed, into everlasting fire, prepared for the devil and his angels" and "cast them into a furnace of fire where there shall be a wailing and gnashing of teeth." He went on to describe Jesus dying on the cross for their sins and began quoting Mathew again, "For as Jonas was three days in the whale's belly, so shall the Son of God be three days and three nights in the Heart of the Earth before rising for our sins." He began chanting over and over expressions of how everyone must now accept Jesus as their savior in order to be forgiven or face the warning from Revelations that sinners "shall be tormented with fire and brimstone."

In a loud, pained gasp, he then became prostrate on the floor and called on his followers to do the same. "We are not fit to stand up and face Jesus, the Son of God, until we have confessed our sins to him. Let the spirit of Jesus go through each and every one of you….do not let Satan win." He began to thrust himself back and forth as he chanted for Jesus to save their souls.

Gina squatted down behind the back of the desk but Dickie, loudly endorsing the preacher's admonition, began rolling around on the school floor and chanting everything the preacher said and adding some of his own. It was when one of the Holy Rollers, after loudly confessing his sins, rolled under the school bench in the front of the classroom, and tried to get up that Dickie's actions were questioned. The prostrate Roller trying to get up kept hitting the bottom of the bench. He began wailing that his sins were so heavy that the Lord would not let him up. He began crying out in pain as he bumped the bench bottom. It was then that Dickie in his enthusiasm, got up and pushed the bench aside and said, "Rise, I am the Lord. Yours sins are not that bad." Dickie and the still-crouching Gina were immediately thrown out by the preacher as Satan's children.

It was not long before their parents heard about it and punished Dickie for disobeying them by going to the service. However, Dickie's father was not as disturbed over what his son had done as the others were. He had his own problems with the visiting Holy Roller preacher who had supposedly saved one of his hired hands. The itinerant preacher's literal interpretation of the Bible included 10% tithing of everything they had. As was the custom in the valley, the farmers provided total housing for their hired hands. When the Holy Roller preacher drove up with a huge truck to take 10% of the furniture in the tenant house, Dickie's dad called the sheriff.

While that was the end of the Holy Roller back then, there are still different religious groups that come and go seeking souls to save. As for Dickie, who grew up to become a farmer like his father, he learned not to take things too literally. After all, when he was four he had learned that curiosity killed his cat.

Farm Sentinel

Life not only changed for all us when my father died, but the farm seemed to lose its will to live, too. The corn he had planted a month before was still trying to shoot its way up through the dirt even though he had thoroughly cultivated and pulverized the soil. There had been plenty of rain although not the downpour on the day he died. He had gotten all of his sun-cured hay in the barn just before it hit. He was so attuned to nature that other farmers used to do as he did . . . they had only been an hour behind him in getting their hay in.

It was when my mother checked the barn to find out why he was late for supper that she found him beside the tractor. It was still running . . . something was wrong . . . he would never waste gas. She saw the new breeding bull he had gotten attached to; it had belonged to his uncle in the next county who had given up farming because he could no longer compete with the big corporate feedlots in the west. The big Hereford was nuzzling him gently, trying to get my father to move. My mother saw his face, it was peaceful but lifeless. She knew his weak heart was probably the cause.

She called for Mike, my brother. He was sharpening the blades on the mowing machine. My two sisters and I were in the house talking with our close aunts and uncles. Once a year, we would get together for a reunion of those born on the farm. The farm had given us our start in life. When our ancestors settled the valley in 1740s, there had been plenty of land to support the first three generations. But, large families resulted in too many heirs and, thus, smaller farms. So, the English rule had been adopted for the past three generations. The farm would go to the eldest son or barring that to the son that wanted to stay on the farm. The farm would educate the others so they could make a living. It was true that it had to be mortgaged to get my oldest sister through the state university, a comedown from the prior generation when it had even sent my father's sisters through expensive finishing schools.

I was lucky in that four years separated me from my oldest sister. She not only paid off the mortgage but managed to loan me the money to also go to the state university. My middle sister went to a nearby free nursing college.

Our mother had married our father when they were just 18, both graduating from the same high school class. Mike had been the only son, so it was automatic that he would inherit the farm. He did his duty and had even enhanced his hard-working reputation by becoming known for his mechanical ability. He worked part-time at the local machinery dealer to supplement the decreasing farm income. Because of the high cost of farm equipment, the valley farmers had begun sharing equipment such as combines. Mike's knowledge gained him the reputation my father had knowing when it was going to rain

During the past two generations, the farm had supported the education of a chemist, an engineer, a nurse, several teachers and a lawyer with one son staying behind to run the farm. If any of us were ever frustrated in our jobs, we shared this with each other and not the one left to run the farm. Any complaints we had would sound pretty trite in comparison to the never ending chores and risks a farmer faced.

When my mom and Mike came in with the horrible news that my father was dead we couldn't believe it. My two sisters and I had not even seen him this visit as all of us had arrived that afternoon. We had planned on walking the fields with them the next day just to hear how things were going, a ritual that was good for all of us to connect with our past, as providers and beneficiaries. While my mother called the doctor, my sisters and I just looked at each other, stunned. Somehow we felt the farm, daddy, mom, and Mike had become indestructible . . . something we could always come home to. All of us rushed to the barn to gather around my father until the doctor and coroner came. I mostly remember the bull that had been nudging my father. While Mike had tied him to a nearby hay bin, the sounds of his grazing seemed soothing. Yet, he would pause to look over at my father with those huge, dark, unblinking eyes.

Over the next couple of months, the lawyer on my father's side of the family would be called upon to help. It turned out my father had not made social security payments for two hired hands. He had given both his and their contributions directly to them, figuring they would spend it more wisely than the government. Then it was discovered the farm, because it was so close to Washington DC, had tripled in value. It was being taxed on commercial value rather than farm income. The lawyer in our family, as well as many others, had been trying to get this rule changed which did result in a Tax Reform Act. The act based a farm's value on the income it produced, not what it would be worth for commercial development. But it didn't go into effect until a year after my father died. So it was too late for my brother, Mike. To keep the farm, the cattle herd and the farm equipment had to be sold to pay the taxes on a farm now valued at $100,000 instead of $25,000. So Mike went to work as a truck driver which paid better than working on farm equipment at the local dealer.

We went back to our jobs. Mom turned the farm over to our cousin, one of the few farmers still left with a herd and equipment, asking him only to pay the property taxes, knowing that was about all he could make on the land.

Then a near tragedy struck again, just three months after our father's death. Mike had come home from driving the truck to repair a neighbor's tractor and got caught in the power takeoff. If he had not been wearing Daddy's old jacket, which ripped easily, he could have lost his arm or his life.

He and my mother had no sooner come back from the hospital that evening when two tractor trailers loaded with lean cattle arrived with a bill for $8,000. Daddy had cut back on developing his own small herd. He could make more money turning the pasture into corn fields and using the silage to fatten the lean cattle during the winter. Hillside farmers did not have this advantage and eked out a living by selling their new heifers in the fall because they couldn't store enough hay to feed them. Daddy had not told my mother that he had ordered this fall's shipment of lean cattle.

The drivers helped Mom get them penned up in the barnyard while Mike did what he could with one arm. They had just gotten the gates fastened when I arrived, having heard about Mike's accident earlier that day. We would have to work something out to fatten the cattle. The corn crop, though not good, had grown and maybe would produce enough silage to fatten them. Otherwise, it would be a huge financial loss as my brother simply could not, in his condition, handle that many cattle. Besides, he could not afford to lose his job. He was married and had one child with another on the way. A resale of the cattle, as is, would only bring half the value at most, a loss of $4,000.

While we were calming ourselves down at the kitchen table trying to find a positive side, we could hear the restless cattle in the barnyard. This was not unusual. Strange cattle in a new place have to adjust to new surroundings. Mike had noticed several had what Daddy called shipping fever because they were sweaty, frothing at the mouth, and hard to control. Mom had gotten the reluctant drivers to herd the ailing ones inside the barn.

We had just managed to believe that, possibly, we could maybe even make a little money if our cousin and other relatives in the valley could feed the cattle until it was time to take them to the stock sale in February. The corn had not been harvested. But all of us could take whatever vacation we had now to cut the corn and fill the silo. We could take turns coming home on weekends and any other days we could get off to help our mother, cousin and other relatives in the valley feed the cattle.

It was then we saw the spotlight from a car on the road sweep the fields. It was illegal to jack deer at night by stunning them with a spotlight, making them easy to shoot. My mother ran to the phone to call the game warden. The deer were in the field just below the barn. The hunters were out of their cars, now shooting wildly. Mike was quickly on his feet as the sound of gun shots rang out. But it was too late. We both heard the nervous cattle stampeding. Not only did the 60 steers in the yard break through the gate, but the sick ones busted out of the side of the 100-year-old barn when a gun shot went into it.

The cattle were running in circles in the twenty-five acre pasture field. It was a night with just a quarter-moon. I could see some of the darting, whirling white markings on the Herefords. Most of the cattle were black, Angus. All I could make out were running shapes. The ground was shuddering as they thundered around the field. You could hear them breathing hard and loud, losing pounds. We had just been talking about adding fat to the cattle and knew that they were losing weight now as they stampeded. We had to get them back into the barnyard where they could settle down and eat. Mom got in the truck to go to the neighbors for help.

The deer jackers with spotlights had gone, perhaps realizing what they had done. Mike was able to get up on the tractor and get it to the end of the field where he used its lights to back light me so I could see where I was going. I tried driving the cattle to the gate they had broken through, but they simply would not quit running. Mike and I began mimicking my father's soothing sounds. I could hear Mike's voice crack as his broken ribs were no doubt hurting him. He had gotten off the tractor to stand guard in one end of the field, but simply could not keep up with the cattle. The slivered moon threw reflected light off the white bandages around his ribs and arm.

As I darted back and forth to round them up, I could feel Mike's relief as the dark Angus shadows and white faced Herefords headed towards the broken gate. We dared not speak as noise would spook them. Then another gun shot rang out further down the valley. All I could feel was the ground shaking under me as the mass of black and white came thundering towards me. I couldn't speak, hear or even move. They were coming straight at me. I just felt the earth, the movement of the cattle towards me. They were pushing memories, all rushing through me. It seemed like my father was just ahead of them. He seemed to be there in the dark night.

Then I knew what he would do. I had to stand straight up no matter what. If I fell the stampeding herd would not see me. I would be crushed under their feet, pulverized, swallowed by the earth. Did my ancestors want me, would the farm take me, would it like me, use me? I could smell and feel the heavy breath of the cattle as they came straight at me. Then I felt the farm, my father, the growing fields. I reached up just like withered corn does when raindrops begin to fall. I was being whip lashed by the cattle as they began to divide around me and close in behind me. But I didn't fall. It seemed to last a lifetime, but I stood tall, as tall as my father, I said to myself, as I reached up even further. I could still see the tassels of the tall corn in the field next to me as the cattle thundered around and by me. I was still motionless when I heard them behind me.

They were turning again but not towards me. Mike's white bandage was moving and I heard his pain as he struggled up behind them. He had seen that I was safe. The cattle were heading to the river side of the field next to the cornfield. Mike quickly signaled me to close in along the back side so they would follow the fence. The fence led to the broken gate. They followed it. They found the opening. Amazingly, they went through.

Mike and I were right behind them. I propped up the broken gate and Mike brought the tractor up against it to secure it. I looked at the moon; it was just above the cornfield. Back then, corn was not planted by drilling it in rows to get more corn. Seeds were drop-planted in hills so it could be tilled and weeded from two directions. Thus, from every vantage point, you could see the corn standing tall, in perfect harmony, advancing up and down the field. The corn now seemed to be moving in lockstep like soldiers, marching, watching us. I felt my father was there with others before him.

We watched as the cattle settled down, now munching on our best timothy hay strewn around the barnyard by my mother, who had arrived with help. Somehow I knew the farm would be there for the next generation. It was still alive. It had saved me. I hoped I could return the favor.

Fending

When my father died, leaving my mother to rent the farm, there were some people in the valley, the ones she called "riff-raff," who underestimated her ability to fend for herself. They found this out when they decided the farm could now be used for jacking deer at night.

It was accepted that the valley was overrun with deer and my father, like others in the valley, had permits to kill them because of crop damage. That was fine with my mother who understood the need to protect the cornfields by downsizing the deer population. But, it had to be done legally. It was against the law to shoot from a car and to use a spotlight at night to stun the deer, making it easy to shoot them.

When crop damage was especially severe, most farmers would look the other way when the spot-lighters came. But not my mother. She would be cranking up the phone to ring Central to get the game warden on the line.

We had a rural phone system everyone shared. Each farmer was assigned a number of rings. In our case, it was two longs and two shorts. The central operator's number of rings was one long. Everyone in the valley could listen in on this shared party line and often did, sometimes resulting in an entire church covered dish supper being planned.

It didn't take long for my mother to realize the night hunters would quickly disappear when she rang up the operator. So, she started asking Central to connect her to her aunt who was also a law-abiding citizen. She would invite her to some event, a signal for her to use another phone system to call the game warden.

We just had one road in and out of the valley so it only took two game wardens to catch them. After one of the spot lighters killed a big steer in the field, mistaking it for a deer, my mother took great delight in putting up a poster picture of a cow along the road, labeled, "COW." She even convinced the game wardens to put up a plastic deer in the field near a well-known deer crossing from the mountain to the valley. It had been shot so many times it eventually collapsed. Despite getting hate mail from the illegal hunters, particularly on Valentine's Day, saluting her as their favorite witch, she never let up for the next 25 years.

Even a new generation of spot lighters would have to learn she would not be intimidated though she now lived by herself. Once when I came home, I found I had lost the nerve I thought I had inherited from her. We were watching TV when a spotlight streaked through the big picture window of our living room.

"Today's riff-raff is even worse," she said, as she jumped up to the window to see where the light was coming from. "Of all the nerve," she angrily declared, "they have driven off the road and down into the cornfield by the river." Despite it being dark and well past midnight, she ordered me to sneak down through the cornfield and see where they hid their guns. She dialed the game warden directly without fear of discovery, proclaiming the new phone system was at least good for that despite having to learn all those numbers. As I was going out the back door, she went out the front to get the truck and drive it to the head of the dirt road leading down to the cornfield. She parked it sideways to block their exit.

Times had changed. Not only could she get them for illegal hunting but there were heavy fines for trespassing and even jail time for carrying loaded guns. The spot lighters had been known to hide their guns and pretend they were just looking around. Each illegal gun cost as much as $500 each.

As I was trying to make my way in the dark through the cornfield, I remembered a large copperhead snake I had once encountered in that area. I calmed myself by knowing that I had high boots and long pants. I was also grateful for having grabbed a full length jacket as the blades of the tall corn were sharp. But there was a growing fear, as I struggled blindly through the corn rows hoping they would not hear or see me—that was getting worse as I got closer to where the night hunters were. I had gotten used to life in the city where people with guns shot other people, not deer. I asked myself, "What are you doing here in the middle of the night chasing down people with loaded guns? They could even be on drugs for all you know."

Still, I pushed on knowing that I had to be my mother's daughter. Even though I was trying to be quiet as I could snaking my way between the two corn rows, I roused a deer which jumped up just ahead of me. It started thrashing its way through the cornfield.

The sweep of the spotlight soon caught up with it and several shots rang out. I hit the ground flat and stayed there for a while, renewing my question of "What on earth are you doing here?"

It was then the deer jackers saw the lights coming up the valley road and figured my mother had gotten the game warden.

They ran for the bridge crossing the drainage ditch along the field and stacked their guns tightly under it. They jumped in their car to flee and found themselves facing the side of the truck and my mother.

The game warden arrived about that time. He checked their car for guns as they protested that the night was so nice they thought they would just take a walk to the river. In the group was a distant cousin which made no difference to my mother. She just shook her finger at him and said, "Shame on you."

My mother yelled for me to come out of the cornfield which I did, still shaking from the gunshots. I told her where they were and let her lead the game warden to the bridge where they had hidden their guns.

She slept soundly that night, but I didn't. I kept thinking about those loaded guns and the gunshots that landed near me when the deer jumped up. There are some things that are worse than copperhead snakes. But my mother feared neither.

River Deal

"It was a sight to behold," Jess said, as he described Ham Spurling hanging on to his mule in the middle of the river.

Problem was, the mule must not have been able to swim either, Jess said, because it just stopped in its tracks when the water rose up to its bulging stomach. What the mule knew or did not know about the coming flash flood, Jess did not speculate.

But the mule, which had crossed the river before with Ham on its back, must know the water was deeper than it remembered because it would not budge now. The high waters were on their way from a cloudburst up on the Allegheny front. However, unlike the mule, Ham knew that in about an hour the water would be over both of their heads. That was why he was panicking and yelling as loud as he could back to Jess.

"Damn you . . . you can swim . . . get out here and pull us in you son-of-a-bitch."

Jess just sat there laughing under the sycamore tree, knowing he had some time before he had to go into action.

"Tell you what," he yelled back, "You give me half of everything you make in that still over there and I'll be right there."

Ham, now cursing Jess as well as the mule, realized he had been had. Jess had told him that reports from above said the waters would crest at five feet and that was enough to go up the feeder stream and contaminate his still. The river was already turning muddy and if the high waters carried enough limbs and trash it could carry off his still, too.

You're going to burn in hell for this," he yelled back. "How do I know you told me the truth? Maybe, just maybe, this is as high as the river is going to get? He slapped the mule on the side again to try to make it move forward, causing the mule to nearly lose its bearings on the slippery rocks.

Jess, still laughing, displayed a large grapevine which was hanging from a huge sycamore along the high bank. He pulled it out and dangled it in the water upriver from Ham knowing Ham had spent many a youthful summer swinging off grapevines into shallow eddies he could handle. Most of the other kids had learned to swim but not Ham. He preferred to while away his hours fishing and often only used the grapevines to get to tiny islands in the river for better fishing spots.

"You can hang on to this and I'll pull you in. But first you must promise to share your shine," Jess hollered.

Ham thought of the time Bill Kuykendall, who also did not swim, had rescued his tractor which was across the river when a flash flood came through during the night. There was no place to cross because of the high and swift water. Bill had waded out to a tree, tied a rope around it and let the stream carry him down river until he could manage to beat his way to the other side…in water that was over his head the whole time.

He had admired him when he did it knowing the terrifying feeling of not being able to touch bottom in the river. But no one had asked him to give him half either.

"Just throw it out here, you son of a bitch, and I'll get myself in."

But Jess just repeated, "Half of your shine, and you got it."

Jess displayed both ends of the grapevine which he had cut down. You still need me and I need drinks. So how about it" he yelled back.

"Go to hell," shouted Ham. The water was getting muddier and more branches were floating by. Then Ham remembered the time that Jess had saved what he thought was a person in the huge flood they had in 1936. It had turned out be his mother's scarecrow from her riverside garden. Jess and Ham were pulling up their long john boats to a safer higher site when Jess saw the scarecrow being tossed around in the surging rapids. He had chided Ham for not jumping into the water with him and saving the flailing body which Jess had even identified as possibly being Ham's father because the checked shirt was just like one Jess had seen him in. Jess had been mortified when Ham's father turned out to be a scarecrow.

Ham had kept his promise he would never tell anyone about Jess's mistake. Jess had always, and loudly, proclaimed to everyone he did not make mistakes.

"Either you come out here and get me now, or I will spread the word about the Scarecrow in 36."

Ham watched as the grapevine floated down towards him, with Jess holding on. "It is a sight to behold," Ham said.

Riverdance

The news went up and down the valley in whispered tones. It was true, a poet and a dancer from New York City had just bought the old abandoned Kuykendall home across the river and, oh my, they are both male and they say, they are, you know, very close.

The only way to get to the huge stone home, long ago bypassed when the road went in on the other side of the valley, was by crossing the river. You could see the ancient house off the top of the pullover on Breakneck Mountain where the river below took a huge horseshoe turn and isolated the old 18th century house from the road.

For the past 150 years, the valley people had watched the vines climb, but not conquer, the three-story stone house. The ivy had managed to peel off the double-decker porches, envelop the stables in back and completely cover the ice house.

Speculations about the two men would be preceded by general, non-gossiping comments such as: "It will cost a fortune to get electricity to that house. In the old days, they'd get across the river by boat. Or when the river was low they could make it with horse and wagon. Do you think city people can do this? Or live without electricity or TV? They just bought the house; young Isaac didn't sell them the 150 acres around it. He kept that for pasture. Wait until they find out that a herd of cows will be surrounding them a couple of months each year. Hope they like animals, because that's the only thing that's over there."

But, it was precisely this reason that the poet and dancer bought the old place for a summer retreat. They could use it to choreograph new dances during the off-season. They were quite accustomed to the amenities of life in the city and were looking forward to "getting back to nature" as they put it. The place, with panoramic views of the mountains and river valley, would serve as an inspiration for new dances.

Still, they were aware the valley people not only questioned their sanity, but usually ended their conversations with guarded comments about their sexuality. The dancer and poet realized they were coming into an area that had not completely gotten used to black neighbors, much less same-sex partners. While the house was wonderfully isolated with a view of the layered Appalachians set off by the river valley in the foreground, they knew they were vulnerable. They had already found graffiti on the plastered walls, some of which was clearly offensive. The house was accessible from river traffic.

Perhaps this is why the dancer, who owned his own Jeremiah Jones company in New York City, looked up a descendant of the Kuykendalls whom he heard worked at GE in New York State. He and the poet, a Harvard theology graduate who found more solace in poetry than in religious doctrine, decided to find her. It was right after a performance that they got word that Marci Kuykendall, who worked upstate, was currently at a conference at the Biltmore. She was involved in communication news of contract negotiations with the union.

Jeremiah and his poet friend, Jonah, decided that it was best to confront her directly to test her reaction. Because they were well-known in the city, they had no problem being directed to the Biltmore conference room where the meeting was being held. Jeremiah still had on his black leotard suit when he walked into the meeting. He aroused considerable curiousity as he looked into the audience to find her which was not hard because there were only two females there.

When he asked for Marci, the Vice President, not known as an arts patron, gave Marci a reprimanding look and quickly told her, with much displeasure in his voice, that in the future she should have her friends wait for business sessions to be concluded. He added that in this case it was best Marci leave to see her "friend" now.

Marci, not having learned to assert herself under the new Equal Opportunity laws, left the room red-faced but not curious. She had heard that the famous dancer was looking for her.

He introduced her to Jonah and they invited her to an early dinner at the Russian Tea Room which she heartily accepted, anxious to show the two of them their life styles were quite acceptable to her plus she had never been to the tea room. She knew it was an au literati place, certainly not one where skills in company propaganda were admired. She felt intimidated by her lack of culture but determined to make a try at fitting in.

It was there they concocted the plan to become acceptable

community neighbors which they had determined was necessary in an area where people kept an eye out for riff-raff and, most important, in doing so protected each other's property. After all, Jeremiah and Jonah would only be down there a month or two in the summer.

Jeremiah, already aware that most of the gossip occurred after church since that was the only place most families saw each other, suggested they do a free performance. Marci, still amazed that Jeremiah raised no eyebrows when they had arrived with him still in his black leotard suit, nearly fell out of her chair. She remembered that dancing, even square dancing, in church would be even worse than using it as a voting site. She laughed so loud she drew unwanted attention. A couple of Jeremiah and Jonah's friends came over. By then, the realization that she was out of her element was no longer a problem for her. She could teach them something.

Marci described life and culture in the rural, farming valley. She made the case that if they wanted to be accepted the best thing was to reach out to the women first. What they should do is have an open house because many people were curious to see not just what it was like inside, but it would also be good for them to see what good house and grounds keepers they were. Marci had heard the approvals from her mother that the vines had disappeared and local contractors had built the porches back onto the house.

The couple de grace, Marci suggested, would be they hold a bring-your-own covered dish event for everyone in the valley. All Jeremiah and Jonah would have to do was supply the ice tea and lemonade. Drinking simply was not accepted, even socially as they knew it. Marci also explained that the farmers were independent and "beholden to none" and besides that, the farmers' wives loved to show off their favorite dishes.

It would be an adventure. Marci could get her cousin, who still owned the pasture around them, to ferry everyone across the river by tractor and wagon. Jeremiah and Jonah, still feeling they ought to do more than provide the ice tea and sodas, were excited about the idea of having real home-cooked country food. Marci's suggestion they ask for recipes, another "good neighbor technique,." was quickly accepted by Jonah as a great idea. By the time they left the Russian Tea Room, those overhearing the conversation, as well as Jeremiah and Jonah's friends, wanted to be invited to the event.

Marci's mother, well-known as the matriarch of the valley, was pleased someone was finally fixing up the ancient home place. If she did have reservations about the rumors she had been hearing, she wasn't saying. She was one to quickly discount rumors, especially those that were not socially acceptable. When the invitations went out, she was the first to lead the responses of acceptance. The river cooperated with its summer low period so the wagons could go across. It was a warm late July day past the mosquito season. Jeremiah and Jonah had outdone themselves on cleaning the house and making it cozy. Both decks were adorned with hanging flowers and the 18th century tables had been covered with fine linen. Marci's cousin had earlier that morning delivered the supplies they had ordered, including all the bags of ice they would need to keep the ice tea and lemonade cold. Jonah had added his artistic touch to several watermelons sitting in huge, wooden Dutch platters. The biggest oblong melon, cut into two halves, had its sides cut out to form the skyscraper shape of Manhattan Island as seen from the East and Hudson rivers. The center was hulled out and filled with melon balls, banana and kiwi slices, cherries and blackberries.

Even more color was added to the table with some 30 or more covered dishes, ranging from bird's eye peas to sliced hickory-smoked ham to candied yams. Jermiah and Jonah were ecstatic. As each new dish arrived with its maker, they had repeated the owner's name just as if the bearer were a patron of the arts. Ongoing tours of the house, completely furnished with primitive colonial pieces, some of which they had bought at Sotheby's, were especially welcomed by many guests who still had similar pieces in their homes. When the feasting began, names of dish contributors were quickly remembered and the dish described with an especially good artistic adjective.

Jeremiah and Jonah gave Marci an exaggerated bow as guest after guest arrived. Even the Presbyterian minister came. Marci knew they were more than grateful. They were thoroughly enjoying not only the company but the food. She could not believe how much they were eating, how quickly they circulated in the crowd. While the dancer was in fine athletic shape and could handle all the food, Marci saw that Jonah, who was on the thin side, might be overdoing it no matter how small a sample he took from each dish.

She told him it was customary to keep the food, just return the dish. Marci laughed as he kissed her repeatedly on the cheek, an act that did not go unnoticed. It hit her that this would certainly add confusion to the gossipers, so she kissed him back.

While Marci had insisted that no liquor should be served— not even Jonah's favorite wine—she had agreed they could stash some in the old ice house they had restored behind the house in case they needed "bracing" for their guests. But the afternoon had gone so well that neither Jeremiah nor Jonah had given a thought to needing it.

But when the minister, who had discovered that Jonah was a Harvard theologian major, albeit a doubting one, jokingly suggested they should partake of a blessing or two, Jonah could not resist. He knew his lack of fervor for theology was very disconcerting to the Presbyterian minister who had more than his share of theology degrees and considered himself an expert. Each time he had rationalized a scripture to counter Jonah's doubt, Jonah had come back with one to attempt to make the minister doubt his belief.

Marci noticed the two of them go to the ice house and decided she had better investigate. Marci's mother noticed her daughter disappearing and decided she too would investigate.

By the time Marci, followed by her mother got there, Jonah and the Presbyterian minister were in a heated debate. Marci had no trouble concealing the wine decanter because her mother, who had taught Sunday School for years, had joined the debate and was not paying attention to Marci. Even if she had seen her hide the wine, Marci knew her mother would not want to make a scene. She would just yell at her later. Marci's big surprise was how well her mother was holding her own in the conversation. Her mother was simply telling them both to have a little faith and not take things so literally.

But it was when Jonah, either from too much bracing wine before the event or too much food or too much of too much, was about to lose it that her mother stepped in to preserve polite conversation. Jonah had suggested that he and Jeremiah had discovered that God's love could best be found in bed between two people who loved each other. The Presbyterian minister, having been unsettled in his thinking and now irritated, struck back by telling Jonah he was far too removed from normal society to understand godly love.

It was then that Marci's mother gave both of them much more to consider. She told them that when she was a little girl she always had to warm the bed for the circuit rider preacher before he retired for the evening. "Godly love is making your guests feel welcome and part of the family," she said with finality.

The party ended on a high note of success that day, Marci noted, as they were crossing the river. Both the minister and Jonah, who came along for the ride back, had seated themselves beside her mother in a very solicitous manner.

Uncle Henry

"Death is a debt to nature due.
I have died and so must you."

Uncle Henry quoting Ralph Waldo Emerson and probably Thoreau, too.

Folks said Uncle Henry's life style changed when he came back from the Korean War. He sold the 1954 Ford Thunderbird he left with his brother, added to what he saved in the army, and managed to buy an abandoned cabin and forty acres three miles back in the mountains.

He made sure he had enough left over to buy a horse. The dirt road that used to go back to this mountain cabin could hardly be called a path. The creek beside it had washed out most of it. Those who lived back there in the late 1800s had long since left for industrial jobs in the city. What was left was taken over by brush, briars and sycamore trees.

Uncle Henry lived his life alone but he was not a recluse. He rode his horse out once a week to collect his mail and often visited the valley farmers to catch up on the news. Still, he preferred books over most people and he often ordered them along with seed for his garden and items from Montgomery Wards or Sears that he couldn't make himself.

The mailbox, fashioned from the hollow trunk of a dead sycamore tree, was big enough to accommodate groceries he couldn't raise himself, such as sugar, coffee, salt, and occasionally special things like chocolate. The rural mailman was happy to shop and drop these things off for Uncle Henry, especially when he received payment in the form of animal skins that he could sell for much more than the price of the goods.

At Christmas, the mailman would find a pair of deerskin gloves and a jacket. Uncle Henry also made useful things out of horns, such as carved pipes or rack mounts to hang hats, all of which could be seen in valley homes. Everyone liked Uncle Henry even though he would turn down their offers of extended visits or invitations to community events.

Uncle Henry had been the local high school football star before he was sent to Korea. He was still admired for his physique and ability to fend for himself. So when several farmers tried to interest him in their daughters, it was a surprise to them that although Henry was interested, their daughters were not. It was true that he did not have electricity that far back in the mountains. But, many farmers had grown up with outdoor johns and they knew Uncle Henry had running water in his house because he built a stone well house over a mountain spring and had piped some of it through his house for drinking water into and through a stone trough to keep his food cool in containers.

There were at least five women in the valley who ventured on horseback with Uncle Henry to visit his cabin in the mountains. When they came back, they invariably, and with tact, reported that people should not worry about Uncle Henry being lonely. His house was full of friends—animal friends. Some people used to say a good man is one who never met an enemy. Even snakes were among Uncle Henry's friends and had free use of his house. The women complimented Uncle Henry's industriousness in providing running water and the fact that he had screened a section to keep the frogs and fish from having a free run of it. The outdoor john was sturdy, they said, but again, they felt one would never know what animal might be in it or around it.

Uncle Henry used to say, "Live and let live—unless you are hungry—then, never kill more than you can eat. Only man wages war, not nature." Some said this attitude was no doubt developed during the war when he regretted the so-called collateral damage to innocent villagers. Uncle Henry decided man should learn to live by the law of nature.

So even if a rabbit or squirrel or a deer visited Uncle Henry and found itself in a stew or their furs used in a coat, their kin never showed fear of Uncle Henry because he said they had understood the law of nature better than mankind did. Perhaps they knew Uncle Henry would not use the unfair advantage of guns. In addition to the car, he had also left his guns with his brother before the war. But he did not sell them when he came back. Instead he buried them.

When an animal died, it was usually wit against brawn and one against one. Uncle Henry set traps for small game like mink, otter, ferrets, beaver, groundhogs, squirrels, and hares. He would quickly kill them by knocking them unconscious with a rock and then skin them with a knife.

If he trapped a pregnant mother, he would release her figuring he was evening the odds allowing both mother and the unborn to live. He often had to use a knife to kill some animals which he felt was unfair so allowing a pregnant mother to live "relieved" his conscience.

Uncle Henry had the greatest respect for nature's design of making the adult male species more colorful so they would most likely become the meal instead of the mother or their young. He most admired male pheasants, grouse and quail for sacrificing themselves by appearing to be injured and thus easy prey. In the process, the predator would be lured away from the ground nest. Uncle Henry loved to allow the male to think he was being fooled by following it as it limped and scrambled through the brush. He also praised the ganders, who with wings flapping, neck straight out and a menacing, open beak, would try to scare the predator away from the mother and young ones while they fled to the water. The gander, in saving the family, often lost its battle with an unimpressed fox.

Spring was Uncle Henry's favorite time of year, when the peepers at night sang their song of birth in the nearby creek and in mountain terns. To know which plants were edible, all he had to do was watch which ones the animals ate. He did not fear bears and appreciated their guidance by showing which berries to eat. The valley folk used to say it was a good thing that bears did not easily become tame or they would have been eating berry pies with Uncle Henry.

Uncle Henry planted a garden each year and kept a small orchard. He planted it larger than he needed so there was plenty for his animal friends.

It was not unusual for him to be sitting on the front porch with his pile of books nearby watching the insects in his vegetable garden being eaten by small birds which, in turn, often became the prey of hawks and owls. Or he would be observing the deer eating his sweet corn while squirrels were swinging wildly in his hickory and walnut trees reaching for nuts on limbs that sometimes could not support them. He would laugh at their attempts to hang on the branches, saying they were funnier than the young goslings when they were being taught to fly by their parents.

Breaking up this serenity, however, would be warning calls and perhaps a shriek as predator found victim.

If an animal was injured and he did not want it for food,

Uncle Henry would bring it in his cabin to recover, considering that another equalizing of his deal with nature because he had the advantage of wit over brawn.

His cabin indoors looked a lot like the outdoors. However, to protect prey from predators, he would keep them in separate rooms or cages. But most of the animals and even insects were able to run free. Butterflies were a favorite of Uncle Henry's. If it was possible to save an injured one by letting it heal itself with food provided by Henry, he did it. Therefore, Uncle Henry had lots of flowers and plants in his cabin, too.

While one or two of the ladies who visited Henry were known to appreciate and respect nature, there was perhaps just too much of it to contend with at Uncle Henry's. It was not just living without electricity and indoor plumbing. Most snakes had free run of his cabin, yard and gardens because, explained Henry, they are the perfect mouse trap,   He did, however, divert rattlesnakes and copperheads from the cabin if they tried to come in. Poisonous snakes, skunks (which he said only perfume one if it is scared of you) and other less desirable guests were part of nature to him and he respected that animal's privacy and modus operandi to survive.

Snakes, he would explain, were never known to bite unless they were disturbed. So all you had to do was watch where you were going. This, of course, requires one to be attentive at all times but to Uncle Henry that was nature's way.

Once he fell asleep on a bed of moss he liked to relax on while fishing and rolled over on a rattlesnake which was there looking for some insects. Uncle Henry was bitten in the process but did not seek help other than to cut across the bite and suck out the venom. He survived because he knew that only the very young and old did not have the stamina to fend off poisonous venom.

He was drowsy for days but claimed he suffered no pain. That was probably the only altercation Uncle Henry had with an animal and he blamed himself for it. He lived what he considered a good life after the war. Uncle Henry found happiness living with animals, not in working the land like his valley neighbors.

So when they found Uncle Henry, at the age of 88, dead from a rattlesnake bite, no one who knew him believed it was an accident.

Roots

Marci was standing in the attic stairwell dragging the wooden apple crate towards her from under the eave in the attic when an edge caught an uneven floor board. The contents spilled out, falling down the stairwell beside her.

Marci, cursing, backed down the steps to retrieve whatever was in there for either her "save" or "get rid of" pile. Startled to hear music, she began laughing when she saw it was the music box her parents had gotten her when she completed grade school. The box, on its side, had opened. The sideways white-tutued ballerina was laterally dancing on a tiny pink pin cushion to the tune of "Poor People of Paris."

When Marci reached down to upright the music box, she spotted another box which had come apart in the fall. She pulled back the tissue in it to find several brilliantly colored plastic bracelets, a necklace and some loose charms.

After all these years, it seemed appropriate to just sit there and cry. She caressed each piece of the costume jewelry. She went back to herself at the age of eight, nine and 10 when she had been given this costume jewelry. She wondered how much of a brat she had been.

This thought was one of those things buried in dreams, occasionally surfacing when she went to bed feeling guilty about something.

Looking at the forgotten jewelry now brought everything into focus. She was older and now had experience with children . . . from the terrible twos through their hormone-driven teens. No one expected them to step outside of their own worlds. Why should she have been any different? Marci let herself drift back to the time she was in the one-room school. She pushed away the first vision and concentrated on the school which sat on a knoll, surrounded by mountains. The coal shed was on one side of the school and an outdoor privy on another. She was looking out the school windows. But it was not the cows in the pasture which they chased out to

use the field to play ball in at recess that held her attention. Nor
was it the South Branch of the Potomac River coming out of an
seven-mile ravine just below the pasture. She thought she had seen
a figure approaching the springhouse near the river. But only Mr.
Riley, their teacher, had a full view of the springhouse. She was in
a double-seated desk with her second cousin.

Mr. Riley was now looking at her. He had strategically placed
his desk to enjoy the view as well as keep his eye on the exit door at
the opposite end of the room. He had eight grades to teach. When
he brought a grade up to the front row bench for an hour session,
keeping an eye on the other students was difficult.

It was time for Marci and the other three in her fifth grade
class to be instructed. But now Marci was being excused. Mr. Riley
said she had done so well on her state history class the last session
that she did not have to attend this class.

He assigned her to go to the springhouse by the river and get
some water for their Bluebird stoneware cooler, a chore, like filling the
coal bucket for the pot belly stove, served as a reward for those excelling
in his classes. While it was usually an award when not in class up front,
Mr. Riley added that she had done so well she could stay outside the
rest of the morning before she bought the water in for lunchtime.

When Marci arrived at the spring house, the stooped old
woman was waiting for her. She was chanting "Mary had a little
Lamb" in a childlike voice. In her withered hands, she had a gift for
Marci. It was a bright red band which she slid over Marci's small
wrist. The old woman shook Marci's arm and was delighted to see
that it did not slide off.

For the past three years, Marci had become accustomed to
seeing the old woman at the well and now that she was bigger she
had been allowed to stay longer and take little trips though the
mountain gap with her.

Marci also knew that she was not supposed to tell anyone
about the meetings with the old woman, not even the other kids.
Mr. Riley had been quite specific about keeping it their secret, a
pact that Marci enjoyed since it made her feel so special that the
teacher would trust her not to tell.

So when she received the gifts from the old woman, Marci hid
those after showing them to Mr. Riley. She remembered he seemed
pleased as well as amused when she told him how the old woman
taught her to fish, using bright red, yellow, white and blue charms
as lures, which eventually ended up on Marci's bracelet.

Once, she had climbed with the old lady to a cave back into

the mountains where she showed Marci a fish that had been carved into the rock by Indians. Mr. Riley had asked her if it pointed to the river which Marci had confirmed, adding that it looked like a big mouth bass. After that, he had added the study of the Shawnee, Seneca and Susquehannock Indians to the study of West Virginia history. He even went back to the Adena mounds, one of which was just fifteen miles away and predated those tribes by a thousand years. Marci remembered sharing this knowledge with the old woman who just nodded her head with pleasure.

But it was the time that one of her classmates had come down to the river during recess when Marci was late coming back that she remembered the most now. The kid saw her with the old woman, made fun of her and called her a witch when she ran off.

Marci cringed at the memory now, knowing she had been embarrassed being with the old woman, feeling that yes, her clothes were dirty and torn, her hair did look like coiled wire, and that she was missing teeth.

Marci had been advised by Mr. Riley that the kid was wrong and just jealous that Marci was a good student. He advised her not to answer questions and just ignore the kid who would soon forget about it if nothing more was said.

But it was the old lady's feelings back then that Marci was concerned about today. Had she let her embarrassment show? Had she said anything mean like the kid had?

Marci remembered not wanting to go to the spring well again. She also remembered a lecture she had gotten from Mr. Riley about being nice to everyone and not to pay any attention to kids who didn't know better. He had told her to must go to the well again and show him how nice she could be.

She had gone. In fact, she continued to go until the seventh grade. The fall season was almost over when Mr. Riley told her the old woman had left the area and would not be back. Marci saw sadness in his eyes which seemed to be as directed to her as it was for the old woman. It had made her feel bad. She felt the loss of their secret and the hours she had spent with the old woman at the river. Memories of trekking through the gap and into the mountains searching for lady slippers and other flowers in the spring and picking up autumn leaves in the fall months were vivid. She had tucked some of the leaves in her history book much to the delight of Mr. Riley.

Now here she was 40 years later looking at the colorful costume jewelry she had stored away with the music box. She wound it up to play it again. Despite the ballerina dancing to the joyful

French melody, Marci could not shake her wish that she could go back to the fifth grade and make amends. She thought it was ironic that the jewelry, which was Bakelite, was a valuable collector item today. But its value to Marci was the person who had given it to her. It was never going back into that attic again.

Marci found out who the old woman was when she ran into Mr. Riley about 20 years after graduating from college. When the one-room school closed and everyone was bussed to the new countywide elementary and middle school, he retired. They were reminiscing about their youthful days, which for him had started during the depression and for her, memories of World War II picking milkweed pods to serve as down in military jackets. But it was the one-room school which held special memories for them.

It was then that she learned that the old woman was her grandmother. Her mental acuity from syphilis brought home by her husband from World War I had taken its toll. Mr. Riley had known it was not contagious without social contact but he also knew the disease was something society did not accept, including her mother. But rather than have her confined to a mental institution, it was felt she was better off living with remote mountain relatives.

When Marci got over the shock, all she could ask was: "Was I kind?" Mr. Riley had said, "Yes, because she was so happy to be able to see you."

Still, Marci wondered if her teacher wasn't just being nice. After all, she had been so young and she remembered being embarrassed when the kid taunted her.

Marci decided the attic cleanout could wait another day. She put on the Bakelite jewelry and went out into the garden to see how her expensive new, wildflower collection—the pink and yellow lady slippers—were growing.

She had bought them when she found out that the old woman was her grandmother She was the one who first pointed them out as fragile and wild. Marci had gone back to the deep ravine and waterfall across the river from the school to find them again. But they were no longer growing there. A road had been put in and the cliffs were lined with new homes with big picture windows overlooking the waterfall.

Marci had not gone back, preferring to remember the scene as a child. Here she was today, paying over $10 a bulb for these wild flowers and now wearing expensive Bakelite jewelry, which was making a comeback. If only she could go back and spend some time to thank her grandmother for the precious memories.

Killbuck's Reminder

There were still people in the 1800s who remembered, as they called it, putting up with the old Indian who had been left behind by the Shawnees when they were forced out of the northern neck of Virginia in the mid-1700s. They called him Killbuck's reminder.

Killbuck was the Shawnee Chief who led the lethal raid on Fort Seybert in 1758 on their ancestors who dared to settle along the South Branch of the Potomac River. Twenty-three adults were scalped and eleven captives taken, mostly young children which Killbuck wanted to raise as warriors plus several child-bearing age women.

Most of the captives were released in 1764 after the French and Indian wars. Records from these survivors were retold, not unlike what we do today, from different points of view.

Some felt that Killbuck's offer outside the fort that fateful foggy day in April to surrender or be killed was the right one by Captain Seybert to accept because they were so vastly outnumbered. Arguments abounded that if Seybert's son had not tried to shoot Killbuck, even though his father tried to stop him by deflecting the shot, things might have been different. Perhaps the shot would have killed Killbuck and it was known when the Chief died, the raiding party usually left.

However, the ball landed at Killbuck's feet, enraging him and soon the fort was set afire and two rows of those to be scalped and those to be saved were formed.

Stories of individual acts of bravery and cruelty were repeated. Mrs. Hawes, who was on her way to milk a cow, used the sheep shears she had to intimidate one of the Indians. Backing away, he fell over a bank, causing the Indians to call him a squaw man and putting her on the saved list for her courage. Captain Seybert's son who had taken a shot at Killbuck, seeing his father next to him scalped, was a good runner and proved it so much that Killbuck, when they finally caught him, decided to save him because he would become a good warrior.

There were also the written memories of Hannah and her squalling baby on the trail being knifed by one of her captors and left to die in the fork of a dogwood tree. Most captives had to run gauntlets of sticks and stones to prove their mettle, several who did not make it and were scalped.

When the American Revolution came, Killbuck, now forced back into Ohio country, tried to adopt a policy of neutrality between the English, American settlers and French and do what he could to protect what land they had. During this time the Moravian Church had established several missions to convince the natives to adopt Christianity and learn to live like the Americans.

Killbuck resented his grandfather for allowing the Moravians to remain in Ohio Country because they believed in pacifism. Killbuck believed that every convert to the Moravians deprived the Shawnees of a warrior to stop further white settlement of their land.

By 1800, there were no tribes left in the east to resist American settlement. But along the South Branch of the Potomac River and its tributaries, where some 20 forts had been built to protect the settlers, there was this aging Shawnee called Killbuck's Reminder, who still gave the settlers a good fright at times.

Killbuck's Reminder had been left behind many said, because he was like Hannah's squalling baby. He could not keep up and he was of no use. Others suggested he was left because the Indians probably found him to be annoying, too.

While Killbuck's Reminder was not capable of scalping anyone because he was so feeble, he did manage to scare them with some badly aimed arrows. They had gotten on to his trick of taking a cowbell off a straying milk cow and hanging it in a tree branch. When he rang the bell and they came looking for the cow, he would surprise them with a shot from his bow. So they made sure the cow was with the bell first.

His knife had been taken away from him when he was found under a under a swinging bridge over the north fork of the river. He had nearly succeeded in cutting the rope holding the bridge up when the settler was crossing it.

Killbuck's Reminder was able to supplement his diet of native plants, berries and nuts with rabbits and other small animals he found in homemade boxes put there by settlers. Bits of foods were left in these boxes, luring the animal in to walk on a trigger which sprung a trapdoor behind them. Killbuck's Reminder sometimes even took the bait from these boxes, if it was edible, before the settler checked them.

There were those who suspected they were also missing fruit and vegetables from their gardens, and attributed their lack of proof to Killbuck's Reminder's superb night vision. Fortunately, for Killbuck's Reminder, the memories of what his chief had done to their ancestors at Ft. Seybert were not first-hand. He had become more of an amusement than a threat to them. He was left alone. Even the Moravians did not try to convert him. He was too old to be of use.

When he died, he left another question unanswered. They found his body at the old Fort Seybert site which had been rebuilt to honor the dead. His remains were in the ashes of a huge bonfire he had built beside the fort. Had his intention been to burn the replica fort or not?

Aimless

When he moved into Hampshire County in 1970, it was a new leaf in what Arthur "Aimless" Aimhardt thought might be the final chapter of his life.

He had worked at many things, never staying more than a year or two in each job. He had been a mechanic, a mason, a construction worker; an assembler in five different factories, even sold insurance and autos and between those jobs, which he neither liked nor disliked; he just drifted from one county to another. He had also been in World War II, serving in the South Pacific, and had little to say about it other than it was hot there and that everyone would have been better off if the MPs spent all of their time on the battlefield. Aimless had his first run-in with the law at the age of eight for stealing food during the depression.

Ever since he could remember, no one addressed him as Arthur which was his birth name. The Social Security Administration had even made "Aimless" his middle name in their records. Since he didn't like Arthur, he used Aimless as his name. When cornered by sheriffs in at least ten counties for drunk and reckless driving, they would invariably comment that he lived up to his name. He lost his license several times over a 35-year period. It had just happened again and this time the Hardy County sheriff said he was on the computer now and he would never be able to get a license again. He advised him to, "Get a horse; they have more sense than you do."

So, that was exactly what Aimless did. He even bought it from this Hardy County sheriff who advised him to make a new start in the next county and not to answer too many questions. Aimless had already learned to evade the "what did you do for a living" question by simply saying he was retiring from a life sentence. Because he mostly associated with rootless people like himself that is all he had to explain about his past. The sheriff was even there when he rode off into the woods which would take him to the next county and the hunting cabin. The sheriff also handled real estate on the side and Aimless had liked the photo of the cabin so he had paid for it as well as the horse with a little left over which the sheriff had said should hold him over until he got a job.

"Just one road in and one road out of that valley, so you can't get lost," the sheriff had said in giving directions of what he would see through the forest and a narrow hollow until he got to river valley and the hunting cabin. Sure enough, Aimless saw few breaks in the woods except for two small farms cut out of the hillsides where he met Mrs. Smith along the road. She was waiting for a farmer who came by in his truck on the way to the stock sale to take her butter and pies and cookies to market for her. When he stared at the cookies, she gave him one and confirmed the sheriff's directions. An hour later, Aimless came out of the woods into a narrow hollow. He spotted the saw mill and then some sheep and pig farmers making use of the mountain stream flowing through it.

This narrow, rutted trough was bordered by rugged mountains which paralleled the South Branch of the Potomac River where the river burrowed and snaked its way for seven miles through high mountains on each side. That was when Aimless began to seriously look for his new home in Hampshire County.

When he went by a church and through the gap to meet the river, his horse didn't wait for a signal. It took a side path to the river for a drink while Aimless helped himself to one to from his flask. Whether it was the sound of the river or the cool breeze coming out of the long river gap or the big valley view below, Aimless did not know but, whatever, it was he felt he was part of his surroundings for the first time in his life.

He attributed this strange feeling of peace and belonging with the slow pace of the horse. After all, you could hardly appreciate anything from a speeding car window, he thought. The river, which was settling down into eddies from its riffling flow through the mountains, held his attention. Aimless smiled when he looked down the wide, fertile valley with its fields and barns surrounded by mountains which ran in bread-loaf formation with hollows tucked in between each loaf, all rising in layered tiers.

He began looking for the one-room school house the sheriff had told him about. Just a 100 yards or so below it would be a dirt road off to the right leading to the old hunting cabin he had purchased from the sheriff.

The school was not hard for him to recognize even though it had been turned into a fishing camp with a porch added to it. Rubber waders, turned inside out, were hanging off a clothesline.

Several cross-stringed seines for catching hellgrammites were strung up on the porch swing which was loaded with crewels and strainers. The evenly spaced windows on each side and the patched roof revealing what had most likely been the chimney opening for a pot belly stove triggered memories for Aimless.

When he was a kid in Kentucky, he had gone to a one-room school and his teacher was an English major with a penchant for poetry. While she had given him some good marks for math and in the later grades even had even had him check her accounting for school expenses, he had not done well in poetry. He had been excused from writing poetry to keep the Morning Glory stove going in the winter and to keep the windows clean. So he amazed himself remembering a poem he had read by Robert Frost about paths not taken.

Before finding the dirt road just below the school which led up into the foothills to the cabin, he decided to give his horse another good drink of water while he checked the river below the old school for bass. At the river's edge, he was able to look back up into the foothills where he spotted the clearing the sheriff had told him was next to the cabin in the woods. The sheriff had been right. It was an ideal place to pasture the horse, with easy access to both hunting and fishing for him.

Now anxious to get going, it did not take him long to find the cabin or to settle in. He smiled remembering the sheriff had said the former owner was a guy just like him. It appeared he had just taken off and left everything behind, including a bed which was not made up in the corner of the one room cabin. The open cupboard showed different cans of soup, a least a dozen Spaghetti O's and mostly just one of everything, a stewpot, a frying pan, a coffee pot, a towel, dishrag, and a can opener. But there were several plates, saucers and lots of knives and forks. Aimless, having only met one person in the past four hours, wondered who his company had been.

For about a week, Aimless roamed around his hillside and the surrounding hollows. He had just about gone through all the canned food left behind when he decided he should ride to town to get some supplies. It was a ten mile ride and he figured the sheriff would get a kick out of hearing about him reducing his horsepower speed to about three miles an hour.

The thought that he was not going to be a "hazard on the road" as the sheriff had loudly proclaimed him, amused him. Aimless laughed to himself because the sheriff either did not know or neglected to tell him that further back in the mountains from his cabin was a working still. The second day there he met G.W.Culpepper. He got along with him just fine. He could tell he had a mean streak when he talked about how his family had to be kept in line when they complained about how he ran his business. But Culpepper's wrath was not aimed at him because Aimless had quickly become a customer who didn't need delivery services.

Culpepper had advised him that there was no such thing as social drinking among the farmers in the valley so offering someone an illegal drink was the quickest way to find yourself in jail again. In fact, he should avoid farmers who were always looking for someone to help them during harvesting season. Still, Culpepper explained, most wouldn't hire him anyway if they thought he was a drifter and apt to have a drink, that is, except one farmer. He'd better steer clear of Bill Kuykendall who would and could get a hard day's work out of the most worthless of them all, even that Kline who still owed Culpepper for several gallons of shine.

Also, when he went by the Van Meter farm, he would need to make sure his huge overfed Angus bull was in his pen. Some guy named Millard had made the bull mad and he was still in the county home recovering from it.

As Aimless rode toward town, enjoying the view even more than he had when he first entered the valley, he decided not to take Culpepper's advice too seriously as he noted there was not one person the grumpy old man had anything nice to say about.

He rode several miles past three farms when he realized Culpepper was right about one thing. The morning sun had cleared the mountains but you could tell the farmers had been out there since sun-up. One corn field, probably about 100 acres, was nearly half harvested. Two wagons were lined up at the cutter at the silo, an empty one heading out to the field and another loaded wagon coming in to take its turn at the cutter.

Cattle were everywhere grazing on pasture and he had no trouble spotting the Van Meter bull when he rode by that farm. The Angus was by himself, which made sense since the cows were still with the calves they had that spring, but Aimless could tell it was prized by its owner. It had its own grassy penned-up lot with a shiny new water trough and a bin full of silage, while the other bulls shared a pasture in a lot the same size and had to get their water in an old cut-out, rusty steel barrel.

Aimless could also tell the farmers were making every good acre count by the fact he was riding on a road to town which ran up and down the low foothills on the east side to preserve all flat, fertile land along the river for farming. The thought of all that heat down there in the fields made him thirsty so he rested under a huge black oak tree along the road and let his horse have a drink from a nearby stream. It was cool there and Culpepper's brew was better now that he had earned the old man's trust enough to let him mix up his own at the still.

A cool, soothing breeze was coming out of the creek's hollow stirring the leaves on the trees as far as he could see. Then he recognized several were hickory trees. Boyhood memories rushed back to him as he remembered foraging for food during the depression. He told himself to remember these trees in the fall because he much preferred them over walnuts, even though they were harder to crack open in halves with less nutmeat inside. He remember that squirrels seemed to like them better, too, seldom letting them fall to the ground although he supposed a big walnut might be too bulky to carry across a weak limb. He didn't see any butternut trees and didn't care to. They were even harder to crack with even less nut. He hoped he would never have to work that hard for food again.

He could tell it would not be long before noon as the eastern mountains could no longer throw shadows into the valley. He knew he still had a long road ahead before he got to town and figured he better get back on his horse—although, with the comforting breeze and warm taste of the booze absorbing his senses, he felt like a nap.

As he was leaving this spot reluctantly, an old woman was coming through the field in his direction with a basket under her arm, gathering berries he assumed as he had noticed they were ripening. He figured this must be Old Sarah who lived in the huge house in the middle of the field and, according to Culpepper, was the sanest one in the valley. She knew how to live off the land without working yourself to death cultivating it.

Next, he rode by what he immediately knew was Lucy's place from the description of it being a good place to camp because of all the produce being grown along the river. Aimless admired it as the biggest outdoor grocery market he had ever seen. Much of their bottom land was taken up with fields of sweet corn, an acre or two each of tomato, bean and melon patches, and other plants in rows he couldn't make out from the road. They definitely worked for their food and made money doing it because their house looked as well-kept as their barns.

He had gone about another mile when he saw the mailbox for the Kuykendalls and remembered he was the one to avoid at all costs. Still, when he saw a freshly mowed lawn bordered by the biggest, prettiest flowers he had ever seen, he couldn't resist. He just had to find out what they were so he could get some for outside his cabin. Besides, he could see that Kuykendall was cutting corn in his field with perfectly straight rows that ended right at the river. Aimless didn't even see a road between the fences and then realized he had cut his way into the field to use as much land as possible. Culpepper had said he could squeeze water out of a rock and took great pride in having the straightest rows of corn in the valley even though they were cut down every year—pointing out that Bill and that drunk Kline would even reseed by hand if he thought they were not straight enough, not that Kline could tell the difference most days. Culpepper added that Bill always bailed him out after he got drunk on Saturday night and deducted his wages for it but he had been downright nasty when he asked him to collect the money Kline owed him.

Still, Aimless had no beef with him and he was in the field. So, still a little wobbly from his creekside drink, he was just about to knock on the door to ask about the flowers when Mrs. Kuykendall opened it so quick, he lost his balance and fell face first into her living room. She gave him a stern look, he struggled up and quickly introduced himself as Aimless at which point she declared, "That's for sure." Opening the door wider for him to leave, she added, "And you're not welcome here in that condition either."

However, Aimless, profusely excusing himself and now on the porch explaining his great admiration for her beautiful flowers and the best-trimmed lawn he had ever seen, and what a good person she must be because no one had as many hummingbirds circling a feeder as she did on her well-swept porch, was soon led to the hibiscus rows where he could take his pick of each color.

When he got back on the horse, with the hibiscus samples secured to and straddling the saddle horn so he could continue to wonder at them as well as inhale their scent, Aimless began whistling a song he remembered from his youth which now seemed appropriate, "Down in the Valley," although he recalled his boyhood home was in a hollow which he had gotten out of as soon as he could. Still, he began thinking of it now as a small valley.

He rode on for another hour and was at the top of another foothill mountain which he decided must be the one called, Breakneck, because that was where the river made a huge horseshoe-bend in the middle of the valley before it returned to follow the west side of the mountains. He paused to give his horse some rest and found himself further drifting off into old memories as he surveyed a full view of the valley below.

From here you could see the beauty of the hard work of the farmers below even though he recalled Culpepper saying he had learned early on that it was better to look at than be involved in. Still, it was like a painting. So he traced it with his hands which were steadier now since the encounter with Mrs. Kuykendall.

As he left this scenic view and wound down back into the valley, he rode by acres and acres of pastures dotted with Hereford and Angus cattle. The valley was starting to narrow again and this farmer was using most of his land as pasture, some of it trapped by the river which was horseshoeing again through the valley. He was amazed to see how nonchalantly the cattle would swim across the river—to get to the greener side. As he rode on, he saw this farmer also grew enough corn and grain to feed the cattle as well as the hogs he had seen lounging in a backwater section of the river.

Aimless was probably only two miles from town when he spotted all the camping trailers along the river that Culpepper had mentioned. Some farmers still had fields between the road and the trailer parks and Aimless wondered if they had to supplement their income by renting to campers since the farming was getting tougher in this narrow end of the valley. When he read a sign announcing "No ATVs," he remembered being warned about another Kuykendall who had a farm and, like his Uncle Bill, rented whatever was available from other farmers in a mad rush to work himself to death.

The sign, he remembered from Culpepper's laughing about it, was up there because one of the new campers, who knew nothing about farming, had used the rented 20-acre field beside the campsite to try out his new high-powered ATV. The wheat was probably three inches high when the he left it ruins; it would not recover from the deep ruts, some circular and other zigzagging so that year's crop was lost. Word had it that when this young Kuykendall caught up with the vandal, he had added a few ruts on his chin.

When Aimless left the dirt road to get on U.S. 50 just a quarter-mile from town, he realized he had not gone three miles an hour but had taken most of the day making the trip to town. He got his groceries, packed them in the saddlebags, fed the horse, and was heading back when he spotted the Moose Club that Culpepper mentioned. Aimless checked his watch and knew he only had about four hours of light left which meant he would be riding in the dark, even if he hurried. It would be a tough ride back in the dark. But he was thirsty, so he decided to have one for the road. Besides, he could easily make it to that hickory tree grove before dark which had been very comfortable and the horse liked it, too.

He ordered a beer and asked to chase it with some of Culpepper's brew which he knew they carried, figuring his moonshine mentor would appreciate that. It was then he met Kline who introduced himself upon hearing Culpepper's name.

"Is Culpepper making his stuff out of flowers now?" he said pointing to the Hibiscus-clad horse outside the club. "You'll never have a clear head drinking his stuff," he declared.

For the next several hours they enjoyed each other's company and their chats with Kline's lady friends. Aimless also felt the husband who came in to collect his wife was unreasonable and came to Kline's aid. That night as they were both in jail, the sheriff called Bill Kuykendall. "Say Bill, I think I have what could be some good news for you. There's this new fellow hanging around with Kline now and he's got quite a bit of Kline in him. He was going on about how beautiful the farms are and how he loves that valley. He also has a horse. I believe you are going to want to bail him out, too."

The Good Belle Snickel

She's crazy good! That's what we kids would say as we dived into the treats old Belle Van Meter would leave us a few days before Christmas during the 1950s in the eastern panhandle of West Virginia. A tap on the door with her cane would alert us if we had not first spotted her coming up the flagstone walk.

Little did we know then she was following the tradition of belsnickeling, sometimes called Christkindeling, a custom that went back to Germany's Peltz Nickel, who was said to have gone from house to house at Christmas to give each mother a beating rod with which to discipline her children during the coming year. During the Middle Ages in Holland, the Dutch version of a Belsnickel was clad as a medieval page in black plumed hat, doublet, gloves and hose and carried with him a yawning black bag in which to stuff exceptionally naughty children. Fortunately for us, Christkindeling had evolved into Kris Kringle to today's jolly Santa Claus. We were glad that her ancestors had been open to changing the custom to more benevolent visits in Appalachia.

Belle, who always dressed herself up in a long cloak and fur hat, did use a walking stick which she only waved at us in a friendly manner as she asked the traditional belsnickeling questions, "Do thee obey thou mom and dad, go to church, repeat thy catechism, say thy prayers when yee go to bed and do everything which good children should do?"

Naturally we answered in the affirmative. Belle would then cast her walking stick aside as if she no longer needed it and dole out the nuts she had cracked out from her fall harvest along with tiny fruit cakes she had made. There would also be peppermint candy which she called hard tack, telling us it was often the only thing the Continental soldiers had to eat at Valley Forge. Then she would wave her cane at us again and leave, reminding us that we had better continue to be good or Bells Knickel would get us on New Year's Day and if we were naughty put us in a big black bag.

While our parents would agree with us that Belle was odd, we found they were quick to back up her admonitions to be good. They would quote her even when her comments were directed to them. When they were paying bills in town, they would often repeat Belle's advice of, "There's no reason you can't live off these mountains and valley."

Belle did a fine job of it, picking early burdock and fiddleheads, poke, ramps, wild collard and mustard greens in the spring, later on gathering blackberries, raspberries, and huckleberries as well as picking apples, cherries and peaches from her well-cared-for trees and finally ending her natural harvest by gathering walnut, hickory and butternuts.

Anyone that drove by her flourishing garden in the summer knew she had a pantry full of canned goods for the winter. And when she needed cash, you could find her stand next to the A&P in town. For her, the hard-to-find valuable ginseng and sassafras was plentiful, a business she conducted by mail.

While most of us just associated her with her annual Christmas visit, I especially remember meeting her once when I was about 10. I was coming out of the woods near her cabin. It was spring, the banks were covered with Dutchman's britches, the redbud was out in full bloom and the mountain laurel buds were swelling. She had a bag full of early green moss, the kind that ends the summer with tiny-red headed blooms, often described as British soldiers marching through the green. I asked what she was going to do with it.

She invited me to her home to see, but it was not to her cabin. I followed her into a blackberry patch thicket to find out that she had made herself an imaginary split-level house in the center. It had rooms divided by rows of stones and huckleberry bushes. She had made use of the flat boulders to serve as tables and stumps as chairs. And yes, there was a real stone fireplace and on the lower level near the creek was a springhouse she had dug out. But, the real treats in this playhouse were the moss beds she had cultivated. After swearing this Eden-like playground to secrecy, I went back several times to lie down on this soft bed of sweet smelling moss and earth and watch the clouds take on recognizable shapes, which were much easier to discern than trying to connect stars into constellations.

It has been 50 years now since Belle left us for what we hope are just as green pastures. There are still many of us who remember her Bellsnickel gifts. I have seen peppermint candy left at her gravestone. But in memory of her, I have sworn not to tell anyone why there is a bed of moss atop her grave.

Whose Mother Was It?

They might call it tough love today but to the teenagers at Hampshire High School, the mad mother of Breakneck pretty much stopped all the moonlight activity on that mountain overlooking a scenic valley horseshoed twice by the winding river that ran through it.

Parking and necking was what they called it back then. Every Monday morning if you looked hard enough you could see the "hickie" marks on the necks of those who were dating. There were some who tried to cover them up with a turtleneck and a few, like Lo Ann, the head cheerleader and her quarterback boy friend, Eddie, who sported them like a badge of honor.

Marci wondered if they at least left their house with a scarf around their neck. She certainly knew her mother would have had a fit and confined her for who knows how long had she come home with those telltale marks. But then again, it was not likely to happen as she was what the nicer people called a late developer and awkward. She had even earned herself a tomboy reputation which she had decided she would probably never outlive. Boys simply ignored her unless they wanted her to do their homework or get something off a high shelf for them.

Marci was long legged and lean all over. Her height had gotten her on the basketball team but she had failed to become a favored forward. In those days, girl could only be guards or forwards, so her long arms were put to use keeping the other team from scoring. Much to her dismay, her nickname became "Windmill" but at least she was popular with the forwards on her team as she often snagged the ball in a whirlwind frenzy and passed it to those who usually lined up near her side of the court.

Marci's mother would try to boost her confidence by predicting that one day all those petite, full bosomed blondes with lots of cleavage on the cheerleading team would one day envy her as a model. Marci wasn't buying it. She, like most of the kids, was in awe of the cheerleaders and football players. Every Monday morning they would hang around them to look for hickies and hear about their weekends.

But there was one Monday when Marci was not looking to see who had been out Saturday night. When she was not in class, she was hiding behind the lockers in the girl's room. She did not come out until the class was just ready to start so she could set in the back without being noticed. When the bell rang she was the first out of the room.

It was after home-economics class—which Marci was no longer in because her father had forced the principal to let her in shop class instead so she could make farm gates for him—that Lo Ann showed up with the girl she had declared to be her best friend. Marci stayed behind the row of lockers and braced herself. But to her great surprise and relief, LoAnn, who she now knew was on Breakneck that Saturday night, was telling her best friend about Eddie's crazy mother.

"Would you believe she actually reached in and pulled Eddie out by the back of his shirt and hit him?"

"What were you all doing?"

"We were enjoying a beautiful night. The moon was full and you could even see the cows in the field below it was so bright. It was right in line with the river, too, and you could see it shimmering on the water. We were just having fun."

"Sure you were, Lo Ann. I met his mother once, hard to believe she would do that."

"You should have seen her. She was so angry. She even asked me what I would do if I was pregnant."

"What did you say?"

"Nothing. I was so stunned I didn't know what to say."

"What about Eddie?"

"He was embarrassed. She even zipped up his pants when she yanked him out of the car."

"Wow, would I have loved to have seen that."

"No, you wouldn't have. He was not the Eddie we know. He was this meek guy who wouldn't say a word to me on the way home. Just stared at me. I don't care if I ever see him again. Maybe I should just feel sorry for him, having a mother who would do that."

Marci was glad that they left the locker room as quickly as they came in. Surely they would have heard her very audible sign of relief. Her mother had not been recognized, she happily declared to herself.

Marci could still hear her father laughing when they had gotten home that Saturday night and seen what they assumed to be her brother's car—one just like Eddie's that she watched him get out of the parking lot at school as soon as she got there.

It happened after she, her mother and father had left their usual Saturday night trip to the movies in town, a drive that took them by the infamous Breakneck Mountain.

Her brother Mike was a senior and had worked hard to buy a car with the help of an older sister. Having a car almost gave you as much status as football players. Her grandfather had been against it saying that cars, just like TV, were causing kids to grow up way too fast. But Mike had gotten a sporty red Chevy with white sidewall tires which was only five years old. The car that Marci and her parents spotted near the trees on the Breakneck overlook was just like the one her brother had. They assumed it was Mike.

"Stop the truck," her mother, the first to spot the car, demanded.

Her father, who had to slow down for the turn, tried to ignore her. "I will talk to him. Don't go making trouble."

"That is what he is doing," she declared. "I said stop the truck."

Her father slowed down momentarily as if he were going to and then started down the other side of Breakneck at which time her mother reached over across Marci and pulled the emergency break. "I Said Stop The Truck" she declared as she bailed out. They watched her as she strode back to the car half hidden by the trees.

When she came back, she was strangely quiet. Because Marci's father was mad, he asked no questions. Ten minutes later as they approached their house, there was Mike's car where he usually parked it, facing the road for all to see. The moment of silent recognition was quickly broken by Marci's father who roared, a laugh that was still going even after he promised not to tell Mike, who they had found was fast asleep.

Marci, after realizing what would happen if people found out it was her mother, was very quick to assure her mother she was not about to tell anyone about it. Neither she nor her father asked questions about what happened as they knew by the don't-you-dare look on her face they would get no answers.

Now, the time of final reckoning had come for Marci. It was near lunchtime at school. Marci decided it was safe to go to the cafeteria even though she did not know if Eddie knew who it was. When she went in, she could tell Lo Ann's friend had spread the word because groups were clustered around giggling and looking at Lo Ann and Eddie who were not seated together as they usually were, holding hands.

Now that it appeared her mother was not named, Marci decided not to skip Shop Class. She would listen in on what Eddie had to say there. Shop was an informal activity and the guys paid little attention to her, giving her the moniker "Beanpole" when they wanted her to reach something they couldn't.

The instructor had barely left them after inspecting their work when the boys started in on Eddie: "Hey Eddie, Lo Ann is calling you a Momma's boy . . . Be glad Big Momma didn't break your neck on Breakneck . . . ha, ha . . . bet you won't be going back there for awhile . . . " on and on went the comments.

Eddie spun around, face flushing in red like the cherry table he made for his mother which he was now priming for a final coat. "It wasn't my mother. It was Lo Ann's mother, you S.O.B.s. What a bitch. She even tore off my shirt collar when she yanked me out of the car. For a minute there, I thought she looked confused. But then she tore into both of us with both barrels. LoAnn didn't even apologize for her mother. She just looked at me on the way home like it was my fault."

The group gathered around Eddie then to hear more about what Lo Ann's mother had said and done but Marci had heard enough. A catastrophe for her had been avoided. Besides, she really didn't want to hear anymore about what her mother had done and said. She started up the band saw to cut out heart-shaped ends for a walnut magazine rack her mother had asked her to make. Their house was beginning to fill up now with walnut star-shaped what-not shelves which she quickly made until the locust lumber was dropped off by her father for more gates.

Still, Marci knew that it would not take long for Lo Ann to hear that Eddie said it was her mother so she was still uneasy. Her next class was Health and Phys Ed, where she would be practicing for upcoming basketball games with the team while the other girls just did floor exercises. All of them had to first listen to a lecture or film on body functions and health.

Even before the teacher got started, Lo Ann threw a fit when it was whispered to her that Eddie said it was her mother. She declared him a liar and soon the whole story spilled out as Lo Ann tried to explain that it was not her mother...that she would never do such a mean thing. She reiterated that she guessed she should feel sorry for Eddie who had a mother who would do that.

It was then the health and physical education teacher slowly looked each girl in the eye and said, "You should be happy to have a mother like that who cares enough about you to keep you from making a huge mistake that you will have to live with for the rest of your life. She went on to outline dire scenarios from unplanned pregnancies, praising concerned mothers who were trying to get their sons and daughters not to repeat mistakes they perhaps had made.

During the rest of the school year, Marci did notice that there were seldom any cars parked on Breakneck as word went around about the crazy Breakneck mother. She also noticed that the health teacher was getting a more attentive audience with her lectures on health and body functions.

She overheard her tell another teacher one day that she believed this might be the first year in ages that a girl would not be able to walk across the stage and get her degree because she was pregnant.

George N. Parker

It didn't make any sense to people that George N. Parker would go out of his way to hit an animal crossing the road.

He was the richest man in the valley and always drove a huge Lincoln town car. People talked about his giving a million dollars to his alma mater, Washington and Lee University.

Even though he traded in the Lincoln for a new one each year, it didn't take long for the bumper and fenders to show signs of hitting deer. People had even seen him veer off into ditches to get a fast-moving squirrel, groundhog or a raccoon. Even though he could stop and pick up a slow-moving turtle, he would aim directly at it. Some said he liked to hear the shell popping while others said he was making it easy to get the meat.

George N. Parker ate road kill. Bypassers were amazed to see him struggle with the bloody carcass of a deer to get it in the back of his town car. Some would even stop to help just to see if he minded what the blood was doing to those plush leather seats.

Some people gave him roadkill recipes. But if they hoped to shame him, it was to no avail. George N. Parker would thank them with all the graciousness he had learned at the gentleman's school in Virginia.

They tolerated him at the homeless shelter where he went for meals. When he came to the church festivals and went through the food lines set up for cash only, he would tell them to send him a bill. He didn't carry cash. Few ever bothered taking the time to do it for so few dollars.

At the drive-in movie, he would walk in with a fold-up chair and sit by a speaker, tipping his hat to those in the car beside it.

To save gas, he would drift down the mountain roads to take him up the next hill as far as he could before he hit the gas again.

He always parked his car in the free grocery store lot rather than put change in a meter even though he would have to walk several blocks to get where he was headed.

He had a dog. When he stopped by restaurants and asked for leftovers, people wondered if the dog was getting it all.

He got his clothes at the Salvation Army store. Yet, a stranger might not know it because his taste was impeccable.

He became the talk of the town, a legend for the next generation when he died, leaving another million dollars to Washington and Lee.

The guy running the homeless shelter probably summed it up best when he died. "We are going to miss George N. Parker. He made all of us feel better about ourselves."

Firsts

"So what do you do at that Memoir Writing Center," joked my husband. "You live in the past, you become the past," he grinned. "I bet all of you just sit in an easy chair and go back to your second childhood."

I thought about it, and decided it was not a bad idea to regress if reality was having a discussion with him in this mood.

So, I moved over to the Lazy Boy chair he usually occupies in front of the TV set, closed my eyes, and let him think I was in regression. He could sit in my hardback rocker and amuse himself with Dave Letterman if he wanted to. Maybe that was where he got the irritating habit of repeating himself when he thought he was funny. He kept digging up the same old sarcastic bones.

I decided I would, indeed, regain my childhood and a way to do it was to search back for my earliest memories. I would categorize them as: first happiness, first fear, first sadness, first Christmas, first school memory, first love and so forth.

Happy thoughts first, I said to myself. I visualized myself at about age 4. I was introducing my ducks, Duckie and Daddles to two people who were visiting my mother on the front porch. It was probably Lucy Belle and Aunt Susan. They always sat in the porch swing and they were giving me their full attention, which I know today I always got from them. Mom was explaining that she let me bring the ducks on the porch because I agreed to clean up after them which I liked doing because I could use the water hose at the side of the porch. Because my sister was allowed to bring her two cats in the house and even sleep with them, I had wanted to do the same with my ducks. But Mom had quickly pointed out that would be impossible because the ducks could not be toilet trained. Not to be deterred, I tried to get them to back up to the cat sandbox which they over-squirted. I even tried using some long ice trays no avail. I soon found out that leading a duck to water was a lot easier than trying to get them to go to the bathroom in an orderly manner.

Unlike cats, they didn't even give you a sign they wanted to go and had no intention of doing so.

So, I joined their world and became an outdoor kid. At first, I called them Duckie I and II but my dad renamed the male one Daddles because, he said, Duckie wasn't enough for him. Daddles' straying testosterone often sent him in the hen house looking for more action, a noisy affair which not only interrupted the egg production, but was also irritating the lone rooster. Still my father tolerated him or as my mother used to muse, probably admired him. It was my job to let them out of the coop in the morning so they could trundle off to the pond for their food and then close them up in the coop at night. All of our pets had to earn their keep and my sister frequently offered mice as proof of what good cats she had. While no one liked duck eggs for breakfast, Lucy Belle said they were great for baking and insisted on paying for them—money which went into Mom's egg money jar. My brother had two barns full of at least 25 outdoor cats which not only kept the barns rat free but also served as a genetics lesson for us all. Within about ten years, most of them were all black with white tails, and I won't repeat my memory of what happened to the kittens born without this trait.

My first fear came when I was going to the pond to get Daddles and Duckie to pen them up for the night. It was nearly dark. I stepped on a big black snake which we called racers because they humped in several places to get away fast. This one was about six feet long, my father said, and I had been so scared I fell on it. Evidently, I was so terrified I passed out and the snake kept biting me trying to get out from under me. I don't remember my dad freeing me from the snake, but my mother would later say that I learned my lesson too well when they had earlier tried to make me afraid of snakes. It seems that not long after I had learned to walk, I came in the house with the front of my skirt bunched up with a lot of baby copperhead snakes in it.

My earliest sad memory came the morning I went to let Duckie and Daddles out of their coop and saw the screen front was torn open. Even at that age, I knew Daddles and Duckie were no longer in there, and I remember seeing some of their feathers stuck in the screen. I knew the dreaded foxes that had plagued the hen house from time to time had found my ducks. My mother said it took me several weeks before I would even speak about it. They had tried unsuccessfully to get me to give up the two big long yellow bills I found near the apple tree behind the barn where Daddles and

Duckie had been consumed. I carried the bills with me in the pockets of my red corduroy pants. Rather than hand-me-down dresses from my sister, I was now getting pants from an older cousin. Not only would they be difficult to carry snakes in, but more useful for me as I often assisted my little brother in digging bathtub size trenches by the house where he could play with his trucks. We would spend hours in the pit building roads up and down the sides of it and then racing his equipment made out of wooden blocks in and out of the pit. Mom used to say it was a replica of the mountain roads we used to take to town in our 1938 Ford truck.

While all of our Christmases growing up were pretty sparse as far as presents, we never lacked for good food as farm kids. We even had steak for breakfast with our eggs and lots of vegetables and fruit. Mom's egg money was saved for a special Christmas treat—a gallon of shucked oysters brought over from Chesapeake Bay that to this day none of us can fry as deliciously as my mom did. She never shared the recipe, so that has given the following generations a challenge still attempted. My first Christmas memory vividly jumps out. No matter how tough things were, we always had one present under the tree which was usually a toy. But, I won't forget what happened when I opened the box and, even though it had a new dress on it made by my mom, I recognized my sister's old doll and cried. Obviously, my struggling parents were pretty disgusted with such ungrateful behavior. It only took my father a few minutes to go down to the tool shed and bring back a hoe. He attached the red ribbon from the box on it, and said, "There you are. If you don't like being a little girl, I have something for you to do in the fields."

From then on, I became not only an outdoor kid with chores, but one that was soon working the field and, to her delight, loving every minute of it. I preferred it instead of washing dishes and scrubbing the floors like my sisters were doing. I was assigned a 10-acre cornfield and kept it clean of weeds for at least eight summers before I grew up and was old enough to work with other kids in the produce fields. Sweet corn, bird's eye beans, tomatoes, melons and other perishable crops thrived in the rich, fertile soil of the South Branch of the Potomac River valley. Such crops had to be picked fast which meant we had to have the stamina to work from sunup to sundown to get them ready to be trucked to markets.

But I digress in my regression. The first day of going to school was also a traumatic event. For me it was getting on that big yellow school bus with older kids, who I knew would be teasing me, and there would be no way of running away from them. There was also the fear of that two-room schoolhouse which had the first four grades in one room and the four higher grades in the other room. So I stayed overnight with my bigger cousin in the fourth grade who promised to defend me and to this day, I look on him as a protector of my youth. Even when the teacher asked me to give my name, he answered for me. I am told it took a week before I said anything in class, a happening that many today simply cannot believe.

Then there is the first love. There is no feeling like that one. I guess some of those hormones Daddles had surfaced in me. I was working in the produce fields under a big elm tree by the river bagging corn. He was picking corn with the older men, and every time the fifth sled of corn came in for us to bag, I looked for him. He was as shy as I was. We would just stare. But I knew he liked me. He had given me a rabbit box for my birthday. My father let me keep it, but demanded that I catch rabbits in it and give them to his father. What I didn't realize then was that his family was so poor the only thing he could give me was a rabbit box. His family used those to obtain meat. Later in life, I realized what a sacrifice that had been, and that his father and mine had decided I could keep it, but that it should be useful. I proved to be true to my first love. I probably cleaned out our 500 acres of all the rabbits it had and presented them to him and his father.

He died in Viet Nam. Like so many poor boys in our county, the service was the only way out of poverty. I went on to other loves, and so did he. But his memory stays with me.

Even when I am jostled out of my regression with the Dave Letterman show and my husband says to me, "Hey, snap out of it. Talk to me. I didn't mean what I was saying about your memoir writing center. Tell you what, tomorrow night let's go out to dinner."